The Crow Queen

Elaine Conrda

Novels by Elaine Corvidae
Published by Mundania Press

Lord of Wind and Fire Series

Wolfkin

The Crow Queen

Dragon's Son

Tyrant Moon

Heretic Sun

The Crow Queen

Lord of Wind and Fire BOOK TWO

ELAINE CORVIDAE

Mundania Press

A Mundania Press Production
Mundania Press LLC
6470A Glenway Avenue, #109
Cincinnati, Ohio 45211-5222

To order additional copies of this book, contact:
books@mundania.com
www.mundania.com

Cover Art © 2004 by Stacey King
Book Design and Layout by Daniel J. Reitz, Sr.
Production and Promotion by Bob Sanders

ISBN: 1-59426-058-3

First Trade Paperback Edition • April 2004

Library of Congress Catalog Card Number 2004100303

Production by Mundania Press LLC
Printed in the United States of America

10   9   8   7   6   5   4   3   2   1

Prologue

The Crow Queen crouched in darkness, feeling the cool whisper of a breeze touch her cheek. The plants that grew in the garden stirred restlessly with the wind, the soft scrape of their large leaves against one another enough to cover the faint sound of her steps. The stone wall of the mansion in the heart of the garden lay to her left, half-hidden beneath climbing vines. A torch flickered wildly above a recessed entrance onto the lower floor. A quick motion of one hand, and the light died.

A soft oath came from within the recess. A guard stumbled out, fumbling in the darkness for tinder and flint. Only a few moments later, he succeeded in restoring the comforting light of the torch. Cursing the wind and the night, he went back to his station and took a sip from the cup of mulled wine waiting there for him, having never seen the slender figure that had slipped in and out while he was otherwise occupied.

Within moments the guard was slumped on the floor, a thin rivulet of wine trailing like blood from his dropped cup. The Crow Queen stepped over him, pausing only long enough to ransack his belt for keys. She would return them before she left, and no one would ever be the wiser, not even the guard who would awake the next morning with a splitting headache and no recollection of the previous night.

"You take too many risks," Yozerf had said once, his voice angry and bitter. *"Dead men cannot remember your face. Why*

don't you just kill them and be done with it?"

"*Finesse,*" she had replied disdainfully. To spare the lives of the guards and servants who unwittingly crossed her path—that was the mark of the professional.

He had not said anything—had not needed to for her to know that he believed it the mark of a fool.

The door into the mansion yielded to one of the keys from the guard's belt. The Crow Queen ghosted up the stair inside, her passage barely a flicker of black amidst deeper darkness. She'd heard rumors that claimed she could hide the shadow cast by a poker, and the conceit had pleased her. She wished it were true.

Most of the mansion slept, except for the few guards set about the perimeter. Their master had no true fear in him, believing that his wealth would be enough to keep him safe, and so the Crow Queen found herself able to move unimpeded through his home. Following the route she had memorized, she came at last to the door of his study.

As his wife had promised, he was up late, scribbling in his ledgers. The flames of the candles might have bent slightly as the door at his back opened noiselessly, but if so he never noticed. The Crow Queen's boots made no sound on the sumptuous Undish carpets that covered the floor. No premonition of danger caused him to look up or shift position.

Her gloved hand knotted in his hair, jerking his head back hard. A curved knife sharpened to a lethal edge sliced through jugular and windpipe before he had a chance to cry out. A torrent of blood splashed across the papers on his desk, obliterating whatever had been written there. His eyes went wide with shock, and his hands scrabbled helplessly at the terrible wound in his throat for a moment before his life bled out. Then he slumped in the chair, the look of surprise still stamped across his features.

So many of them looked surprised, and it never ceased to annoy her. She wondered if the gods would tell him that his wife had hired an assassin to kill him after he had raped their daughter on her tenth birthday. Chances were he would still miss the point.

A few sestarrii gleamed golden amidst the papers and blood, and she took them without guilt. Let the city watch believe that he had been murdered during a robbery. They would never learn the truth anyway.

≈≈

She had only walked three streets away from the mansion when the wizard found her.

One moment, the night was empty, silent except for the near-noiseless whisper of her feet on the cobblestones. The next...there was something *more* to the shadows, as if they had gained a weight and depth that they had previously lacked. She froze instantly, all her senses attuned to the night around her, straining to unravel any possible nuance.

White robes caught the faint light of torches locked beyond manor gates; the flames turned them red, as if they had been washed in blood. Between the ivory bristle of beard and hair, his face looked dark, his expression lost to her. "I have come to ask of you...a favor," he said.

The Crow Queen slowly rose from the defensive crouch she had dropped into, but her daggers remained in her hands. Not that they would defend her against magic, she thought bitterly.

"What do you want, Ax?" she asked, her voice as cold and expressionless as she could make it.

"To retain your services."

"No."

He chuckled softly. "You have not even heard my offer yet."

"I don't need to." She would have walked away, if she'd trusted him at her back.

"There is a lord coming to this city. An important man. I want you to keep him safe."

She laughed. "I kill. I don't save."

"If you do not, you will be the last of your kind."

Ice slid through her veins, and she hissed softly. "If you threaten—"

"I merely prophesy. Auglar of Kellsjard must live through all that is to come. If he does not, your son will die as well."

"What could the fortune of a lord of Jenel possibly have to do with my son?"

Ax smiled briefly. "You will see, Londah Jonaglir. You will see soon enough." And with that, he was gone.

Londah stood alone in the street, her fingers gripping her knives so hard that her knuckles had gone white. Then, with a curse she had learned from the sailors who frequented Segg's port, she slammed her weapons back into their sheathes and stalked off.

Damned wizards.

Chapter One

Suchen bit back a hiss of frustration as her opponent easily evaded the fist aimed at his nose. Before she could recover, he grabbed her wrist, his deceptively slender fingers trapping her in an iron grip. She snapped her knee up at his groin, connecting only with thigh as he out-maneuvered her again, and then dropped her weight to pull hard against the joint of his thumb. His grip broke and she leapt back, bringing her forearm up in a fast block to fend of the quick snap of a fist. A second time she blocked, then a third, and then went on the offensive, whipping her foot up in a kick that should have knocked the wind out of an attacker, possibly breaking ribs on the way.

He moved aside with an incredible, animal speed and grace, gray eyes tracking her foot so that when her leg was fully extended, he caught hold of her ankle and used her own momentum to send her tumbling to the ground.

She hit hard, the wind huffing out of her lungs, and sent one hand scrabbling in the dirt beside her head. Catching up a handful of mud and rock, she threw it at his face. Her aim wasn't true, but it forced him to dodge, giving her the opening to get back on her feet. But she was still too slow, and an instant later she found a sinewy arm snaked around her throat, the other poised to grab her head and snap her neck.

"Dead again," he said in a voice like velvet and midnight.

"Damn it!" His arms loosened their hold, and she pulled away, kicking at a loose rock and glowering at the churned mud of the yard where the soldiers of Kellsjard routinely practiced the arts of warfare.

"You did well," Yozerf protested.

She glanced back over her shoulder uncertainly. A cloud of blood-red hair straggled wildly about Yozerf's shoulders, blowing lightly in the wind. The only spot of color in a monochromatic landscape, it contrasted sharply with his black clothing, his bone-white skin, and his sleet-gray eyes. Despite the inhuman size and cant of those eyes and the sharp bones of his triangular face, he looked beautiful to her. Beautiful and entirely unflustered.

Damn him—he could at least be polite enough to look a little winded.

"I didn't land a single blow," she pointed out irritably.

"It takes time to learn a new way of fighting," he said reasonably. "We haven't been practicing that long. And none of the Sworn would have done half as well—you're quicker than they are, more flexible. This isn't sword-work."

Suchen sighed and pushed a stray strand of blonde hair out of her eyes. No, this was certainly nothing like the measured pace of swordplay, with its repertoire of attacks and responses. This was the dirtiest kind of fighting, where there were no rules, no boundaries, and no set forms. It was a style that Yozerf excelled at, having learned it at an early age on the streets of the city he had been born in.

Having seen how deadly and effective his unconventional style of combat could be, she'd asked him to teach her as well. It had been something to do to get them through the long, harsh months of winter, when snow had fallen heavily enough to isolate Kellsjard from the outside world. Something other than watch the stores in their larders dwindle and wonder what was happening in places poorer and less well-supplied.

"How long did it take you to learn?" she asked.

He shrugged, an easy movement of his thin shoulders that he still managed to make look graceful. "Too long." One white finger lightly tapped the heavy padding that hung over his shirt to protect him should she somehow—against all likelihood, it seemed—manage to hit him. "And of course I didn't have this."

The door leading into the keep opened across the yard. Yozerf turned to look, and Suchen saw his nostrils flare sharply. Over time, she had come to appreciate what a truly keen sense of smell he had. It was one part of his divided heritage: half Aclyte, half Wolfkin shape-changer.

At any rate, the gait of the man who stepped out into the yard identified him at a distance, even to one without a sharp eye or nose. He moved slowly, leaning heavily on a wooden staff topped with a dull globe of steel. The mace head turned the staff into a weapon, at least theoretically, and perhaps took away some of the sting of having to use such a prop in the first place.

"I thought I might find you here," Gless called when he was close enough. His golden hair blew loosely about his face in the biting wind, no longer kept in the dandy's curls that he had once been so fond of. His clothing was sober, at least for him—gone were the wild colors, the flamboyant cuffs and ribbons. Lines of pain framed a mouth that still smiled often, but the smile was wan and drawn, as if every joke was bitter.

Yozerf watched him come, then cocked his head slightly, as if considering. "You may join us, if you wish," he offered. Suchen flashed him a sharp glance—surely, such an offer to a man who needed a staff to walk was nothing but cruelty. But Yozerf's austere face was impassive, a white mask that gave nothing away.

Still, he was not cruel by nature. Many other things, yes— hard, bitter, ruthlessly practical, and at least slightly insane. But never cruel.

Who knows? Maybe he thinks Gless could do it.

Gless gave Yozerf a quizzical look, as if wondering the same things as Suchen. Then a strained smile touched his lips. "No, thanks. You two play too rough. You're the only couple I know who never quarrel and yet still try to kill each other on a regular basis."

Suchen grinned. "That's us—two of a kind." She slipped one arm around Yozerf's waist, beneath the protective padding. Although he had actually gained a little weight over the winter, she could still feel the curve of bone through a layer of tough muscle. Glancing up, she saw surprise and pleasure touch his gray eyes at her comment. His arm went around her shoulders, pulling her in tighter to his side.

Gless rolled his eyes at them. "I didn't come out here to watch the two of you make cow-eyes at each other. Auglar sent me to find you. He's calling together the Sworn and a few other trusted advisors."

"Is this about his bid for the kingship?" Suchen asked softly.

Gless shrugged. "I don't know. It would make sense, though. Spring is here and the roads are finally clear. There's nothing to keep him from going to the Conclave of Lords in Segg."

Yozerf's eyes narrowed slightly at the mention of the city he had grown up in, but he made no comment. They followed Gless back inside, pausing a moment to store their protective padding in the small training hall that formed one wall of the courtyard. Then, confined to Gless's limping pace, they made their way to Auglar's study.

When the keep was first built, back when the Empire of Kells still held dominion over all the lands between the Dragon Mountains in the North and the Undish desert in the south, the fortress of Kellsjard had been a simple square tower made for defense rather than comfort. It occupied a high hill on the very edge of the great plain of the Kellsmarch, situated so that any invasions from the kingdom of Shalai would have to pass by it before penetrating farther. But over the intervening centuries, its lords had added on to the original keep. Most often, this additional architecture matched the fashion of their own times, in blithe disregard of anything else around it. As a result, Kellsjard had evolved into a lunatic's dream of sealed-off courtyards, corridors that went nowhere, and rooms whose purpose had been changed so many times that they were no longer useful for anything. Visitors were well advised not to stray, and even inhabitants who thought themselves familiar with the structure's every twist and turn sometimes became confused. If any enemy were ever to breach the walls, they would find battle in the corridors a nightmare.

Auglar's study was in one of the oldest sections of the keep. The walls were of unfinished stone that held in the chill even in high summer. Tapestries struggled to enliven the setting, although their colors had faded through countless decades. Although the air outside was beginning to feel of spring, a fire burned in the enormous hearth, perfuming the room with wood smoke.

Auglar glanced up as they entered. Black hair straggled into his face and framed a pair of startlingly pale blue eyes, and ink stained his slender fingers. Although he had come young to his lordship, and had fought a bitter war of succession to gain it, scholarship was still his first love. "Ah, that's everyone, then," he said with a smile that failed to hide the worry that lurked in his eyes.

The small room was crowded, Suchen saw. On Auglar's right sat his wife, Sifya, her belly swollen in the late stages of pregnancy. Sifya's brother, Brenwulf, was also present. The Sworn—Buudi, Gless, and Suchen's brother Peddock—were arrayed about the room. Garal, Suchen's assistant, sat nervously at the far end of the table, along with Wildstorm the scribe and Jiara the healermage.

Three empty chairs remained. Gless sank into one with an audible sigh, his bad leg stretched out before him at an angle. Suchen sat in the next one, expecting Yozerf to slip in beside her. But instead he stopped just inside the door and leaned against the wall, his chill eyes taking in the gathering dispassionately, an outsider observing a scene that had nothing to do with him.

Suchen frowned uncertainly, wondering what this deliberate distancing could mean. But before she could motion for him to come closer, Auglar rose to his feet.

"I suppose that there's no mystery about why I summoned you all," he said. Clasping his ink-stained fingers behind his back, he wandered over to one window, then stopped and stared out. "Most of you know the events of last fall and winter."

"Only too well," murmured Buudi, the first among the Sworn. Although silver had begun to streak his black hair some time ago, he seemed to have aged years over the course of the last winter. The lines on his rough face were deeply graven now, and the decades looked out sadly from his brown eyes.

Auglar cast him a rueful glance. "Yes. Last fall, the wizard Ax came to Suchen and asked her to escort a young woman here. Little did we know then that she was Queen Rozah, fleeing in disguise from her Regency Council, which had kept her prisoner and usurped her power. The Council was destroyed, but not without the loss of Rozah's life as well."

No one said anything. The Sworn had been charged with keeping Rozah safe, but they had not been able to save themselves from treason within their own ranks. Although no one could blame them—they had done all that they could—Suchen knew that they held themselves responsible for the Queen's death.

For that matter, so did she. What she would have done differently, she didn't know, but there had been many nights when she had lain awake in Yozerf's arms, wondering if she could have done something—anything—to save Rozah.

As for what Yozerf felt, who had last seen Rozah alive...not even Suchen could say.

"Since then, Jenel has been without a monarch," Auglar continued at last. "This is a dangerous time for the kingdom. Ax warned us that Jahcgroth of Argannon plans to conquer Jenel, as cold and ice threaten to destroy his own kingdom. Yozerf has confirmed this."

Yozerf nodded once, shortly, but said nothing.

"Jenel cannot afford to remain leaderless for much longer," Auglar went on, pacing restlessly back across the room to stare now into the fire. "I am related to the royal line, and so have decided to present my claim to the throne. Unfortunately, word has reached me that Lord Fellrant intends to do the same."

Brenwulf's eyes narrowed. "This is the lord who attacked you when your father disappeared?"

"Yes." Auglar shook his head at old memories. "Fellrant saw an opportunity and took it. He has a reputation for being ruthless in pursuit of what he wants, and if I may judge by the siege he lay around Kellsjard, that reputation is well deserved."

"But we prevailed," Buudi added firmly.

"Yes." Auglar smiled briefly. "And we will this time as well. Both of our claims are too distant for it to be immediately obvious which of us should take the throne. Therefore, we have been commanded to present ourselves before the Conclave of Lords at Nava Nar in Segg." He cast a rueful glance at Sifya's belly, then reached out to take his wife's hand. "The timing is dreadful, of course, but if I want to have any chance against Fellrant, then I have to leave as soon as possible. Sifya will command the keep in my absence."

"The thanes won't be happy about that," Sifya pointed out, her accent giving away her peasant origins.

"The thanes can go to Hel's domain," Auglar said bluntly. "After last winter, they should be glad I don't hang the lot of them." He squeezed Sifya's hand fiercely, then let go. "The Sworn, of course, will accompany me. Jiara will remain here with you." His expression turned wistful. "If I can't be here for the birth of our first child, at least I can be assured that the delivery will be safe and easy."

"You have nothing to worry about, my lord. Either of you," Jiara added, nodding in Sifya's direction.

"Excellent." Auglar rubbed his hands together. "Then that is all, for now. We'll leave as soon as we can. Suchen, see to the supplies we will need for the journey. And if Brenwulf and Yozerf could stay a moment longer?"

At last, Suchen thought with satisfaction. She glanced at Yozerf's face, to see if he guessed what was coming. But wariness lit his gray eyes from within, and a slight frown touched his sculpted lips, quickly hidden.

She rose with the rest, pausing a moment to touch Yozerf's arm. "Don't be so paranoid," she whispered, feeling the tension in the muscles under her fingers. "At least until you know why he wants to talk to you alone."

He nodded sharply, but she could still sense his trepidation. With a sigh, she dropped her hand away and followed everyone else out the door, leaving the three men in privacy.

～⁓

Yozerf remained where he was, his back pressed hard against the stone wall. Dread pooled in his belly, for he thought that he knew what Auglar wanted to ask from him.

The human lord paused a moment to stoke the fire. Brenwulf glanced briefly at the flurry of sparks, then turned his steady gaze back to Yozerf, no doubt scenting the Aclyte's unease. Yozerf pointedly avoided his stare, a wolf's gesture of submission. He and Brenwulf had never been easy with one another—two males, one an interloper, the other jealous of his place in the pack.

Auglar turned so that his back was to the fire. The flames leapt up behind him, framing him in gold and throwing his face into shadow. "You both know that I lost two of my Sworn last winter," he said at last, grief edging his words. "Uzco was killed and Dara-Don...Dara-Don betrayed me and everyone else. Until now, I have done nothing to rebuild the Sworn, partly out of respect for Uzco's memory, and partly out of fear. I kept asking myself how I could have judged Dara-Don so badly."

"He was true when you made him Sworn," Brenwulf said soothingly. Yozerf said nothing—the bonds of the Sworn were forged from trust. And he had learned long ago that trust was the most dangerous trickster of all.

"Perhaps. But I fear that leaving a void in the Sworn has done more harm than good to those who remain. It's been a constant reminder to them of the defeat that they suffered, of the friendship that they lost. I think it's past time to remedy the situation.

"Brenwulf, Yozerf—I am asking the two of you to become Sworn to me."

It was the highest honor any lord could offer a retainer, short of raising him to the nobility itself. Brenwulf immediately came to his feet, smiling. "Of course, Auglar. You're my sister's mate—part of my pack. I would do anything for you."

Auglar clasped his hand warmly. "I knew that already, Brenwulf." Still smiling, he turned to Yozerf. "And you, my friend? You saved my life last winter—I haven't forgotten that, and now at last I have an appropriate reward."

For a long moment, Yozerf simply stared at him, surprise holding back any motion or word. And it came to him with a sudden clarity that he knew two things.

One: that Auglar was offering him a place. A *real* place.

No more sulking on the edges of their comradeship, watching from a slight remove that he could never quite seem to cross. No more the outsider that no one really knew what to do with. No more the unsheathed blade that was too useful to throw away, but never really trusted.

A place. Belonging.

The Sworn were the men that a lord trusted above all others, even above his own kin. Their obligations to him were clear: to protect, to advise, and in the end perhaps to die. Their lord valued them above all others, but in turn they valued him equally. Their bond went deeper in its way than that of blood or marriage.

He already had a sort of bond with them—didn't he? They— all of the people who had gathered in this room—were his pack. But that deep instinct, informed by the wolf's understanding, meant less in human terms than what Auglar offered now. Or perhaps it was simply that humans needed words for these things to make them real, and that was what Kellsjard's lord wanted to give him. Acknowledgement of the bond from both sides, not just his.

It was more than he had ever thought to be given, more than

he had ever dreamed of having in the long, hungry years when he had wandered alone.

But he also knew a second thing. Auglar wanted to be king.

Yozerf meet Auglar's expectant gaze and held it for a moment. "No," he said clearly, then turned and walked out the door.

~~

Yozerf took the nearest stair he came to, following its windings until he reached a window that let out onto a rooftop. Unseen by anyone, he slipped out onto an expanse of blue slate tiles, following them until they gave way to copper sheeting, then red pottery. Gargoyles offered convenient handholds, their smooth-horned heads cold under his thin fingers. Fragrant smoke belched from chimneys, occasionally blowing into his face and blinding him.

At length, he came to a high tower at the North end of the keep. He had discovered it by accident one night, its crumbling masonry giving him the handholds he needed to haul himself up through its single, high window. A heavy wooden shutter had blocked the way, but the iron hinges holding it in place had rusted almost to nothingness, and he had found it easy to push through.

Kellsjard had many rooms and corridors that had been sealed off during later building sprees, and at first glance he had believed this tower to be one such forgotten nook. A single rotting table and chair stood in the center of the tiny room, adrift in mounds of dust and cobwebs. The round shape hanging on one wall had proved to be a bronze mirror, lost beneath centuries of grime. Curious, he had let himself down through the trap door in the floor of the room, following a spiral stair until it ended abruptly in the solid wall whose construction had led to the tower's abandonment.

She had been lying at the bottom of the stair, curled against the unyielding wall, as if she had tried at the last to force down the stones with her bare hands. Time had not left much of her: a few mice-gnawed bones, a red layer of dust that might have been a dress, and the dull glitter of gold at her ears, throat, and waist. Yozerf did not know who she had been, or why she had been sealed away in the tower and left to die. A rival, a mistress, a sister? With humans, the possibilities for cruelty were endless.

A few questions to the servants revealed that the portion of the keep near the sealed tower was said to be haunted by a woman's ghost, although no one knew her story. Yozerf briefly considered telling Auglar of the old bones he had found, then decided against it. Better to leave the unknown woman her silent monument.

Since then, he had made the tower his sanctuary, a place where he could escape to be away from humans and where he could plumb the depths of his own secrets in solitude. Only once in all the months that he had been coming here had he glimpsed the ghost of the dead woman. Shortly after deciding to make the tower room his own, he had entered to find her standing by the table: a thin, transparent shape in a red dress. She had started towards him—then flung up her hands in an expression of horror and fled, vanishing before she reached the trap door.

"*Shadows,*" Telmonra had whispered with a nasty chuckle.

And what are you? he had asked in that silent space in his mind where she could hear him.

"*Vengeance.*"

Now, Yozerf hauled himself in over the windowsill and carefully replaced what was left of the broken shutters behind him, blocking the thin, gray light of the overcast afternoon. The darkness in the tower was nearly absolute, but he had supplied it with tallow candles filched from the storerooms. Recalling their shapes and placement in his memory, he reached into the silent space once again.

The candles burst into simultaneous flame, flooding the small chamber with yellow light. Cobwebs that he had not bothered to clear away streamed wildly in the sudden flow of heated air, like the rotted banners of dead armies.

Yozerf sighed and ran a hand back through his hair, absently tugging out the snarls the wind had worked into it. It was a trick, that was all, just a damned trick. A trick that had taken him long practice to perfect to the point where he wasn't in danger of setting himself on fire as well as the candles, but still nothing compared to the feats of a real wizard. Nothing compared to what Auglar needed.

And even if it had been what Auglar needed…would he—dared he—admit that he could perform such tricks?

The single chair creaked dangerously under him when he slumped into it. The candles glowed in his sight, threatening to become a blur. Suddenly feeling tired beyond words, he propped his boots up on the ancient table and tilted his head back, staring unseeing at the wheel-spoke rafters.

He was tired, so very tired. The look that he had glimpsed on Auglar's face just before he walked out came back to him: shock, confusion…and hurt. Strange beyond words, to think that any gesture he could make would hurt a powerful human lord. Before meeting Auglar, he had thought that the mighty were beyond such things because they cared for nothing save themselves.

He didn't want to imagine the look on Suchen's face when she found out.

"They are humans," Telmonra whispered scornfully, as if that damning statement should be all that was needed. At one time, it would have been.

He was not entirely certain that all changes had been for the better.

∼≈∼

Suchen sat in her favorite chair in front of the fire, unable to concentrate on the book she had been trying to read for hours. The candles on the small table at her elbow had burned down, spilling long loops of melted wax over the silver of the candelabrum. The wind moaned around the cornice outside the window and caused the fire to gutter slightly.

The heavy, oaken door swung open on near-silent hinges. Setting her book aside carefully, she looked up at the shadow that filled it. The firelight snagged on his mad tangle of blood-red hair and lent unnatural color to the pale skin of his face and hands. His large, canted eyes reflected it like the wolf's, an eerie incandescence that stole her ability to read his expression.

"Why?" she asked simply, careful not the make the word an accusation.

Yozerf's mouth tightened slightly. He shut the door behind him, then drifted past her to the window. One hand lifted, pressed lightly against the glass. "Do you have to ask?"

"Obviously I do."

He sighed and slumped a little. "Suchen...think. Auglar wants to be king. But right now, his fate is largely in the hands of a group of southern lords who only want a reason not to like him. The first of Auglar's Sworn is a disgraced nobleman who lost his inheritance because he was having an affair with another man. Peddock is the disowned son of a merchant. Gless is a peasant. And Brenwulf is a constant reminder that Auglar is married to a commoner." Yozerf's mouth quirked into a sudden half-smile. "That motley assortment alone might give the southern lords all the excuse they need to send Auglar packing. Add an Aclyte to the mix, and I assure you that it would."

She started to deny his words, then caught herself, forced herself to think about all the things she had encountered traveling with him. And, although she didn't like it, forced herself to remember her own childhood in the south, a life that had included Aclytese servants who were viewed as little more than trained dogs whose performance had long ago lost its novelty. "Perhaps."

"Perhaps nothing. Yes. You know it. Auglar isn't thinking like a southern lord."

"Auglar isn't a southern lord."

"He must become one if he wants their approval." Yozerf shook his head, hair sighing softly against black-clad shoulders. "Auglar and Fellrant are both used to doing things as they wish. Until now, no one paid much attention to the demesnes of the Kellsmarch. Who cares about a land of herdsmen and farmers, where there isn't anything to be found but grass and wind?"

"You're overstating the case."

"Maybe." He shrugged. "It doesn't change my point."

"No." She sighed and looked at her hands. "Auglar wants to leave as soon as possible. Within the next few days if he can."

"Good luck to him, then."

"I'm going with him."

Yozerf's back stiffened sharply. She saw the hand that rested on the glass curl very, very slowly into a fist. When he spoke, his voice was like the winter come inside. "No."

"Yozerf—"

"*No!*" He spun around, and his gray eyes were wild with desperation. "You aren't going to Segg!"

She bit her lip, hating the mix of rage and fear in his words. "The decision is already made. Auglar needs me. If he is to become king, he will need a Steward."

"Let Garal go."

"Garal isn't as good at this as I am!" she snapped, temper suddenly fraying. "I am the Steward of Kellsjard. No woman has ever done what I've done. If I become Steward of Nava Nar...can you imagine what it would mean?"

His expression went blank, face a white, inhuman mask that allowed nothing to escape. "Then this is what you want."

Suchen hesitated. "I...I don't know. But Auglar has asked me to come with him, even if only for a while. If he does become king, he will need my help, at least at first. There's no telling what sort of mess the Council left behind them—he'll need someone who can look through the books, who can understand what the numbers mean and where they don't add up. For a little while."

Yozerf said nothing. For a moment, he stood very still, as if weighing her words against some unknown criteria. Then, without warning, he turned and smashed his fist through one of the glass panes of the window.

"No!" Startled by the suddenness and violence of the motion, she grabbed his arm. Through layers of black cotton and wool, she felt muscles tense as wires. But he made no movement to repeat the act, only turned his hand over slowly. The glass had cut his knuckles deeply, and streamers of blood the same color as his hair ran out over white skin.

"I'm sorry," he said softly. He closed his eyes for a moment, as if in response to some pain. "I just...I can't...."

"Shh. It's all right. No one's asking you to do anything." She tugged on his arm gently, and he allowed himself to be led over to the light of the fire. Suchen carefully picked out shards of glass from the wounds, then fetched a pewter ewer filled with water to wash them. When she shoved his sleeve back to keep it from getting wet, her fingers encountered the ridges of old scars that crisscrossed the great veins of both wrists.

Those scars had been made in Segg, she knew, although it was not something he spoke of often or in detail. And she had known that he would be upset when she told him that she was going there herself. "I'm not asking you to go," she said quietly as she bandaged his hand with cloth torn from an old shift. "You know that you are more important to me than anything—even my duty to Auglar." She glanced up, met his wild, inhuman eyes. "I am going because I have to, but if you want to stay here, then I will return to you as soon as I may. Someone else can be Steward of Nava Nar."

"I don't want you to die."

It was such an unexpected response that she stopped in mid-motion. "What? Why do you say that?"

"Because that's what Segg is, Suchen. It's death, death in a thousand forms." He pulled his hand away and ran it back through his hair. "Death for the unwary, death for the foolish, death for the young, death for the weak, death for the poor, death...death." Yozerf stood up abruptly and stared down at her, a crazed look in his eye. "It will swallow you. It will swallow all of you."

Grief for him touched her. "Yozerf, my love, no. You say that because of your own experiences. But things will be different for us. We'll be staying at the palace, not on the streets. We'll be safe."

He looked at her sadly. "You're wrong."

"No." She put her hand on his unwounded one, drew it close to cradle against her face. "I'll be all right. You stay here—I'll be back soon, you'll see."

"I can't stay here," he said raggedly. "I *can't* stay here. You're my mate; you're my pack. Where you go, I must go as well."

The desperation in his gray eyes tore at her heart. "Do you mean that?" she asked, uncertain what instincts might be ripping him apart. If he'd been human, or even purely Aclyte, she would have thought that he was exaggerating. But the way he said *mate* and *pack* made the words sound less like concepts and more like something felt in the blood and the bone.

He pulled away from her and went back to the window, despite the cold evening air flooding in through the broken panes. His head leaned wearily against the casement as he stared blankly out. "Yes."

"I don't want to hurt you."

"It doesn't matter."

"Yes, it does!"

He only shook his head, not looking at her—not looking at anything as far as she could tell. "No. I'll go with you. I don't mind." And the way he spoke the lie told her that she would get nothing more from him.

Chapter Two

Yozerf stared out the window, watching as the caravan made ready in the courtyard below. The cold, gray light that precedes sunrise touched the sky, outlining the shapes of men and horses. Their breath steamed in the cold morning, and lacy frost glittered from stones and roof tiles. In the south, he knew, frost would be nothing more than a memory by now.

In the south. In Segg.

He closed his eyes tiredly and wondered if he would ever see Kellsjard again, despite Suchen's assurances. Voices whispered to him; memories of the dead and the damned.

"You will do as I tell you, you stupid git, or I'll beat you until there's not a scrap of hide left to keep you warm!"

"What's wrong with you? Emasculated whore!"

"I have failed you, my son."

He had not thought of them in years—had deliberately shunted them away, buried them down in the dark places—but now they seemed more clear than what had happened yesterday. He could remember them all: Daryn's calculating cruelty, Sweet Gin's desperate need, and Londah's pitiless gaze.

Most of the faces he had known would be gone now, swallowed by one of the many deaths that stalked the streets. Londah would be there, though; few things walked the night more dangerous than she. It had been over three years since he had last seen her, but she would come to his side if he asked.

If he could figure out a way of explaining a human mate and a human pack to her. If she didn't think that he was nothing more than a gullible fool.

And, Hel, who knows, he thought darkly. *Perhaps I am, at that.*

Suchen emerged from the bedroom they had shared, her pack slung over her shoulder. "Ready?" she asked, smothering a yawn behind her hand.

For a moment she looked vulnerable to him, with her disheveled blonde hair and blue eyes like wells onto midnight. But that was ridiculous; there was nothing delicate or fragile about her. Her body was wiry and tough from years of sword practice with the Sworn and from the harsh Northern winters. She was determined, defiant, strong, and free, and just looking at her made his heart ache.

Perhaps Londah would love her, after all.

He bent and picked up his own pack; although light, at the moment it felt as though he lifted the weight of the world itself. "Yes, I'm ready," he answered, but it was a lie. He would never be ready for this.

✿✿

The journey was both too long and too short to Yozerf's mind. He had never traveled with a large group before, and the slow pace of the oxen pulling the wagons was a frustration to him. On the other hand, the caravan could stick to the easy road of the Great Trade Route, rather than take the more furtive paths that he had always been consigned to. Bandits still lurked on the Route, of course, but the size of the convoy along with its contingent of armed soldiers ensured that any highwaymen would stay far away.

He spent the days riding by Suchen's side and trying not to think of the destination that lay ahead. Buudi, Peddock, and Brenwulf were more reserved with him than they had been in many months, doubtless because of his refusal to join their ranks. If no one had been quite sure what to do with him before, it was doubly true now that he had confirmed his status as an outsider.

Despite Auglar's original request that all the Sworn accompany him to Segg, Gless had remained behind at Kellsjard, ostensibly to watch over Sifya. Although no one had spoken of it aloud, Yozerf strongly suspected that the true reason was that Gless no longer felt of any use to his lord. The wound that had crippled his leg had also crippled his spirit, as if all of his worth had depended on his ability to walk unaided. To his surprise, it had saddened Yozerf to see the cheerful soul replaced by a withdrawn, embittered shell.

But then, perhaps that happens to us all, in the end.

The day before the caravan was set to reach Rhiaht, the first true city on their journey, outriders came back with the report of another large convoy before them. As they drew closer, they saw that the other party had stopped and awaited their arrival. Several flags whipped and cracked in the breeze, displaying a black eagle on a purple field.

"Lord Fellrant," Buudi observed unnecessarily.

Auglar nodded once, sharply. "Raise our own colors."

Banners bearing the white horse on a blue field quickly rose, as if answering a challenge. Once they were within shouting distance, Auglar called a halt. Silence fell as the last wains creaked into place, and the two convoys sat staring at one another like opposing armies. Yozerf felt the hair on his neck stand up instinctively, and his lip twitched with the urge to growl.

Three men rode out to meet them. Two of them were clearly retainers, but the third caught Yozerf's attention instantly. He was young, possibly several years Auglar's junior. Raven-black hair streamed to his waist, bound back from his eyes with a fillet set with dark blue stones the size of a man's palm. Sumptuous purple and black fabrics covered a small, lithe body. His features were delicate, almost feminine, with a sensuous mouth and seductive eyes. Yozerf frowned and glanced at Suchen, wondering if he should be jealous of the other man's beauty.

Auglar urged his horse out in front of his caravan, Buudi and Brenwulf flanking him. "Fellrant," he said, voice flat with distaste.

Yozerf felt a flash of surprise. Was this *youth* the fearsome Lord who ruled from his keep of Vorslava with an iron hand? The man who, it was rumored, had first terrorized the bandits of the Kellsmarch, then forced them to work for him? Who had laid such fierce siege to Kellsjard that everyone inside had truly feared that the keep would fall for the first time in its centuries-spanning history?

Fellrant smiled, apparently at ease. "Ah, Auglar, I thought that might be you hurrying to catch up."

Auglar didn't return the smile. "Let me remind you that *both* of us are expected to arrive at the Conclave. I doubt that the southern lords will look with favor upon any attempts to diminish that number."

Fellrant arched a perfect brow, still unperturbed. "Such harsh words."

"I haven't forgotten your little war against me."

Fellrant waved a languid hand. "The folly of a boy, Auglar. I was only fifteen at the time, after all. Youth is known for its impetuousness."

"Somehow I don't find that to be an excuse for your behavior."

"As you wish." Fellrant shrugged. "But our demesnes have been at peace ever since then, have they not? And seeing that you and I are traveling the same way, there's no reason that two neighbors can't make the journey to the Conclave together."

Auglar scowled, but there was nothing he could say to counter Fellrant's gracious attitude. At his stiff nod, Fellrant turned his

mount back to his own convoy and signaled for them to begin
moving once again. The two lords fell in beside one another, their
respective Sworn mingling nervously, with many a hard glare exchanged. As the caravan once again began its lurching progress,
Yozerf urged Windshade closer to Suchen.

"I didn't know he was that young," he said.

Suchen's mouth quirked in distaste. "Yes. He became Lord of
Vorslava when he was twelve. I gather that no one thought he would
survive for long, given the back-stabbing and conniving that was
going on there at the time. But he not only survived—he pros-
pered. It only took him three years to have his demesne so completely under his control that he could start thinking about attacking his neighbors." She shivered. "He must have been a monstrous
child."

"Perhaps."

She gave him a sharp glance. "Surely you don't admire him?"

"No. No, of course not," Yozerf said. It wasn't quite a lie, he
thought. Rumor attributed every kind of ruthless tactic imaginable
to Fellrant, down to burning entire villages whenever he believed
they might be harboring rebels. He allowed no challenge to his
authority, no matter the source, and was pitiless when it came to
scouring the countryside clean of any potential rivals.

But...he had managed to survive when the odds were clearly
against it. He had acted ruthlessly when the situation called for it,
not allowing sentiment or folly to cloud his mind. If an accident of
birth had determined his status, it was Fellrant himself who had
earned that status by managing to keep it.

And would I have done anything differently?

The ghost in his head stirred, apparently intrigued by his
thoughts. *"Of course,"* she whispered, then laughed softly. *"You
are Jonaglir. You would have been a hundred times more ruthless and cruel than Fellrant could ever dream of being. My pretty,
pretty boy."*

Despite the warmth of the spring sun shining on his black
cloak, Yozerf shivered.

☙❧

When the caravan halted that night, the two lords set their
tents on opposite sides of the encampment. The convoys mingled
at the mess, servants talking and laughing with one another, uncaring about old wars that had been fought by their supposed betters. The soldiers were more ill at ease, and tried their best to stay
apart despite being assigned watches together. Auglar's Sworn clung
to his side like burrs, as if they expected assassins dressed in

Fellrant's colors to spring out of the shadows at any second.

Yozerf and Suchen shared a small tent pitched near Auglar's. After a quiet supper, Yozerf headed out to stand the first watch of the night. The hours passed uneventfully until another of Auglar's guards relieved him. Leaving the man to fight back yawns, he slipped through the camp like an invading shadow.

The camp was a maze of half-seen tents and tether ropes. The air stank of humans, horses, oxen, and cooked food. Yozerf threaded his way between tents, supply wagons, and latrines, habit making him careful to avoid the revealing firelight of the few groups still awake at this late hour.

The scent of lavender touched the breeze unexpectedly, and he slowed, his eyes making out a still, slim shape standing alone between two supply wains. Moonlight flashed off blue gems as the figure turned towards him. Startled, Yozerf stopped, all his muscles going tense. A growl tried to crawl up his throat, but he bit it back hard. Foolish as it seemed, his behavior would ultimately reflect on Auglar, and he would not give this man any more weapons to use than he already had.

"Good evening," Fellrant said pleasantly, as if they were meeting in a comfortable study instead of a mud-churned slot in a sleeping camp. "Yozerf, isn't it?"

Yozerf's eyes narrowed. He was used to being anonymous in the eyes of the powerful, merely a nameless bit of scenery for their eyes to skip over. To be honest, the change now did not sit well with him at all. "How do you know my name?"

"I've made it a point to learn the names of all Auglar's chief retainers. As a courtesy, of course. Although I'm not entirely certain what your status is."

Yozerf ignored the question. "Shouldn't your Sworn be with you?"

Fellrant made a dismissive gesture. "Oh, they're about someplace, I'm sure. Why? Do you think I'm in some sort of danger here?" He smiled as he spoke, sensuous mouth curving. His beautiful eyes studied Yozerf curiously.

"You are among your own kind, Lord Fellrant. I'm certain that I don't have to tell you the danger of that."

To his surprise, Fellrant chuckled. "No. No, you don't. Although your candor surprises me, a little. Most would hurry to flatter my ego, tell me that of course no one would ever think to harm me. As if I were fool enough to believe *that*."

The conversation was going nowhere. *What can he want?* Yozerf wondered. Aloud, he said, "It's never been my habit to bandy words."

"So I see." Fellrant paused, still studying him thoughtfully. "They tell me that you saved Auglar's life."

Yozerf cocked his head, feigning surprise. "They?"

"Servants talk while the mighty argue. I'm not so stupid that I don't know the value of gossip. Is it true?"

Yozerf hesitated, then wondered what it could possibly matter. "Yes."

"Ah." Fellrant nodded slowly. "I hope that Auglar at least offered you a gift of land."

Yozerf stiffened, anger slicing through him. "Don't taunt me. Aclytes aren't allowed to own property in Jenel."

Fellrant tilted his head back and met Yozerf's baleful stare squarely. "True. But clever people have figured out ways around the restriction before. One of my thanes is, in fact, merely a legal fiction who allows an Aclyte to 'manage' his land for him."

Their eyes continued to hold, indigo versus dragon gray. Although Yozerf had long ago discovered that most humans couldn't meet his gaze for more than a few moments, Fellrant showed no sign of looking away. Disconcerted, Yozerf yawned elaborately, breaking the stare. "A tenuous position at best. He could lose all that he has in a moment."

"That's true of everything in life, isn't it?" Fellrant shrugged. "He thought it worth the opportunity. But perhaps you didn't. I'm assuming that Auglar did offer you the same reward that he would have given a human man, of course."

Yozerf held himself very still, refusing to allow any emotion to show on his face. "Of course," he lied.

"Good." Fellrant smiled. "Very good. Well, I'd best be off to my bed before my Sworn become worried. Give my greeting to your lady."

The young lord turned and walked away, his gait lithe and graceful. Yozerf stared after him, wondering what the point of the conversation had been. Fellrant had deliberately waited there for him...but why? What possible motive could he have for seeking out an Aclyte with no real position or power?

"Looking for any advantage, any weakness, of course," Telmonra said. *"You are in Auglar's inner circle...but not. Fellrant wishes to find your anger, to turn it to his cause. He does not know that we will have our revenge."*

Her words made him uneasy. *What do you mean?*

But she gave him no reply.

※

In his dreams, that night, he saw her memories. They came

slowly, like the gradual rise of dark water, filling the spaces of his own sleeping thoughts, until they burst suddenly into being, a scene clear and sharp as no dream could ever be.

The mountain wind was bitter, carrying the taste of winter even in the midst of spring. The wildflowers that covered the lower slopes could find no purchase here, not in this world of rock and wind and merciless sky.

The wind tore at Mazande's hair as she walked slowly towards the Stone, her gait as even and inevitable as doom. Her dress whipped about her legs, as if seeking to halt her steps. Telmonra searched her face as Mazande walked past, seeking some flicker of apprehension, some spark of regret. But Mazande was Jonaglir, and her gray eyes were like the mountain slope: bleak, hard, and lifeless.

The entire clan had gathered, as tradition required. The entire clan save for Jahcgroth, at least; he had gone into the North many years ago, before Telmonra was born, and no one looked for him to return again.

Small children not yet honed by blood and magic stared bewildered at Mazande, not understanding what they saw. One of them called out her name and was quickly hushed by an impassive adult. They would learn soon enough, Telmonra thought; everyone did. Born into a clan of sorcerers, where madness threaded through their genealogy like a malignant growth...they did not have much choice.

Mazande's path led her to the foot of the Stone, where she stopped. The Stone dominated the glade, commanding attention, its dark surface seeming to drink in the clear light of the day. Twice the height of a horse, so wide that twenty men with their arms outstretched could barely join hands around it, the enormous stone was the remnant of whatever violence had given birth to the mountain. Its rough black basalt was the same as that which formed the rest of the two ranges, which enclosed Caden in protective arms. Born of fire, the mages said, one with the mountain. And through magic, one with all the land.

Mazande's eyes scanned its surface, as if seeking the blood left behind by earlier Sacrifices. Those not of Jonaglir, who had never seen the Stone, claimed that the spilled blood of Osha the First King could still be seen atop its dark mass. It had taken him nearly three days to die, the killing slow so that as much of his life as possible could soak into the Stone and the magic his wizards had set about it.

Blood to bind to blood, blood to bind to earth, blood to bind to power. Forever, until the world's ending.

*Girith flinched suddenly and looked away. Blood-red hair—
a gift from a Trihychyl grandfather—whipped into his eyes. Court
gossip said that he had begged her to reconsider her Sacrifice. If
rumor was true, he should have known better, Telmonra thought.
Changing one's mind was not a trait their clan had ever held to
be valuable.*

*King Osha, the fourteenth of that name, cast a sharp glance
at his youngest son's unseemly display. Then, stepping past
Girith, he went to stand beside Mazande. He raised his arms,
dark blue sleeves flapping in the wind like wings. A slender fillet
of gold held back his pale lavender hair, lending him an air of
formality even in this family gathering.*

*"Do you, Mazande Jonaglir, come here of your free will, to
make Sacrifice for your land and your people?" he intoned. His
baritone carried clearly even over the moan of the wind, the
cawing of the crows.*

*She nodded once, stiffly. "I come here to give my life to the
Stone, so that I might rise up anew to protect this land and this
people."*

*It was an old, old ritual, originally spoken on this very spot
by Osha the First and his wizard daughter over three thousand
years before. A tingle went up Telmonra's spine, causing the
hair on the nape of her neck to prickle. It was as if, she thought,
something had heard the ancient words, and stirred to sluggish
wakefulness. She felt it along her veins, along her nerves, an
odd sense of anticipation that was both elating and frightening.
Girith jerked his head up and moaned, as if to deny the feeling
that moved in his blood. And Osha...her father's eyes burned
like stars, bright and wild with power.*

*There was no more to the ritual exchange; Mazande had
spoken the last words she would ever utter. In silence, she
stripped out of her simple dress, tossing it aside to stand naked
and shivering in the cold air. Osha reached into his robes and
withdrew a silver-hilted dagger. Its edge gleamed razor-sharp
as he slipped it from its ornamental sheath and offered it to her.*

*Mazande took it and moved past him to stand directly be-
fore the Stone. The Stone was not completely vertical, and water and time had carved out a shallow basin at its foot. Mazande
crouched down over it, her raven-black hair spilling down to either side. Then, with a single, quick motion, she drew the edge
of the dagger across her throat.*

*Blood gushed from the wound, a torrent that poured into the
basin. Even as it touched the Stone, however, its substance vanished, as if swallowed into the mountain itself. As if swallowed*

by whatever consciousness lay beneath the Stone.

Tendrils of golden light lifted from the basalt, washing over Mazande. The cut at her throat sealed closed, and for a moment she stared back at those watching, as normal as if nothing had ever happened.

Then, suddenly, her body contorted as if racked by excruciating pain. A scream so anguished it sounded more animal than Aclytese burst from her throat. Even as her family watched in horror, fascination, and awe, she began to change.

Her slender body writhed, bones shifting under the skin. Muscles altered their dimensions, found new points to attach to the deforming skeleton. Her hair fell away in great clumps, revealing an elongated skull. The skin atop it stretched, until suddenly a pair of spiral, back-swept horns burst forth, to be joined moments later by two shorter, straighter horns. Delicate features became a long muzzle, and tough hide replaced ivory skin. Nails became talons, and a long tail whipped out behind.

Her body began to swell, growing until it was the size of a horse. A hump formed on her back as new muscles grew, until a pair of bat-like wings suddenly unfolded, thrashing madly in the air.

And then it was over.

Gods, she's beautiful, *Telmonra thought in awe.*

The new dragon rose up on shaky legs. Her vast wings spread out to either side, gleaming in the sun. Her hide was an incredible hue of slate-blue, flawless. Talons gouged the earth, and muscles rippled with proud strength as she levered herself away from the basin and the Stone.

Lids opened, revealing a pair of gray eyes that were so like Mazande's own that Telmonra felt a stab of unexpected pain. The dragon looked about, and there might have been confusion in her gaze. Or regret.

But it was too late for regrets. Dragons were impervious to outside magic; that and their fiery breath were their great strengths. The most powerful wizard in all the world couldn't give Mazande's Aclytese body back to her.

An imperious call, like three harsh barks, rang off the cliffs. Telmonra looked up, saw the other four dragons circling high overhead. They were beautiful, and exquisitely graceful, yet she who had been Mazande Jonaglir visibly hesitated to join them.

Three harsh barks, repeated. Do they tell her to come, to forget her life as a woman? *Telmonra wondered, her stare locked on the muzzled countenance that had once been her cousin. No one knew whether dragons even spoke to one another, or merely*

*made primitive sounds like any other animal. The only thing
known for certain was that, over time, even the most reluctant
and uncertain of them gradually lost whatever it was that had
made them Aclytes, and became wild creatures of wind and fire.
In time, Mazande might not even remember that she had ever
been anything save a dragon.*

༄ ༄

For the next two weeks, they traveled through the light forests
and open fields of southern Jenel. As they continued to make their
way south and east, spring advanced and the days became hotter.
Northern-bred men and women sweated uncomfortably, stripping
off all the heavy clothing they had and wondering if they would be
reduced to their undergarments by the time they reached Segg.
Having grown up with the heat, Yozerf laughed silently at his companions. If they thought this was uncomfortable, they didn't want
to be in Segg during high summer.

He encountered Fellrant several more times during the journey. Not every day, but frequently enough to suspect that chance
was not involved. The lord's words were briefer to him than they
had been the first night, but were unfailingly polite and pleasant.

I know a seduction when I see it, Yozerf thought darkly after
once such encounter. *But of what sort? There would be better
ways to get to Auglar, surely, if that is what he intends. And if
it's the other kind...he implied the first night that he knows I am
Suchen's mate. There are always plenty of camp followers to
choose from—why me?*

"*Because none of them are you?*" Telmonra suggested. He
couldn't tell whether the comment was meant to be amusing or
serious. "*Either way, the words he's spoken to you have been
nothing but truth, have they?*"

He didn't know how much of his thoughts she could share,
but he tried to keep any acknowledgment of her words hidden.
Instead, he countered, *You've been talkative lately. Why? Why
now?*

A soft sigh hissed like the wind through his head.

Yozerf wondered whether he should be frightened by her more-
active presence as of late. She had grown stronger over the months,
but much of that might have come from his own acceptance of her
gifts as he learned to utilize the magic she gave him. But either
way...should he be worried? And if so...of what? Telmonra spoke
to him, yes, but that was all the power she seemed to have.

Desperately, he wished he could talk about it to Suchen, ask
her what she thought. But of course he had sealed that path off

from himself months ago when he had neglected to tell her about his initial suspicions that something strange had returned with him from the other side of death.

It wasn't worth the chance, he reminded himself. What if he had told her—had told any of them—that he had killed a man with sorcerous fire, but was unable to actually recall it happening? Would they have believed him? Or would they fear him? His relationship with Suchen was so new, so unexpected, so precious…nothing was worth putting it at risk.

And later, after Rozah's death…he had not been able to tell them the truth then, either. If he had told them everything he had held back before, had revealed that he had awakened fully to the strange powers the ghost gave him and used them to destroy the Council, they would have wanted to know the truth about what had happened to Rozah as well. And if he had said that she had not been killed by the spell at all, that she had given her own life to save his…well, who would believe such a thing? Queens did not die for lowly Aclytes.

It was my fault she died. For a moment, his memory of Rozah's pale, heart-shaped face altered to become a darker, though no less lovely, countenance.

But no. He would not think of Ginny now, not with Segg so near.

✦

Suchen's first glimpse of Segg was not at all what she had expected.

On a hot morning in late spring, the caravan finally came down out of the low hills that covered southern Jenel. Before them ran a wide, high road paved with crushed shells bleached white by the sun. The road had been built up to keep it above the level of the thick marshes that stretched away to either side as far as the eye could see. Shadows lurked beneath dense stands of cypress, and strange mossy growths dangled from the trees like the beards of ancient men. Birds called from the mysterious depths of the swamps, and the buzz and hum of insects filled the air. Already, everyone was slapping at exposed skin and cursing the army of mosquitoes that had descended upon them.

Segg was nestled directly in between the two halves of the swamp. Although still distant, Suchen could see the faint gleam of white marble on the highest points of the city, fading into a gray-brown blur as it descended towards the docks. Beyond, she caught her first glimpse of the sea.

The air smelled of salt, decay, and living things. Whether the stink came from the city, the ocean, the swamps, or all three, Suchen was unsure. Glancing over at Yozerf, she saw his nostrils flare sharply. Then he turned his head away, eyes closed, as if to deny some pain.

"Love?" she asked softly. After a moment, he looked her way. His face was pale, his expression distant and cold. She could feel him withdraw into himself, like a snail retreating into its shell. "Will you be all right?"

He hesitated for an instant, then shrugged carelessly. "I'll have to be, won't I?"

"You don't have to do this."

"It's too late to turn back." He sighed, and the corner of his mouth quirked up into a half-smile. "Too late for a lot of things."

Troubled, she reached out to take his hand. He gave her fingers a brief squeeze, then let go.

The two lords had agreed to enter the city together, as equals. Their Sworn clustered nervously about them, and their banner-carriers rode in front. Fellrant dispatched a herald to go before everyone, blowing a horn periodically and announcing the approach of the two lords.

The high road ran in a straight line that ended at the city wall. Unlike most other city walls Suchen had seen, this one was made from baked mud brick rather than stone. The gate piercing the wall was enormous, large enough to let several ox-drawn wains through at once, and guarded by two massive doors of blackened iron wrought into fantastical patterns. On the other side, a crowd of merchants and farmers milled amidst bleating livestock, their progress out the gate impeded to let the lords through. As the caravan entered, men in what Suchen guessed must be the livery of the city guard snapped to attention, but their eyes were jaded, as if they saw nobility every day. Considering that most of the southern lords visited Segg routinely, perhaps they did.

The city exploded around them as soon as they passed through the gates. The air rang with the thunder of wheels over cobblestone streets, the shouting of vendors, the bray of donkeys, and the rumble of conversation. The humid air was full of the smell of cooking food, combined with perfume, incense, rotting fish, dung, and unwashed bodies. Sumptuous litters curtained in silk carried women dressed in all the colors of the rainbow, while tumblers in motley performed on the corners. Men in the doublet, cape, and hosen costume of southern Jenel passed Undish merchants clad in flowing robes, while sailors wearing little more than pantaloons and vests stepped around beggars in rags. Even the people themselves looked different; amidst the skin tones she was used to seeing, Suchen caught a glimpse of a man as dark as mahogany.

Feeling utterly overwhelmed, Suchen bit her lip and tried to hold her head high. "Is it always...this busy?" she asked uncertainly.

Yozerf glanced at her briefly, his expression unreadable. "We're near Market Square," he said. "And this is one of the main thoroughfares. Other parts of the city are quieter...at least in the daylight."

Soon after entering the city, they turned to the right, heading North. Although some of the wild commotion of the marketplace fell away, people still thronged the streets, many of them waving scraps of cloth in either Auglar's blue-and-white or Fellrant's black-and-purple. A few adults held children on their shoulders, so that they could catch a glimpse of the two contenders for the throne. Both lords smiled and waved pleasantly, as if the opinion of those watching could possibly make any difference.

The character of the streets changed quickly once they were away from the main thoroughfare. Shops and warehouses gave way to residential buildings, which themselves gradually went from townhouses to small mansions surrounded by walled gardens. Eventually, the wide, tree-lined avenue came to a sudden halt, and the palace and its grounds opened up before them.

Nava Nar, the ancient seat of power, was as unlike Kellsjard as Suchen could have imagined. Sunlight flashed on marble and gleamed off a copper dome. Wide colonnades let in the breeze from the sea. Expansive gardens rushed outwards from the palace, dark hedges and tall trees haunted with the cries of strange birds and beasts. In the distance, she caught sight of a lake speckled with swans, a golden barge at rest beside them.

A great crowd had gathered outside the palace. As the caravan approached, grooms and other servants broke away, hurrying to take horses or direct the wains. The servants and guards within the convoy fell back, until at last only a small contingent consisting of the two lords, their Sworn, and a few other high-ranking retainers remained. Suchen saw Auglar straighten his back and take a deep breath, as if preparing himself for battle. Beside him, Fellrant looked utterly at ease, a faint smile on his beautiful lips, as if all this was a play put on for his benefit.

Seven men stood at the front of the waiting crowd, a line of guards behind them. They were all sumptuously dressed in furs and silks, with jewels flashing on fingers and around throats. Sweat gleamed on their faces, and Suchen reflected that the layers of ostentatious clothing they wore were not well suited to Segg's climate.

One man took a quick step forward and offered a perfunctory bow. The fringe of gray hair that still ringed his head and been trimmed brutally close to the skin. He had a long, hawk-like nose, sharp cheekbones, and deep-set eyes that looked like chips of obsidian. "Welcome to Nava Nar, my lords," he said in a voice that suggested he would just as soon they had both succumbed to mishap on the road. "I am Lord Igen of Segg. A banquet has been planned for this evening to welcome you both properly. For now, I am sure that you want to wash the road dust away. My steward will see to the quartering of your parties. I am afraid that, with so many lords and other important folk attending the Conclave, little room is left within the palace. Your chief advisors will have to share quarters with others, but the rest must to seek lodging elsewhere."

Auglar nodded graciously and dismounted. "I understand."

Igen's steward, an officious little man whom Suchen immediately disliked, bustled forward. The gaze he turned on Suchen and the Sworn was one of disgust, as if they were barbarians likely to steal the silverware. "Come with me," he ordered, then turned away and started towards the palace, obviously expecting them to scramble behind him in order to avoid being left. Suchen hesitated, glancing worriedly at Yozerf. But he only gave her a wry look, tilting his head slightly to indicate that she should go.

"Later," he mouthed at her.

She paused a moment longer, then nodded sharply and hurried away.

Chapter Three

Suchen followed Lord Igen's steward through Nava Nar's wide hallways, her packs banging uncomfortably against her back. Her boots tapped echoes from the marble walls, in sharp contrast to the whisper of his soft-soled shoes, making her feel like an untutored barbarian lumbering after him. As they walked, they passed by small groups of courtiers, most of whom stopped to stare after them. Knowing that their shock was reserved for her mannish clothing and the sword hanging from her belt, Suchen felt a blush scald her cheeks.

I'll never fit in here, she realized in dismay. *No more than I did back home.*

She had spent her early years in the company of other young women of her class, and the experience still burned in her memories. Their conversations had focused on what man they would marry, what fashions were in style, and who had assassinated the character of whom. Tongues sharp as embroidery needles had mocked Suchen's clumsiness, her flat chest and narrow hips, and her inability to sew a straight seam.

I'm not that girl anymore, she told herself fiercely, trying to ignore the whispers that followed her. *I am the Steward of a powerful lord, and will soon be Steward of the King of Jenel. I have more freedom than those twitter-heads could ever dream of. I have a beautiful man who loves me for who I am—who thinks I'm beautiful. There's no reason to be ashamed.*

But of course the words didn't help.

"Here," said the steward, his disapproving voice breaking her out of her bleak thoughts. Startled, she looked around and discovered herself midway down a long corridor on the second floor of the palace. "You will be sharing this room with Lady Cybelen and her chaperone."

Without another word, he turned and left, his stiff posture proclaiming his distaste with this entire affair. Suchen found herself staring at a heavy wooden door, its surface elaborately carved and etched in an abstract design. Taking a deep breath to steel herself, she pushed it open.

Either Nava Nar truly had no room left to house its guests, or else the Lady Cybelen was in as much disgrace as Suchen. Two beds and a small cot had all been crammed into a tiny room that at one time had probably been a storage closet. Gauzy curtains enclosed each bed, doubtless to keep out mosquitoes. The heavy coverlets were wildly mismatched, one a deep scarlet embroidered in gold thread, the other a modest sky blue without decoration. A candelabrum stood on top of a trunk jammed in between the beds, and a small lantern hung from a wall sconce originally meant for a torch. The heavy branches of an oak filtered the sunlight coming through the single small window, tinting the interior of the room green.

A young woman sat on the edge of the far bed, reading a book. She looked up when the door opened, and Suchen felt an unexpected spasm of envy and trepidation. The maiden was dressed in the style of the southern wealthy. A bodice fitted with whalebone staves clung tightly to her torso, revealing rounded breasts framed by frothy lace. A small ruby in a simple gold setting hung about her neck, perfectly offsetting her smooth throat. Layers of petticoats enshrouded her legs down to her small, delicate feet in their tiny slippers. Hair the color of honey was elaborately coiled about her head, held in place by jeweled clips. Despite the heat of the day, no sweat beaded on her flawless skin.

"What is the meaning of this?" snapped a harsh voice. Startled, Suchen shrank back as an old woman advanced on her. The crone's withered face was set in a harsh scowl that looked as if it had become permanent years ago.

"I—I'm Suchen Keblava," she stammered, blushing. "I'm supposed to be staying here for now."

"Outrageous!" the old woman proclaimed. Sharp, beady eyes focused on Suchen's breeks, sword, and tunic. "I will speak to Lord Jehnav immediately!"

The younger woman rose gracefully to her feet. "That won't be necessary, Mila."

"But, my lady, this woman is some sort of barbarian! Your reputation—do I have to remind you that you're supposed to be looking for a husband?"

"Sit down, Mila." When the older woman had slunk back to her cot, muttering angrily under her breath, the maiden turned back to Suchen with a smile. "Please forgive her—she takes her role as my chaperone very seriously. I'm Cybelen Jehnava."

Suchen nodded, recalling the family name of one of the southern lords. "I'm sorry to intrude on you like this."

Cybelen's small, bow-like mouth curved into a genuine smile. "I'm more than happy to share my broom closet, such as it is. You're Lord Auglar's steward, aren't you?"

"Scandalous," Mila muttered from her corner.

Cybelen rolled her eyes.

"Yes, I am," Suchen said with a smile of her own. Mila might not spare anyone's feelings, but it seemed that Cybelen might not be so difficult to get along with as she had at first feared. "I didn't think I was important enough for anyone to recall my name."

"Oh, Father made sure I could recite the courts of all the lords by heart. As Mila said, he wants to use the Conclave as an excuse for husband-hunting." Cybelen made a dismissive gesture, as if she considered the whole business silly. Clearly, she had long ago accepted that she would have no say about the man she would marry and wasn't going to let that fact worry her unduly.

The sound of bells drifted in through the window, borne by the wind from someplace deeper within the palace complex. Mila looked up from where she was working on a bit of embroidery, stabbing the needle into the cloth as if it had personally offended her. "Seventh bell, girl—the banquet's in an hour! You'd better stop yammering and start getting ready if you don't want to be late. You know how your father would feel about that."

"I know, I know." Cybelen turned back to Suchen in a swirl of skirt and petticoat. "What about you, Suchen? Shall I help with your hair?"

⁂

When Auglar's delegation walked into the great hall, Suchen realized that she was not the only one who appeared out of place.

Auglar, Suchen, and the Sworn had all dressed in their best clothing. For Suchen, that consisted of a simple, form-fitting dress in the northern style. Unfortunately, its long, clinging sleeves ensured that sweat trickled down her neck and crept along the line of her bodice. Most of the men wore breeks and tunics, the cloth expensive but largely undecorated and showing signs of wear.

A virtual army of courtiers, merchants, and lords awaited them in the great hall. The scents of sweat, patchouli, and lavender hung on the air like an invisible fog. Even the lowliest courtier was dressed in brilliantly-colored hosen and tunic, with elaborate embroidered heraldry to proclaim the wearer's lineage. The women wore layers of petticoats, and lace frothed about whale-bone bodices that left their shoulders bare and their breasts nearly so. Jewels flashed at throats, wrists, and fingers, trailing light as the crowd milled about.

Three huge mirrors in gilded frames hung above a dais at one end, reflecting back the glory of the court.

Auglar's step hesitated for an instant as he entered, and Suchen knew him well enough to sense his utter dismay. Compared to this crowd, his delegation dressed like servants. He had meant to impress the southern lords; instead, he would be lucky if they didn't laugh in his face.

But that single hitch in his step was all the emotion he allowed himself to show outwardly. As the heralds announced him, he walked proudly into the hall, his head thrown back. The Sworn followed him closely.

Suchen hung back, hoping to blend into the crowd. As Auglar's steward, she was not needed for any of his official functions. Trying to disappear as best she could, Suchen glanced around the room, searching for a glimpse of red hair and pale skin. None of the Sworn seemed to know where Yozerf had gone after they had parted in the courtyard, but she had expected him to appear by now.

Then again, she thought, looking at the glittering human lords and ladies, *perhaps I ought to hope that he doesn't come.* A gathering such as this one was almost certain to provoke Yozerf's volatile temper, a situation that would benefit no one. Which might be why he had not come in the first place.

A herald's strident voice sounded from the other end of the hall, and Suchen glanced nervously in that direction. Through the crowd, she caught glimpses of Auglar standing before a group of men whose finery made the bejeweled courtiers look like paupers. *The southern lords,* she thought with dread. Gods, there was no chance that they would look at Auglar and see anything but a poor country cousin.

"Isn't this dreadful?" Cybelen asked, appearing as if by magic at Suchen's elbow. She took a sip from a wine glance and fanned herself with a lace handkerchief. "Everyone standing about and talking, while I'm absolutely *starving.* I thought that a banquet would have something to do with food, but obviously that was a misapprehension of great proportions."

"Obviously," Suchen agreed wryly.

Although she had declared herself to be husband hunting, Cybelen showed no inclination to leave Suchen's side. Instead, she pointed out members of the other lords' courts, made acerbic comments on their bad taste in clothing, wine, or lovers, and gossiped scandalously. Her voice was light and airy, and her hands flitted animatedly as she spoke, as if they would turn into doves and fly off her wrists at any moment. Despite the cold looks she got from other members of the crowd, Suchen felt some of her tension ease, and she found herself deeply grateful to the younger woman.

After a time, Peddock made his way to them. Even from a distance, he did not look good. His face was pale, and his hand trembled as he lifted his wineglass and took a generous gulp from it. One of the courtiers bumped him, and he jerked, spilling wine on his tunic.

"Your brother seems nervous," Cybelen commented softly as he approached. A little line of concern sprang up between her brows.

"Yes." Suchen touched Peddock's shoulder lightly when he came up. "Are you all right?"

His eyes went to Cybelen and he nodded stiffly. Suchen hurriedly introduced them and watched her brother come up with a pale smile as he bent over Cybelen's hand.

"It is a pleasure," Cybelen said, but some of the lightness had unexpectedly gone out of her voice. "I think I see my father waving at me—perhaps he has discovered where they are hiding the food." Her hazel eyes lingered for a moment on Peddock's face, then she turned quickly and vanished into the crowd.

Peddock watched her go, then turned back with a sigh. A servant approached with a decanter and refilled his glass. "Gods, I hate this," he muttered when he had finished draining the goblet to its dregs.

Suchen winced. "How...how are things going?"

"About as you might expect. Did you know that there's a contingent from the merchant's guild here?"

Her blood went to ice in her veins. "Father?"

"No. No, thank the blessed gods. They've made him the godsdamned head of the guild, did you know that? He's too important for the preliminaries—he won't be along until there's a clear winner."

There was darkness in his eyes, years and years of darkness. Suchen sighed and tried to hook her hands into her sword belt, only remembering belatedly that she wasn't wearing it. "Only last fall you were trying to marry me off to one of them."

"That was different. Staafon would have protected you."

"I didn't want to be protected."

"It was different for you," he insisted belligerently. "You know it was."

He wasn't speaking of the present or future anymore. "I know."

Peddock looked away for a moment; when he turned back, he had pasted on a false smile. "I think they've finally decided to feed us. Let's find someplace to sit, shall we?"

Suchen and Peddock found themselves about halfway down

the room from the high table of the lords. Their companions at the table were mostly court officials of one sort of another, all of whom were probably deeply offended to have been seated next to a pair of Northern bumpkins, and who spent the meal trying to pretend that Suchen and Peddock weren't really there. Fortunately, dinner provided a welcome distraction from Suchen's gloomy thoughts.

Lord Igen had not stinted in laying the table for this feast. A stream of servants poured continuously between the banquet hall and the kitchen, bearing platters heaped with food and ewers overflowing with wine. There were tarts of mixed fruit, rosemary, and basil; meat-filled pastries shaped like hedgehogs; omelets with almonds, currants, and saffron; roasted fish in wine sauce; pigeons stuffed with cheese; chicken glazed with honey, mustard, and nuts; herb cakes; and apple fritters. The wine served changed with every course as well, beginning with a sweet aperitif and ending with a heavily-spiced red. Entertainment was not neglected, either: tumblers performed on the outskirts while musicians wandered from table to table.

As she ate, Suchen tried to get a glimpse of the high table. Auglar and Fellrant sat in places of honor, both accompanied by beautiful young women she guessed to be the daughters or unmarried sisters of the other lords. Auglar's escort was dressed in enough red silk to beggar a demesne, and constantly leaned over to touch his hand, showing off a great deal of cleavage as she did so. The young lord looked vaguely embarrassed, and Suchen wondered if he wished that Sifya were with him. Although he'd had his affairs— he had in fact been Suchen's first lover, during the siege of Kellsjard—he had never been as free with women as most men in his class. Certainly he had not so much as looked at another woman since marrying Sifya.

Fellrant, on the other hand, had a faint smile on his sumptuous lips, as if he was enjoying a joke unknown to any but him. The woman at his side appeared to have fallen silent shortly after the feast began and sat staring fixedly at her trencher, making no attempts to flirt.

Odd, Suchen thought with a touch of unease. *Fellrant isn't married yet—I would expect her to at least make an attempt at seduction, no matter how unpleasant she might find his company.* Indeed, an older man whom she guessed to be the woman's father was glaring at her constantly, as if demanding an explanation for her behavior. The girl would be lucky to escape a beating tonight.

As if feeling Suchen's scrutiny, Fellrant turned suddenly and looked across the room. For a moment, their eyes met. Fellrant's brows raised, as if in question, and he glanced meaningfully at the men seated to either side of her. Unsure what he wanted, she looked away. When she dared turn her eyes back in his direction, he was talking to the lord beside him.

He was looking for Yozerf, she realized suddenly. But that was ridiculous—what possible interest could Lord Fellrant have in her lover? *Perhaps he was only curious to see whether I would endanger Auglar by flaunting my relationship with an Aclyte and causing a scandal.*

But somehow, the explanation did not sit well with her.

⁓ ⁓

Home, Yozerf thought. His belly clenched, and it was everything he could do to keep his hands from shaking. *I'm home.*

It was the scent, really, that transmuted the abstract idea of returning to Segg into a cold, visceral reality that could not be denied. The salt tang of the sea and the organic rot of the swamps provided a faint background to the more overwhelming smells of human waste and decaying garbage. The metallic stink of blood mingled with the sour perfume of starvation and the cloying ripeness of old sex.

He closed his eyes and stood swaying for a moment, half-hidden in the shadows on the outskirts of the great marketplace. The smells made him want to sink to the slimy cobblestones and weep, or start screaming like a madman, or run wild through the streets, attacking everyone in his way. But instead he forced himself to stillness, knowing how dangerous it was to just stand there like a fool, advertising his weakness to whatever predators might happen by. He had to start moving again, had to at least act like he knew where he was going and what he would do when he got there.

He had left the palace before the scheduled banquet, intending to go to *The Wyvern,* a tavern on the outskirts of the Old Quarter. After parting with Suchen and the Sworn, he had found his way to the servant's quarters and spoken to the Aclytes he found there. He had told them a truth, that he needed somewhere to sleep where he would not disturb any of the humans, and a lie, that he feared enclosed spaces and needed a window in whatever closet they found for him. At last, a sympathetic chambermaid had shown him a tiny storeroom, so cramped that he could barely stretch his height out all the way on the floor. But it seemed largely unused at this time of year, stuffed full of winter hangings and blankets. And the window let out onto the kitchen gardens, where his comings and goings would likely go unnoticed by anyone. Satisfied with the arrangement, he had slipped out the narrow window as soon as the opportunity presented itself, scaled the low palace wall in a gap between the patrolling guards...and found himself in Segg once again.

He had made it all the way to the marketplace, his steps growing slower and heavier the closer he got to his goal. He should go to *The Wyvern* and talk to old Jarvin. It was the only reliable way he knew to find the Crow Queen, should she fail to find him first. But he had not set foot in the small tavern since before he had left Segg. Since *that night.*

The image came to him unbidden: tangled hair spread across the dirty floor, a torn bodice soaked in blood, the stink of rage and semen.

No, he thought, turning his head away sharply. He could not go there, would not go there. But he had to find the Crow Queen. He needed her help.

"You do not need anyone," Telmonra whispered unexpectedly, from the other side of that blank space in his mind. *"You are strong. You are powerful."*

How can you even think that? he wondered incredulously. But she did not answer.

After a moment's hesitation, he began to walk again, passing through the great expanse of the Market Square. Most of the vendors had left for the night, but a few were only just beginning their commerce. Yozerf caught a glimpse of a sly-looking man selling love-philters, an exotic woman dressed in gauzy veils, and a hunched and wizened fortune-teller. At the edge of the market, the gibbets creaked in the evening wind off the ocean. A decaying corpse leaned to one side within the cage where it had died from lack of water. Nearby, a man hung in the stocks, either dead or unconscious.

Yozerf's feet carried him through the market and away, almost of their own volition. So many years away, but he still knew the path so well that he didn't even have to think about it. It was as if he had never been gone at all, he thought, and a chill touched him. As if every moment in between leaving and returning had been nothing but a dream. Suchen, the Sworn, Auglar...none of them were even real.

Stop being stupid, he told himself, a little desperately. He had left. He had changed.

Hadn't he?

"Vengeance."

At length he reached the edge of the Old Quarter. The wall surrounding it marked the original boundary of the city, and its stone surface had been crumbled and pitted by centuries of weather.

As the city outside grew, more and more streets had cut through the wall, until any defensive capabilities were long lost. Its only function now was to mark the boundary between the rich and the poor.

As he walked towards the wall, he could feel all the past defenses slipping into place, familiar and worn as old clothing. His shoulders went back, his stride became a prowl, and his eyes moved constantly, touching faces and shadows and doorways, always looking for an attack that if he was lucky might never come.

The smells of the Old Quarter rose up about him in a dazzling variety: foreign spices, rotting garbage, dung, beer, vomit, sex. A voice called out in Aclytese, and another answered. Laughter erupted from a group of wealthy young toughs, standing on a corner with their bodyguards around them as they kicked a cringing man with their hard-soled shoes. Prostitutes stood on the street, or leaned out of balconies, or beckoned from windows, their clothing as bright as they could afford, their faces smeared with paint. Torches lit the scene, washing everything in red and orange, the colors of rage or damnation.

Yozerf's pulse quickened until he could feel it pounding in his throat. He navigated his way around a fight, brushed past hucksters offering games of chance with shells, and shook his head politely to an old woman selling meat pies. The further he went towards the docks, the rougher and dirtier the streets became. Light shone out through the warped boards of the buildings, garbage made the cobblestones slimy, and rats and wild dogs peered out of alleys, their eyes bright and mad. The prostitutes became thin, their clothing—what little they wore—ragged. His eyes lit briefly on a familiar corner, one that he had worked with Ginny, and he saw that it was still a way station for those seeking to buy the bodies of children.

At last he found himself in a section composed mainly of crumbling old tenements. The packed-together buildings seems almost to lean on one another, like old drunks unable to stand on their own. He had lived in such places for the first twenty years of his life, sleeping away the days in the crowded, flea-infested rooms, spending the nights in allies or the beds of others.

Why did I come here? he wondered. Not to find the Crow Queen—surely she no longer lived in such a place. Surely the business of killing was better than that.

A muffled scream interrupted his thoughts. Startled, he looked around, but saw no one. A faint groan sounded from one of the dark slots between buildings, and he felt the hair on the back of his neck stand up suddenly. Something bad was happening in there, he knew, and his gut clenched in the ancient fear that he might be its next victim.

He turned quickly away, intending to put as much distance between himself and the little alley as possible. There came a sudden oath, followed by a louder scream, and in his mind's eye he imaged a woman fighting desperately against her attacker, seizing the chance to cry out no matter how hopeless her predicament was. No one was going to come to save her, after all.

No one had ever come to save *him*.

Yozerf stopped, his heart pounding like a mad thing in his chest. Fear and rage both raced through his blood, tightening in bands around his chest and making his hands shake. For a moment instinct warred with old knowledge. Then, with a sudden snarl, he spun and ran back towards the alley.

His wolf-sharp eyes had no trouble picking out the scene within the filthy alley. Two figures struggled between mounds of garbage and filth. The woman was on her back, the man on top of her, laughing as he drove his fist into her face in time with the jerking of his hips. There was too much blood and shadow to see the woman's features, but for an instant Yozerf *knew* that she would have curly black hair and dark skin, *knew* that she would have those beautiful brown eyes that burned with a hunger he could never satisfy.

With a sudden scream of rage, he struck. The wind arose around him, birthed from a tide of white-hot anger, and slammed into the man, hurling him across the alley and into the opposite wall. Dazed and shocked, the man looked up, and Yozerf saw blunt human features, an unshaven face, and dull eyes that were only beginning to show signs of fear.

Humans running through the streets of Cade Kwii, the smell of blood and smoke obliterating the scent of stone. The city burned, the citadel burned, her cousin, little Rishia screaming as her young body was violated, Calaevrion's blood bursting forth in a fountain...

Telmonra's memories, but her fury tasted the same as his, and for a moment he could not sort them one from the other. The past was unalterable for either of them...but there was always revenge.

"*Burn,*" he whispered with a smile, though whether he spoke to the man before him or an army long dead he did not know.

Pleasure shocked through him as the power rose and poured out, tingling along his nerves and sending a tide of euphoria through his entire body. The man erupted into flames, his hair and clothing igniting in a firestorm that flung the alleyway into bright relief.

He began to scream hoarsely, body flailing.

Still caught in the grip of the power, Yozerf tilted his head back and moaned with pleasure, only half-aware of the smell of roasted flesh, the howls of agony. Within moments, the fire died away, leaving behind only an inert, blackened husk and the pungent smell of roasted meat.

Yozerf stood very still as the flames died. Elation filled him, bubbling up slowly from the depths of his soul, and he found himself laughing on the edge of hysteria. He turned to see if the woman had noticed, but she had fled at the first opportunity and had not witnessed her attacker's death.

"You begin to see," Telmonra crooned.

As he made his way back towards the palace on the hill, Yozerf's steps were light. The afterglow of power wrapped about him, and he grinned insanely at passersby, pleased when they avoided his gaze and hurried away.

He *had* left. He *had* changed.

The last time he had walked these streets, he had been at the mercy of larger, stronger, more numerous predators. But no more. That frightened boy was dead, and in his place was someone powerful. Someone who could protect not only himself, but his pack as well.

"Vengeance," whispered Telmonra.

Chapter Four

Londah crouched high up in a tree that decorated one of the palace's formal gardens. Gaining access to the grounds had been sadly easy, and the sprawling, open layout of the palace itself presented a multitude of ways inside. *Little challenge for a professional,* she thought. Especially with so many strangers within; it would be harder to recognize the face that didn't belong.

The moon slid out from behind the clouds, bathing the open grounds in bright light, and she shifted back deeper into the shadows of the leaves. The rigid lines of the gardens struck her as very human, the attempt to transform what grew wild into something tame and safe. Even the water was controlled, spouting out of precisely-placed fountains.

And what has any of this to do with Yozerf? she wondered. Not for the first time, it occurred to her that Ax was likely lying.

It was impossible to regret her association with the wizard entirely; she was too practical for that. When he had appeared amidst the agony and blood of an unending labor and told her that she and the babe would both die without his intervention, she had known that he spoke true. And his contention that, by saving their lives he thus owned their lives...well, it had not seemed such a high price then.

She did not trust him, that went without saying. *But surely he could have come up with a less outrageous lie.* Yozerf despised humans in general; certainly he wouldn't care which of them claimed lordship over Jenel. And even if he had, she could think of no reason that he would be here, in the heart of human power, amidst all the symbols of human domination.

She had done her best to stay out of Yozerf's affairs, even when he was a child, afraid of becoming an interfering, domineering woman like her own mother had been. So the fact that she could think of no reason for him being here didn't mean that there wasn't one. He was, in many ways, a stranger to her.

The Crow Queen sighed and moved from her crouch. Sitting

in a tree and observing the comings and goings outside had gotten her nowhere. Perhaps she would have better luck within.

Yozerf prowled the corridors restlessly. Although he had returned to the palace intending to find his closet and sleep, his encounter in the alleyway refused to leave his mind. The wild energy he had felt at the moment that his power was unleashed thrummed in his veins, making him edgy and restless. He wished that he could go to Suchen, perhaps even spend some of that energy in her arms, but nothing would scandalize the court faster than an Aclytese man knocking on the door of Auglar's female steward in the middle of the night.

So he paced the corridors like a ghost, staring awed at the grandeur of the palace. Even Kellsjard had intimidated him when he first found his way there, but Nava Nar made Auglar's keep look like the provincial court that it actually was. The amount of marble and gold in even the smallest, most out-of-the-way nook staggered him. The contents of a single room would make any thief rich beyond his wildest dreams.

The many niches and alcoves that housed works of art made it easy for him to slip into shadows every time he heard the soft pad of other feet. By far he was not the only one to stir abroad in the night, not with so many guests packed into such a small space. No doubt the court was rife with intrigue of every sort, and he found himself heartily glad that he was not Auglar, who would have to deal with such things.

Eventually, he found himself in the uppermost story of the palace, a place that had once been reserved for kings. Moonlight streamed in through a wide window at the end of the corridor, like a silver scarf lying on the floor. Hoping for a cool breeze to soothe some of the restlessness from him, he went to the casement. The window looked out onto the wide gardens that surrounded the palace. The moon turned the leaves of the low hedges silver, and made strange shadows out of sculpted topiaries. The white, marble-chip paths glowed like lines of cool fire.

There was a man standing on one of the paths, Yozerf saw, another restless soul who could find no peace tonight. The man was dressed in garb that could have belonged to any off-duty soldier—perhaps he simply wanted a look at the gardens that would be restricted to his betters during the daylight hours.

Then he lifted his head and looked straight towards the palace, and Yozerf felt his breath catch in his throat.

Dara-Don.

For a moment, Yozerf thought that he had to be mistaken.
Dara-Don had once belonged to Auglar's Sworn, until he had betrayed them all to the Council last winter. It was impossible that he
should be here, where Auglar or one of the other Sworn might so
easily spot him.

But there was no mistaking those broad, plain features that
had once seemed so open, nor the sad puppy eyes that stared at
the palace with an expression of intense grief and longing.

Yozerf held himself very, very still, hardly daring to breathe,
as the implications tumbled through his mind. Then, with a short
oath, he turned on his heel and raced down the corridor with all
the speed he could muster.

There was a man walking down the hall outside of Suchen's
room. He might have been simply a servant, or someone on the
way to an assignation, or even a hapless guard who had just finished his duty shift and was headed back to barracks. Yozerf didn't
take the chance to find out. The wind came to him like a weapon
to his hand, and he flung the startled man into the nearest wall.
There came a muffled thud and the snap of bone, before the man
collapsed into a soundless heap.

Ignoring the body, Yozerf raced past and tried the door, only to
find it latched. With a soft curse, he tripped the latch with the
knife from his boot and let himself in.

Two beds and a cot filled the small space. Even as Yozerf opened
the door, one of the sleeping shapes jerked into wakefulness, and
he felt a momentary rush of pleasure at Suchen's alertness.

"Who's there?" she demanded, blind in the dark. The other
two women also roused, the eldest clutching the blankets to her
neck.

"It's me," he said, hoping that the old woman didn't start
screaming. "We've got to get out of here. Now."

"Why?"

"We have been betrayed. I saw Dara-Don in the garden outside. And there was a man in the hall, just outside your door."

Suchen moved instantly, sliding out of the bed and grabbing
clothes in haste. The old woman's eyes widened in indignation,
and she made a strangled sound of protest. "This is outrageous!
I'm going to call the guards! I'm—"

"Be silent, Mila," snapped the other woman. She had a low,
modulated voice that bore an aristocrat's accent. In the dim light
that came through the window, Yozerf could see that she looked
surprisingly calm. "Suchen, what is this all about?"

"It's a long story, Cybelen. Dara-Don was one of Auglar's Sworn,
but he was a traitor—working for the Council," Suchen explained

as she slid her packs out from under the bed. "If he's here, now, then someone in this palace must be a traitor, too. Auglar's life is in danger—maybe all our lives are."

Deciding that Suchen had things in hand, Yozerf dropped back out into the corridor. All his senses were hyper-alert, listening for the faintest scuff of a foot, smelling for the slightest betraying scent of an approaching assassin. A few moments later, Suchen joined him—followed by Cybelen and an extremely indignant Mila.

"We need to get to your father," Mila told her young charge angrily.

"There's no time," Cybelen said firmly. "If someone planned to murder Suchen in her bed, then they had to have included us as well, or else there would be witnesses."

Surprised that the young noble showed so much sense, Yozerf nevertheless wished she had stayed behind. "Be quiet and follow me," he said in a low voice, then started off without waiting to find out if they obeyed.

Suchen flanked him as they hurried down the corridor, going as quickly as they could without making too much of a commotion. The deserted hallways suddenly seemed sinister, and Yozerf half-expected to turn a corner and find himself in the middle of a band of armed assassins. But for once luck was with them, and they met no one on the way to Auglar's quarters.

Peddock opened the door at Suchen's knock without first checking to see who was there. "Idiot," Yozerf snarled, shoving his way past and into the sitting room.

"What in the name of Hel are you doing here?" Peddock snapped irritably, trying to block Yozerf's progress. The other Sworn were sleeping on makeshift pallets on the floor, and they roused groggily at the intrusion.

"We're in trouble," Suchen said grimly. She shut the door as soon as Mila and Cybelen were inside, then shot the heavy bolt home. "Wake Auglar. We have to get out of here now."

As Suchen explained, the Sworn quickly divided themselves, with Peddock gathering their packs, Buudi waking Auglar, and Brenwulf standing guard on the door. Once she had finished, there was a brief moment of silence.

"I'm not certain that we should leave," Auglar said uneasily. His black hair was mussed from the bed and his hastily-donned clothes were wrinkled, but all sleep was gone from his sharp blue eyes. "We knew that there might be traitors among the lords. Just because Dara-Don is here doesn't mean that anyone is going to kill us in our sleep tonight. I believe that the best thing would be—"

At that moment, the outer door rattled softly, as if someone tested whether or not it was bolted.

Silence fell. No extra lights had been lit save for the single lantern that Peddock had been keeping watch by, so Yozerf immediately faded back into the shadows behind the door. The Sworn and Suchen drew their weapons, forming a protective shield around Auglar, Cybelen, and Mila.

The latched rattled again, and Yozerf's sharp ears caught a muffled curse from the other side of the heavy door. Silence fell, and the seconds stretched out as he strove to catch any indication of what was happening in the hall outside...

Something heavy smashed into the door, ripping the bolt free and sending it clattering across the floor. Yozerf skewered the first man coming through before he had the chance to look around, and then kicked the second hard enough to send him falling. Then there was chaos, with armed men swarming into the tiny room. Blood spattered the rich carpets and draperies, and a priceless glass vase crashed to the floor in an explosion of dagger-like shards.

The assassins had come expecting to take the Sworn by surprise and kill them before they could get out of their sleeping pallets. Instead, they found themselves facing armed and alerted men ready to die defending their lord. The first ones in hesitated, but their fellows pushed from behind, trapping them.

Yozerf let out an ululating howl, sweeping his sword through the gut of one, then whipping it around to take another through the neck. Telmonra rose within him, and his lips formed her battle cry. For a moment, a breeze whipped through the room, ruffling his hair and threatening to slip loose of his control.

"Yes, kill them," Telmonra moaned, like a lover in the midst of passion. *"Kill them all."*

No! I can't lose control, not now, not where everyone can see! To fight blindly, letting her rage take him, would be insanity.

"We've got to get out of here!" Buudi shouted above the clang of steel. "If we give them the chance to get reinforcements, we'll be trapped in this room!"

"Agreed!" Yozerf said. Casting about, his eyes lit on a small table that had been overturned onto the floor. Snatching it up, he slammed it into the men still blocking the doorway, shoving them back. Seeing what he was doing, Buudi and Brenwulf both threw their weight behind him, and the three of them managed to break through.

Everyone else followed hard on their heels. There was chaos in the hall, with armed men running back and forth. No one seemed to be coming to Auglar's aide, however, and dread pooled in Yozerf's gut. Quietly slitting Auglar's throat in the middle of the night was one thing, but a large armed conflict was not something that could be ignored or easily covered-up. The fact that they were willing to take such a risk suggested that they weren't *concerned* about anyone finding out.

Meaning that most—or even all—of the other lords knew about it already.

At that moment, the sounds of fighting came from farther down the hall. "Reinforcements!" Peddock shouted in relief.

But Yozerf shook his head grimly. "No. They're after Lord Fellrant as well. It seems that the southern lords decided they didn't want a Northern king after all."

Indeed, the knot of struggling men was clustered tightly around the entrance to what seemed to be Lord Fellrant's suite. Even as Yozerf watched, men in Fellrant's black-and-purple livery were cut down in the hall, their blood pooling darkly over the pale marble floor.

"We have to help him," Auglar said.

Yozerf cast him a look of disbelief. The young lord's mouth was set in a tight, grim line, and he held his sword in his hand.

Brenwulf seemed to have the same idea as Yozerf. "Auglar, you can't be serious! Fellrant—"

"Obviously has the same enemies," Auglar interrupted. "Which makes us, at least for the moment, allies. Come on."

Auglar charged down the hall, forcing his Sworn to race after him. It was a brave gesture on Auglar's part—but also a foolish one. Even as he rushed to Fellrant's rescue, a contingent of guards dressed in Lord Igen's livery appeared around the corner. Auglar's step hesitated a moment, as if he thought that these men might have come to his aid after all.

The lead guard lowered his pike and drove it straight for Auglar's chest.

Time seemed to slow in that moment. Yozerf saw the gleaming metal of the pike and knew that there was nothing any of them could do to prevent it from finding its target. Buudi's cry of fury and anguish echoed weirdly in the hall. Auglar tried to take a useless step back, bringing up his sword far too late to make any difference.

For an instant, Yozerf felt a flicker of anticipation from Telmonra, and he saw a throne room littered with dead Aclytes.

A dark shape dropped from the arched ceiling. Its boots impacted hard with the guard's chest, hurling him and his pike backwards, away from Auglar. The figure sprang nimbly away from the falling guard, and Yozerf caught the quick flick of a wrist that sent a tiny knife into the guard's neck, dispatching him before he even struck the floor. Then Auglar's mysterious savior dropped to the ground, sweeping one leg around in a kick that knocked most of the lead guards off their feet.

A moment later, the Sworn closed with the guards, and the sound of fighting again filled the hall. At first, it seemed that the guards would hold their formation—then they abruptly fell back, cursing and tripping over the bodies of the fallen. Even as they fled, three more collapsed, blood pumping out of necks and eyes as throwing knives found their mark.

A false silence fell. Auglar's savior stood in the middle of the hall, her entire body tense, held in a pose that promised violence at any second. She was very tall, easily six feet, but she moved with a soundless grace that belied her height. Her clothing clung to her like a second skin—she wore nothing that would tangle or snag—and was a uniform charcoal-gray to blend with the shadows. Long black hair swirled to her waist, framing a sharp, inhuman face and a pair of fell gray eyes.

"*Gods,*" Peddock whispered in a voice that held more than a little trace of awe.

A mixture of relief and gratitude flooded through Yozerf. "It's about time you got here," he said lightly, as if he had never doubted.

She laughed, sheathing the two knives she held ready with a flick of the wrist. "And I thought Ax was mad when he told me that your safety depended on protecting a human lord. You keep strange company these days, my son."

"Imminently," he agreed dryly. "Do you know a quick way out of here?"

"Of course."

"Wait a minute," Auglar said, looking dazed. "What—I mean, who is this woman?"

Yozerf ground his teeth impatiently. Humans would stand and talk while the world ended around them if given the chance. "Weren't you listening to anything? Her name is Londah. She's my mother. And we need to get out of here, not ask foolish questions."

"I say we listen to the Aclyte," suggested a low, shaken voice. Startled, Yozerf looked over and saw Fellrant standing in the door to his suite. His indigo eyes were wide as he stared at his dead Sworn, and his face was pale, but nevertheless he held himself with a surprising amount of composure. "I don't think we have much time, and if anyone knows an easier way out of here than fighting our way through the front gates, I'm all for it."

"Well, then." Londah's lips twitched into a familiar feral smile that lightened Yozerf's heart. "Let's go, shall we."

They went as quickly as they could, down the hall to a small, almost-hidden stairwell that was meant for the use of servants. Yozerf dropped back to the rear, where Suchen was, and fell in beside her. As they clattered down the narrow stair, he heard the approach of boots in the corridor above, and prayed that the returning guards would not realize that their quarry had thought to take a passage normally used only by the servants.

Suchen looked pale in the dim light, but she the way she moved told him that she was unharmed, and he could smell no blood on her. He found her hand for a moment, giving it a quick squeeze for comfort, and she flashed him a weak smile in return. No one would harm her, he swore silently to himself, not while he was alive to prevent it.

The stair let out onto a short corridor that ended in a door. When Londah pushed it open, fresh air streamed inside, carrying with it the scents of flowers and damp earth. "This palace is secure as a sieve," she murmured. "Which is fortunate for us. Follow me, and do not stray."

They found themselves in the back corner of the garden. The chips of white marble that lined the path crunched hideously loud under their boots, and Yozerf swore mentally. Glancing back over his shoulder, he saw the scores of windows lining the palace wall, any of which could host watchful eyes.

As if in answer to his thought, he heard a faint hiss and felt a stir of air on his cheek a moment before an arrow buried itself in the ground beside him.

"Ware the archers!" he shouted. He grabbed Suchen and shoved her in front of him, shielding her body with his own. Arrows rattled in the hedges all around them, and someone let out a strangled scream.

"Mila!" Cybelen shouted, stopping and turning back.

Peddock grabbed her arm, pulling at her desperately. "There's nothing you can do!"

Whether that was true or not, Yozerf didn't know; the old woman was still moaning and thrashing on the path. But he did know that stopping to help her would only result in the deaths of them all. Fortunately, Suchen seemed to realize it as well, for after only a slight hesitation she broke back into a run, passing the dying woman by.

They raced through the garden, the hedges flashing past and foiling the aim of the archers. Shouts rang out in the distance, and Yozerf got a confused glimpse of torches rushing across the wide lawns, making for the gardens. The noose was tightening from all directions, and he sincerely hoped that Londah knew where she was going.

He should not have doubted. The gardens came to an end, and Londah shoved her way through a break in the hedge that he suspected was a bit too convenient to be natural. On the other side, the land sloped sharply down. The trickle of running water came to him, along with the pungent scent of sewage.

"Gods!" Peddock exclaimed, coming to a sudden halt. "You can't expect us to go down there!"

"Then stay here and die," Londah suggested mildly, never pausing in her own scramble down the slope. Cybelen followed her with a determined look on her young face, and after a moment Peddock came after. The rest picked their way down the slick slope after.

The watercourse at the bottom of the slope was too small to be a river, but large for a stream. The refuse of the palace swirled thickly in the dark water, on its way to join with the river outside and thence to the ocean. The stench was strong enough to make a human gag, and as for Yozerf he found himself struggling to breathe lightly through his mouth. Trying not to look too closely at the water, he waded in, proffering a hand to help Suchen on the slick stones. The sounds of pursuit had faded behind them, and he hoped that there would be enough time for them to escape without anyone breaking a leg from hurrying in the slimy water.

Fortunately, the palace wall was not far, and scraggly shrubs lining the stream protected them from view for most of the short distance. Here, the wall was pierced by a low arch, through which the stream exited. Rusted iron bars formed a grate across the opening, denying entrance.

"Now what?" Peddock demanded in a low whisper. "We follow some madwoman down here into the gods-forsaken sewer, only to be trapped!"

Londah ignored him. Instead, she went to the grate, bent down—and pulled it free. In the moonlight, Yozerf's sharp eyes could see the marks of the chisel where she had broken it loose from the mortar at some earlier time.

How long did she plan this? he wondered. More than a day, that was for certain. But then, perhaps she'd had business here before. Given the events of this night, he felt sure that assassination was hardly a new technique for the southern lords.

She crouched down to enter the low tunnel, then cast a glance back at him. "Pull it to once we're through. It might fool them, at least for a while."

Yozerf nodded. One by one, they went through the tunnel, holding their weapons and packs above their heads in an attempt to keep them clear of the filthy water. Striving to hold his breath,

Yozerf went last, pulling the grate back into place behind him. His height forced him to bend low, so that the ends of his long hair trailed in the stinking stream. The interior of the tunnel was utterly black, and he went slowly, feeling with his feet as best he could before putting his weight down. The rocks under his boots were thick with slime and other substances he preferred not to think about. Then the faint glow of the moon grew stronger around him, and with relief he passed out from under the wall and into the city.

Chapter Five

Suchen felt some of her tension ease when they emerged from beneath the palace wall into the moonlit night beyond. The stream continued its course towards the river, flowing between the high walls that marked the mansions of the rich or the noble. Londah led them up the embankment, out of the murky water, then down a narrow slot formed between the two walls put up by neighbors who apparently didn't like the idea of sharing one.

Londah. Suchen watched the Aclytese woman closely and wondered if her mind deceived her. Yozerf said that this woman was his mother, and, despite her seeming youth, Suchen did not doubt the claim. They both had the same gray eyes, the same bone-white skin, and the same high, sharp cheekbones. And they moved the same way, all predatory grace and savage quickness, as if they might explode into violence at any moment.

But Londah was also the same woman Suchen had seen standing outside the kitchen door one morning ten years ago in Iddi. The same woman who had come in through her bedroom window that night and asked if she wanted to learn the sword. The same woman whose teachings, however rudimentary, had ultimately saved both Suchen's and Peddock's lives and given them their freedom.

It can't be her. I must be mistaken.

As if anyone could ever forget a woman like her.

Because, despite the air of danger that echoed in her every motion like a warning, Londah was *beautiful*. Not the sort of beauty men smiled at and tried to talk up over ale. The sort of beauty that they killed to possess, the sort of beauty that the tales spoke of when they told of whole nations going to war over the favor of a single woman. There couldn't be two women who looked so similar that Suchen could possibly mistake them. It had to be her.

The narrow slot let out onto what looked to be a side street. Londah led them along it, her graceful stride full of confidence, despite the fact that anyone who saw them couldn't possibly think that a bunch of filthy, armed warriors who smelled rather strongly of a sewer belonged in such an exalted quarter of town. *Not to mention Cybelen,* Suchen thought, casting a glance at the young noblewoman's ruined gown. No, they were all far too obvious for comfort.

They left the side street for a series of alleys and byways. As they walked, the area around them declined from genteel to shabby, echoing the slow slope of the land down towards the sea. Finally, Londah halted in a small alley that looked similar to every other they had passed through. Garbage littered most of its length, and rats rustled in the shadows. The faint sounds of revelry came from somewhere nearby, but no one appeared to use the alley as a short-cut, leaving their little group undisturbed.

"We need somewhere to hide," Yozerf said. His black clothing blended into the darkness, but his eyes caught the light from a distant torch, glowing an eerie green.

"Agreed," said Auglar grimly. He turned to Londah and inclined his head slightly. "Thank you for helping us."

She shrugged carelessly, her attention seemingly more on the other end of the alley and anyone who might disturb them than on Auglar's words.

"We must get out of this city," Fellrant said. He looked haggard, his fine clothing ruined, but there was a grim determination in his eyes that chilled Suchen's soul. "The southern lords have tried to murder us. We must get back to our own demesnes and prepare for attack."

"They aren't going to let you simply stroll out of Segg," Yozerf said, his deep voice like a velvet touch in the darkness. "As soon as they realize that you have escaped, they will begin the hunt. They can't afford to let you leave here alive, and they will turn all of their power towards finding you."

"We're assuming that all of the southern lords are in on the plot," Auglar objected. Then he glanced over at Cybelen, who stood silently beside Peddock. "Do you know anything of this, Lady Jehnava?"

Cybelen raised her head, and Suchen saw the tracks of tears on her young face. Her hair was tangled and had come loose from its bindings, and her once-fine dress dripped murky water on the cobbles beneath. "No," she said sadly. "My father has only a small holding, my lords. I doubt that the powerful would bother to keep him in their council. And I can't believe that he would have risked my life by letting me be quartered with Suchen if he did know." She sniffled and shook her head. "Poor Mila. She didn't deserve to die."

"Speculation will get us nowhere," Yozerf said. He made a restless movement, and Suchen knew that he must be searching the darkness around them for any sign of pursuit. "For now, we must find new clothes and somewhere to hide. Even with the trip through the sewer, most of you are dressed too conspicuously for the slums."

"We haven't decided to go anywhere," Buudi reminded Yozerf with a little frown. "The lords—"

"The lords are not going to stand around waiting to get their throats slit," Fellrant interjected coldly. "My Sworn did not die so that I could be butchered in an alley. The Aclytes seem to know this city—is that not so?"

Yozerf's mouth tightened into a hard line, but he nodded once, shortly. "*Is* there a bolt hole where we might go?" he asked, directing the question at Londah's back.

She did not turn from her watch. "There are always bolt holes, my son. It would make more sense to split up the group, though."

"No," Buudi said firmly. "We are Sworn—we aren't going to abandon Lord Auglar."

"Then we must rely on chance." Londah shrugged. "Even so, there are places. First baths and clothes."

She started off abruptly, giving no one the chance to argue. *I can see where Yozerf learned his manners,* Suchen thought wryly. As if summoned by her thought, he appeared beside her, nothing more than a shadow until the distant torchlight briefly caught his white face and hands. What little she could see of his expression was grim indeed.

"What do you think our chances are?" she asked softly, so that no one else could hear.

He sighed and shook his head, long hair susurrating against his cloak. "I don't know. I wish we could have gotten the horses. Even if we escape the city, it will be a long walk across the Kellsmarch. And I worry for Windshade."

"I know."

The streets they passed through became more crowded. Laughter streamed out of taverns, and cries of frustration and triumph echoed from gambling dens. Sailors, merchants, and off-duty soldiers wandered from one entertainment to the next, while prostitutes called to them from corners and alleyways. The small group attracted harsh looks from some, while others followed the women—especially Londah—with hungry eyes. Suchen felt her heart speed up, and her hand went automatically to her sword hilt. Gods, they needed to get off the streets, and soon.

Eventually, they found themselves in a slightly quieter neighborhood. Two buildings stood side-by-side: one a public bath, the other a brothel, connected by a short, discreet passage. Apparently the baths were open day and night, for they were admitted after a light knock from Londah. A few coins exchanged hands with an attendant—probably including a jentarrii or two to make certain that they were not disturbed—and they were left alone.

The bathhouse was quiet; at least for now, the brothel was doing by far the better business. Londah led them to a series of cedar-lined closets, each with a low, sunken bath through which water swirled continuously. Suchen stared at them in amazement—in her experience, bathing required much lugging and heating of water by servants.

"A legacy from the old days of the Empire, or so they say," Yozerf said, pausing by her for a moment. "Keep your boots with you and wash them as best you can. Your sword, too. Everything else will be disposed of."

She nodded, not liking the thought but knowing that he was right. After a long time of soaking the sewer scum off in the bath, she emerged to find a small pile of clothes waiting modestly just outside the compartment. All of them appeared to be second- or third-hand at best, and were covered with patches and thin places. The breeks fit well enough, but the tunic was baggy and hung loose on her frame, effectively disguising what little she had in the way of feminine curves. She wondered if that had been Yozerf's intention. A small square of cloth with no obvious function was also included; she tucked it into her sword belt and went in search of the others.

The low murmur of voices came to her from the end of the hall, and she followed them to the small atrium. The attendant was nowhere to be seen.

"You say Ax was involved in this?" Yozerf was saying as she approached.

"Indeed." Londah stood with him, leaning up against the wall in a casual pose that no doubt belied an instant readiness to fight. She stiffened slightly when Suchen appeared, and suspicion flickered through the depths of her gray eyes.

"You may speak freely in front of Suchen," Yozerf said without turning to her. Probably, she thought, he had identified her by scent alone.

Londah did not relax her alert posture. "You have not yet said how you came to be with these humans, my son," she pointed out.

Bitterness flashed briefly across his face and was gone. "Ax again."

"Ah." The Aclytese woman's eyes remained fixed on Suchen, making her feel distinctly nervous. "The wizard has been busy. Perhaps it would be best to leave the humans here and go our own way."

Suchen knew a challenge when she heard it. Her mouth flattened, and she raised her chin slightly. "If you wish."

"I am not leaving," Yozerf said, a trace of amusement in his voice. He detached himself from the wall, came over to Suchen, and deftly plucked the square of cloth from her belt. "Allow me." He turned her gently away from him, then ran his long fingers through her damp hair, fixing it into a plait. The cloth he folded into a triangle, then wrapped around her head, tying it in the back. "There. Now you look like a sailor. No one would ever think that you were the Steward of Kellsjard."

"Steward of Kellsjard?" Londah asked, tilting her head to one side in a gesture that reminded Suchen strongly of Yozerf. "That is a surprise."

Suchen pressed her lips together for a moment. Clearly, Londah did not trust any of the humans. Perhaps she would not have trusted them even if they were Aclytes—after all, she had at least thought that Yozerf's father was human, so she couldn't have been as prejudiced against them as her son had once been.

"Really, Londah Jonaglir?" Suchen asked, and was rewarded with a flinch and a sharp look at Yozerf. It had been generations, Yozerf had said, since the Jonaglirs had been known to any outsiders by their true clan name. "That strikes me as odd, since you are in part responsible for it."

Yozerf's brows quirked together. "Explain."

Suchen did not take her eyes from Londah. "I know you. You were in Iddi, ten years ago. You helped a young woman there."

Londah frowned slightly, but her large eyes were thoughtful. "Ah, yes. I do remember that."

"Why? I mean, why did you help me?"

Londah's frown transformed into a slow, predatory smile. "Because you had the hungriest eyes I have ever seen, child. Because I know a warrior when I see one. And yet you became Steward instead of Sworn."

Before Suchen could respond to the implied question, Yozerf stilled her by wrapping his hands gently around her shoulders. "Suchen has a dragon's courage," he said, and she could hear the pride in his voice. "She is one of us now."

She twisted her head about, intending to ask what he meant by that. But at that moment, the sounds of footsteps came up the hall, and Auglar, the Sworn, Cybelen, and Fellrant appeared en masse. Like Suchen, they were now all dressed in rough castoffs that could have belonged to any poor laborer. Even Cybelen wore a simple peasant dress, although her small pendant still hung about her smooth neck. Her lack of complaints impressed Suchen, and reminded her strongly of Rozah.

Yozerf raked his cold gray eyes over them, then nodded sharply. "Come then."

They left the bathhouse behind, moving swiftly through the streets. They attracted far less attention this time, for which Suchen was grateful. After going a few blocks, they came upon the remains of an ancient wall; houses were built up against it on either side, and ragged cuts had been made in it to allow streets to pass through.

"Welcome to the Old Quarter," Yozerf said, his voice flat and hard. Glancing up at him, Suchen saw darkness gathering in his eyes.

From the boundary wall on, the neighborhood around them rapidly deteriorated, going from poor to the sort of squalor that Suchen had never imagined existed. The gutter down the center of the street was an open sewer, and thousands of mosquitoes hummed above the stagnant water collected in it. The buildings looked as though they had been built lifetimes ago, and had been falling into disrepair and neglect ever since the last nail was driven into place. The people either moved furtively, their eyes averted from the faces of others, or else called out brash offers to all those passing by. A cluster of young Aclytes stood on one corner, like a pack of feral dogs looking for something to savage, and Suchen felt the cold sting of their eyes as she passed. A one-armed man reeking of alcohol staggered out of a building, pulling a girl who looked to be no older than five years behind him.

"An octarii each for an hour with my daughter!" he shouted at them.

Auglar's step hitched, a look of outraged horror spreading over his features. Then Yozerf was beside him, one white hand locked around the young lord's arm. "Keep moving," he snarled, including the rest of the group in his glare.

"But that girl—" Buudi started to protest.

"There's a thousand more like her between here and the docks," Yozerf said bluntly. "Boys, too, for those that prefer them. You can't help her, and trying will only ensure that at least two people down here will have a cause to remember you. *Keep moving.*"

"Heartless bastard," Peddock muttered.

Yozerf shot him a look that should have cut like a knife. Then he quickened his pace, leaving them all behind in a black swirl of cloak.

Anger tightened around Suchen's heart, and she punched Peddock roughly on the arm. "Be silent. You don't know what you're talking about."

Her brother gave her a hurt look. "I should have expected you
to take *his* side."

Suchen saw Fellrant's eyes turn to them and realized that he
was calmly listening and storing away all the information he overheard. Giving the lord a cold look, she closed her mouth on any
reply. There would be plenty of time to argue with Peddock later;
right now, they needed to present a united front.

The smell of the docks, of ocean water, wet wood, and drying
fish, grew stronger as they descended the slope towards the bay.
Eventually, Londah came to a halt before a row of tenements so
decrepit that it seemed impossible for them to still stand at all.
Suchen's heart tightened, and she sincerely hoped that this was
not the place the Aclytese woman had chosen for them to hide in.
But, to her dismay, Londah started for the door.

"Welcome to your new home," she said with a knife-edged
smile. "At least for a little while. Best not to stay in one place for
too long."

The door opened directly onto a flight of extremely rickety
stairs. Other doors faced the small landings, all of them firmly
closed. Trash littered the stair, and the narrow place reeked of
urine. An Aclytese man lay sprawled on one landing, an empty
wineskin in his hand. Londah simply stepped over him, as though
she was used to such obstructions, and the rest followed suit uneasily.

Londah did not stop until they had reached the top of the
building. There she paused long enough to take a tallow candle
from above the door and light it. The pallid flame revealed a single
large room with only a broken chair as furniture. A thick layer of
grime covered everything, and there was a large, dark stain in the
center of the floor that looked as if no amount of scrubbing would
remove it. Nonetheless, Suchen immediately saw the appeal of the
room; its three windows all gave a commanding view of the surrounding neighborhood, and would let them see any trouble long
before it found them.

"Do you...live here?" Auglar asked faintly, looking about the
dirty room with an expression of vague horror.

"Of course not," Londah said.

"At least, not anymore." Yozerf ducked slightly as he came in
through the doorway. The door was half-off its hinges, and he
propped it gently against the jamb. He paused for an instant, long
fingers brushing against something on the wall. The faint light of
the candle revealed old marks in the ancient wood. Drawing closer,
Suchen saw that someone had once attempted to scratch the out-
line of a dragon into the wall with a knife.

"This is as safe a place as any, for now," Londah said. She dribbled some melted tallow on the floor, then used it to stick the candle upright. "But I would advise you not to linger over your decision as to what to do next."

Auglar went to a window and stared out bleakly. "I still can't believe that the southern lords tried to kill us."

"Believe it," Fellrant said bluntly. He went to the chair, tested its solidity, and sat. Somehow, despite his ragged clothes and dismal surroundings, he maintained a regal air.

Suchen felt an unexpected twist of hatred at the sight of him. It had been a long time since the siege of Kellsjard—but not so long that she had forgotten the deprivation and terror of those days. All of that suffering had been caused by this small man, who now had the gall to sit in their midst as if they were lifelong allies.

"And believe also that they might send spies," he added, oblivious to the hard looks many of the Sworn were sending his way. His blue-violet eyes canted about to rest on Cybelen.

"That's ridiculous," Peddock exploded. He stepped in between Fellrant and Cybelen, as if he would protect her from the lord's accusation with his physical presence. "Cybelen could have been killed! Would have been killed, if the assassinations had gone as they were supposed to."

Fellrant remained unruffled by Peddock's anger. "So you say. But you cannot know that is so. There is no reason to think that she would not have been spared."

"I knew nothing of this," Cybelen said. Her voice was level, but Suchen could hear an undercurrent of anger in it. "And I don't believe that my father was involved, either. The fact that a few of the southern lords attempted a coup doesn't mean that they were all involved. Perhaps the conspirators believed that, with the two of you dead, the rest would simply have no choice but to go along with things."

"Perhaps. But we have only your word that you were ignorant of the plot."

Peddock's hands curled into fists, and an angry flush spread across his face. "You have no right to speak to her like that."

Fellrant's large, deep eyes flicked up to Peddock's brown, and he smiled suddenly. "And you have no right to speak to me as you do," he said softly. "You, the disinherited child of a bourgeoisie merchant of no breeding, accepted as Sworn more as a favor to your sister than because of any talents of your own."

Peddock's face went white, and for a moment Suchen seriously thought that he might strike the lord. Then, suddenly, he turned away and went to stand staring blindly out the window, struggling to control both his anger and his fear.

"That's not true," Suchen said quickly.

"I will not have you insulting my Sworn," Auglar put in coldly. "If we must be allies, even temporarily, you will show respect to my people. After all, they are the only thing standing between you and a quick death at the hands of the other lords."

Fellrant bowed his head, but Suchen thought she saw a smile on his lips in the moment before the shadow of his long hair hid his features. "Of course, Lord Auglar. Forgive my rash words."

Auglar stared at Fellrant for a long moment, then ran his hand back through his hair with a sigh. "We are all tired tonight. We have to get out of this city, but it may be a while before we can. For now, I suggest that we all do our best to sleep."

Unfortunately, the only available bedding was a pile of old, musty blankets in a corner. Suchen dutifully distributed them to everyone, on the somewhat dubious theory that they were better than nothing. Most of the humans immediately settled down into whatever comfort they could find on the hard, dirty floor. But Londah remained watchful at the southern window, and Yozerf went to the Northern one, perching in it with one leg thrown over the sill so that his foot dangled above the street below.

He looked up when Suchen approached, his eyes reflecting back the dying light of the candle with an eerie green glow. His pale, beautiful face was impassive, streaked with shadows from his tangled hair, but she could feel the tension in him. He shifted a little, making space for her to sit on the sill between his legs. When she settled in with her back against him, he wrapped both arms around her, resting his cheek against her hair even as he continued to watch out the window.

Feeling suddenly, unutterably weary, Suchen relaxed against him. But his heart was racing against her back, and the muscles in the arms that held her were drawn tight.

"Did you grow up here?" she asked softly, remembering his words, how he had known where to look for the dragon carved into the wall.

"A bit." He sighed against her hair. "I was perhaps ten when we came here. When I was sixteen or so, Mama and I had a falling-out of sorts, and I moved elsewhere. Then I came back, three years later, for a little while."

Suchen glanced across the room to where Londah sat in her own window, beautiful and deadly. "What did you fight about?"

He hesitated, and she knew that she had touched one of those dark places that he almost never spoke of. Her only knowledge of his life before he had met her was nothing but fragments, hints, and guesses, she realized suddenly. "We had...a disagreement over a friend of mine. Nothing that matters now."

Tell me, please, she thought but could not say. There were so many things that he kept locked away from her, but she had never felt the wall between them more acutely than at this moment.

But instead she moved on to a safer topic. "Lord Fellrant knew just what to say to Peddock," she murmured quietly. "How?"

Yozerf's body relaxed slightly against hers. "I don't know for certain, but I can guess. The man is no fool, Suchen. He or his agents speak to the servants and listen to what they tell him. He knows that most of the mighty seem to think that their servants are too stupid to understand the things discussed in front of them, or to put bits of information together. Fellrant knew that Auglar was going to be his adversary, so he no doubt did everything he could to learn as much about him and his chief retainers as possible. I feel sure that, had the southern lords waited even another day to try their coup, he would have known about it beforehand." Yozerf paused, then shook his head, his hair rustling over hers. "He is a very dangerous man."

"I know. I was trapped inside Kellsjard during the siege, remember?"

"Force of arms is one thing. But he has a different sort of strength as well. Even without an army at his command, I think it would be wise to keep a close eye on him."

"You don't think Auglar should have rescued him, do you?"

"No. I don't."

Suchen's mouth tightened. "I don't either," she said, hearing the hate in her own voice. "I think we should have left the bastard to get what he deserved."

Chapter Six

Yozerf sat up all night, watching and waiting, even after Suchen had retired to her blanket. Telmonra watched with him, although she did not speak. The memory of her blood lust hung heavy in his mind, along with the realization that he had come very close to losing control and revealing his powers to his friends. Gods, that would have been a disaster indeed.

But Telmonra had subsided, he reminded himself. He was still in control.

Most of the humans moaned when they awoke, and they all moved stiffly after a night spent on the hard floor. Breakfast consisted of some shriveled apples and a thin porridge that Londah had bought from a cart on the street outside. "Yozerf and I will go out today and see what's afoot and what your chances are of leaving Segg," Londah said while they ate. "The rest of you stay here. A large group of people moving in and out of this place will attract attention."

Peddock's lip took on a familiar, stubborn jut. "You aren't in command here, Aclyte."

"Peddock, be silent," Auglar said. Dark circles ringed his eyes, and Yozerf guessed that he had not slept well. "Londah and Yozerf know this city, and we don't. I'm prepared to trust their judgment."

A faint grin flashed over Londah's mouth. "How unusually wise for a human."

The streets were quieter in the morning light than they had been at night. A few ragged children played here and there, feral dogs rooted in the garbage, and the faint shouts of sailors rang from the direction of the docks, but for the most part the Old Quarter was silent and still.

Yozerf felt his body fall into an old, familiar rhythm as he walked. His hands remained near his belt, as close as possible to his weapons. His shoulders slouched slightly, and he kept his head down, signaling to everyone that he was something that should be ignored. He supposed that if he had been in wolf form, he would have tucked his tail between his legs.

The daylight held different memories than the night. He remembered getting up early as a child to walk to the market with Ginny, spending what little coin Darryn gave them on sweet bread and rotgut. After eating a little and drinking a lot, they would curl their tiny bodies together—she had been ten and he eight—and sleep away the rest of the day until it was time to get up and go out to the streets yet again.

"So tell me of these humans, my son," Londah said, breaking him out of his thoughts.

For a moment, Yozerf felt an odd confusion, as if it was impossible to fit the different pieces of his life together. He shook his head sharply, like the wolf flinging water from his coat. "What would you know?"

"You said that Ax sent you to them. Yet you will not leave them."

"They are my pack."

"Ah." She paused delicately. "And the woman? She seems unlike Sweet Gin."

Yozerf's stomach tightened. He had avoided speaking to Suchen of his fight with Londah over Ginny's presence in his life. Londah had felt that they were bad for one another—that their closeness only served as a constant reminder of their shared past. But who else did he have? He had Ginny had been a pack of two, close as siblings from the same litter.

But she didn't want to be your sister, did she?

No, she didn't. Perhaps Londah had seen it. Perhaps *he* had seen it, but denied it, terrified of losing Ginny. Terrified of failing her.

But he had failed her, of course.

And she had died.

"Very unlike," Yozerf said at last. "Ax sent me to them, to protect another young woman—Queen Rozah, escaping from the prison her Regency Council had kept her in for all her life. I...Suchen...." He trailed off, not certain how to explain the events that had changed his life from a state of hopeless endurance to something precious. "We fell in love," he said finally, spreading his hands apart helplessly. "It was not something I sought."

A faint smile touched Londah's face. "My son in love with a human. If I had not known Sweet Gin, I would not have thought it possible."

"I did not love Ginny. Not like that."

"I know. But you cared for her."

"Yes." Yozerf looked away, not wanting to go any farther down that path. "There is something you have to know." He gave her the

skeleton of what had happened the previous winter, from his encounter with Ax to Rozah's death at Nava Yek, a dry thing with no
detail. No mention of his fall from the tower, no, or Telmonra's
silent presence in his head. Not because he didn't trust her to keep
his secrets, but rather because she had a way of turning every pain
and mistake of his into an indictment of herself.

"I have failed you, my son."

"Jahcgroth is our kin," he said quietly. "He is Jonaglir. I don't
know how that could be, but it's true."

A wide-brimmed hat shaded her features from sight, but he
heard her breath catch in surprise. "There were many things lost
after Caden's fall," she said uncertainly. "It's said...I had it from
my mother that Medelin, Telmonra's son, was brought into Jenel
as a slave. His captors didn't know who he was, and no one who
was taken with him dared speak of it. He was only a child at the
time...there were so many things he did not remember."

A flash of pain hit him, a sense of grief so intense that it stole
his sight for a moment. He remembered Medelin standing solemn
in the courtyard outside of Cade Kwii, looking so grave and helpless, striving to hold back tears. *"You must go,"* Telmonra said to
the boy, her own heart breaking. *"It isn't safe here. I'll send for
you as soon as I can."*

And then only a few days later, the messenger kneeling before
the throne, telling her that the Jenelese had attacked the caravan,
that the son—her only child—was likely dead...

No. Yozerf closed his eyes for a moment, struggling to sort out
his memories from Telmonra's. *He didn't die. He was taken captive, but he lived.*

The grief lingered nonetheless, and he wondered suddenly if,
being a ghost, she was even capable of understanding anything but
the vengeance that drove her. If she could truly know anything she
had not known when she died, or if it was all just an echo...

"And do your humans know this?" Londah asked, jarring him.

He flailed a moment for the thread of their conversation, unable to remember what she referred to. *Jahcgroth, we were talking about Jahcgroth.*

"The traitor..."

"No," he said at last. "No. I...I didn't know how to tell them."
How to say that their great enemy was his blood kin.

"I see. You fear that they would turn against you."

He started to lie, then caught himself. "I don't know," he said
at last. "At the time...it was too difficult. And now, after so
long...wouldn't you ask yourself why I hadn't spoken earlier, if you
were them?"

"Perhaps." She shrugged. "It makes no difference. So tell me, then, now that we are away from other ears...if Jahcgroth survived the fall of Nava Yek, whose side are we on, you and I?"

Yozerf's mouth tightened. "Jahcgroth betrayed us, trapped the dragons and allowed Jenel to destroy Caden," he reminded her.

In his head, Telmonra snarled.

"So he is our enemy. And the human lord and his followers are our allies."

"Yes."

She nodded, content with that. If he'd said the opposite, that Jahcgroth was their ally and Auglar to be put to death, she no doubt would have returned to the tenement and killed everyone there with equal composure.

They walked up from the Old Quarter to the great market near the city's heart. As usual, it was packed with people of every possible description, from the perfumed servants of the wealthy to the mutilated beggars with their wooden cups. The smells of cooking food, animal dung, blood, and incense mingled in the air along with the cries of the vendors hawking their wares. All was a confused kaleidoscope of color: the bright bolts of cloth in the stalls, the ribbons trailing from a young woman's hair, the drab gray of the boys who scraped filth from the cobbles for a fee.

Even so, Yozerf's sharp eyes did not miss the soldiers in Igen's livery circulating through the crowd, nor the increased presence of the city guards. They moved slowly, their eyes watchful, pausing now and again to ask questions of the vendors. No doubt they were hindered by their inability to explicitly state whom they were looking for. After all, they could hardly go around saying "We're looking for the only two legitimate contenders for the throne so that we can kill them—have you seen anything, perchance?"

At least, not on the street. There were plenty in Segg who would sell their own kin for the right amount of coin, and Yozerf doubted that Lord Igen would hesitate to use them.

They passed by unmolested, just two more anonymous Aclytes in a city full of them. Both of them had left their swords behind at the tenement, for openly-armed Aclytes would be too easily remarked on, or even harassed by the watch. For the first time, Yozerf considered dying his hair. Would anyone from the palace remember his blood-hued mane from his brief stay? Other Aclytes, perhaps, but he doubted that any of the lords would be consulting with *them*.

All day, they walked the streets of Segg, pausing twice to buy mugs of ale and listen to the gossip, although naturally they were restricted to taverns willing to serve Aclytes. The sudden increased presence of armed men on the streets was remarked on, but put down to the number of lords staying at the palace. No rumor of the coup had yet reached the streets, it seemed, although it wouldn't be long. The palace servants, many of whom lived in the city or had kin there, would hardly fail to remark on the disappearance of both contenders for the throne and their retainers, after all. By this time tomorrow, speculation on their fates would have run through the city like a fire.

And who then might remember a group of armed men and women walking the streets one night, smelling of the sewers but dressed more finely than the average resident?

The guard on the main gates into Segg had been tripled. On the opposite side of the city, the sailors working the docks gave hard looks to the many soldiers loitering about and asking intrusive questions. Perhaps they thought that Lord Igen had taken it into his head to impress the visiting lords by arresting smugglers, despite the fact that he was neck-deep in many of their affairs.

From one end of the city to the other, the trap had been set, waiting only for Auglar and Fellrant to step into it.

"This will not be easy," Londah remarked when they finally turned their steps back to the tenement and the waiting humans. And that, Yozerf thought grimly, was quite an understatement.

⁓⁓

The long day passed in tense silence in the room at the top of the tenement. The Sworn and Suchen took turns keeping watch out the windows. Cybelen slept fitfully, or talked softly with Peddock, who was unusually solicitous of her comfort. Brenwulf paced the room like a caged animal, although Suchen noted that he kept well clear of the dark stain on the floor. Why, she was not certain; when she had bedded down directly on top of it last night, she had not smelled or felt anything odd.

Through it all, as nerves stretched tight and tempers frayed with waiting, Fellrant sat in their midst like an ill omen. He spoke seldom, but his sharp eyes watched everything. Suchen felt his presence like a knife at her back, and it was impossible to relax.

"Here they come," Buudi said as the sun began to sink low in the west; by his tone, Suchen guessed he referred to Yozerf and Londah rather than the less pleasant alternatives. The intense relief that flooded through her at his words made her realize how worried she had actually been.

Somehow, neither of the Aclytes looked tired, even though as far as Suchen could tell they hadn't slept for well over a day. They had brought dark bread and dried fish from the market for dinner, and passed it around while Yozerf recounted what they had found. The fish had the consistency of leather and tasted abominable, but Suchen forced herself to choke it down nonetheless.

"So we are trapped," Auglar said when Yozerf had finished speaking.

Fellrant carefully set aside his portion of the dried fish, his expression one of disgust. "So what are we to do? I for one don't intend to simply sit here until the other lords ferret us out."

"There are two alternatives," Yozerf replied slowly. He had propped himself against one of the windowsills, and now stared out as if he wished he were back outside again. "You could try to discover if there are any of the lords who were against the idea of killing you, who would be willing to ally themselves with you against the rest."

"And how would we do that?" Peddock asked. "Go the fortune teller in the market?"

"The servants," Fellrant said.

"Yes." Londah drifted across the room like a shadow. "Many of them live in the city, especially those that have families. The rest have kin outside the palace. Some of them would know. But it would be a dangerous venture."

"At least it would let us know who our allies are," Auglar pointed out.

"Perhaps. At the risk of exposing yourselves. Not all servants are disloyal or uncaring of their masters, and it would make an easy trap."

"And our other alternative?"

Yozerf sighed, and for a moment Suchen caught a glimpse of weariness in his gray eyes, quickly hidden. "As this is the only port in Jenel deep enough for sea-faring vessels, you can imagine that smugglers are...quite active...here. You would not be the first persons who wanted to leave the city quickly, without any questions asked. We could most likely find someone willing to get you away from here in secret."

"For a price," Buudi clarified.

A faint, mocking smile touched one corner of Yozerf's mouth. "Of course."

Auglar frowned in concern. "We weren't able to take much with us when we fled. Would we be able to afford it?"

"Perhaps. I can't say for certain yet."

"And this is the course you would suggest?"

"Yes." Yozerf glanced at Londah. "I assume that you know who we should contact to make arrangements."

Londah smiled that razor smile she had. "But of course."

For the first time, Suchen found herself wondering how Londah made her way in Segg. She said that Ax had sent her to them, and that Suchen believed. But she had never mentioned anything else about herself. Clearly she was an incredible fighter, yet she was no mere guard or sword-for-hire. She had been able to walk unnoticed into the palace itself. She had bolt-holes around the city and was familiar with the ways of smugglers, but nothing in her manner made Suchen think that she might be one of them.

Do I really want to know the answer? Suchen asked herself wryly. Whatever Londah did to make her way in the world, it the probability that it was legal seemed rather low. Most likely, Londah didn't care much about human laws; certainly Yozerf seemed to regard them as an inconvenience rather than a moral imperative.

"As a matter of fact," Londah went on, "the best person to contact might be an old friend of yours, Yozerf. Gevannin."

Yozerf frowned. "I would not have called Gevannin a friend."

"Associate, then. He is now the proprietor of a blood pit over on Tallow Lane."

"Ah." Yozerf sighed tiredly, then pushed himself off the window sill. "Very well. I will approach Gevannin tonight. Mama, you can talk to the servants from Nava Nar and see if we can safely learn anything from that approach. The rest of you stay here."

"I'm coming with you," Suchen said quickly. She didn't know what a blood pit was, but it sounded sinister, and she'd be damned if she let Yozerf go into danger by himself.

"Me too," Brenwulf said anxiously.

Yozerf narrowed his eyes. "Your place is by your lord," he said to Brenwulf, his voice soft but sharp. "You chose this path."

Brenwulf took a deep breath. "I'm not used to...to being locked in a cage like this. I need to feel the wind."

"Too bad."

Desperation crept into Brenwulf's voice. "This room smells of blood."

On the other side of the bleak little chamber, Londah suddenly became very, very still. Surprised, Suchen looked at the Aclytese woman and saw that she held herself as if a sudden move might cause something inside of her to break.

"I know," Yozerf said quietly, either ignoring or not seeing Londah's sudden stillness. "But that changes nothing."

Brenwulf closed his eyes and looked away, defeated. Nothing about the exchange made sense, Suchen thought. Brenwulf spoke to Yozerf as if only the Aclyte could understand his need to escape the room. But as Sworn, he should have asked Auglar's leave, not Yozerf's. Not to mention Londah's strange reaction, or Auglar's failure to remark on Brenwulf's odd behavior.

Yozerf turned towards the door, but stopped when Suchen moved to follow him. "You should stay here as well. It is not safe."

"Then it isn't safe for you, either."

"At least I am familiar with the danger."

Suchen put her hands on her sword belt and met his feral gaze defiantly. "Meeting with smugglers can't be safe, and I don't like the sound of this 'blood pit' that Londah mentioned. You should have someone to watch your back."

Yozerf's mouth flattened in annoyance. "I've never had anyone to 'watch my back,' as you put it, before."

"But you do now."

That stopped him. For a moment, he looked torn, and Suchen thought he would find some new argument. Then his eyes softened, and a rueful smile tugged at his lips. "Very well."

"Perhaps I didn't raise a fool, after all," said Londah from the other side of the rooms, where she appeared busy oiling her blades.

Yozerf shot her an annoyed glare, which she ignored. Making a gesture of surrender, he pulled open the half-broken door and started off down the steps. Suchen followed close behind.

The night air was cool compared to the close stuffiness of the tenement. Suchen took a deep breath, then wished that she hadn't when the stench from the privies in back of the building hit her. The sun had set while they debated, and more people were stirring abroad. An Aclytese youth slunk past, his hair an odd admixture of brown and brilliant green. As they passed, he paused, staring wide-eyed at Yozerf. Yozerf, however, bared his teeth in a snarl that sent the youth hurrying on his way.

"What did Brenwulf mean?" Suchen asked after the youth had disappeared. "He said that the room smells like blood, and you agreed. But it doesn't. It's musty and too close to the privies, but that's it."

Yozerf was silent for so long that she thought he wouldn't answer. "There is a stain on the floor," he began slowly.

"I saw it. But I slept on it last night, and it certainly didn't smell like much of anything."

"Nevertheless, it was made by blood."

A shiver worked its way up Suchen's spine. By the size of the stain, then, someone had died there. "Whose?"

"Mine."

It wasn't the answer she had expected. Startled, she stopped in the street. Yozerf kept walking, then paused as well when she didn't move to catch up. "Don't stand in the street," he warned. "It means that you are either selling yourself or looking for someone else to buy. Either way, it's dangerous."

Cursing her own ignorance of this place, Suchen started walking again. Yozerf fell in beside her. His long hair cascaded around his face, hiding all expression from her. "It was a long time ago," he offered, as if that might lessen some of the horror of it.

Once, before they had left Kellsjard, Suchen had waited until he had fallen asleep, then carefully inspected every one of the multitude of ugly red scars that covered the inside of both arms between wrist and elbow. The ones on the left arm were even, straight lines, but the ones on the right were crooked and uneven, as if the hand that had held the knife had not been steady by the time it got to that arm.

And probably it hadn't. The hand had been Yozerf's own, after all, and he must have surely lost a great deal of blood in the first few minutes. That he had survived at all was a miracle.

"I'd brought great harm on someone I loved very much." That was all he had said to explain the scars, sitting in bed with her on the long morning when they first became lovers. He had never explained at all the other scars that troubled her—the ancient, faded outlines of human teeth in the back of his neck and on his groin. Instinct suggested that there was a connection, however indirect, but she had never had the courage to ask.

In any event, now did not seem like the best time to begin such a conversation, not when they would both shortly need all their wits about them. But she reached over and took his hand in her own, squeezing his fingers hard to convey all the things she wasn't sure how to say. After a moment, he returned the pressure, but his eyes remained distant.

✎✎

As they drew closer to the blood pit, Yozerf began to feel as though a ball of ice had formed in the bottom of his stomach. The place they sought was near the docks, in the darkest and roughest part of town. No signs marked it from the outside, but he could hear the cheering of men even from the street, and guessed that it was well known. Rather than go in the front door, which was guarded by a scarred, one-eyed bouncer, Yozerf led the way into the alleyway beside it and knocked on a smaller, more discreet portal. A judas shot back, and a pair of Aclytese eyes looked out at him.

"Who're you?" asked a hoarse voice in Aclytese.

"I'm looking for Gevannin," he said, wishing that he had some better excuse.

The eyes narrowed. "And why should Gevannin want to see

you? I don't know you."

"I'm an old...associate...of his. I've been gone from Segg for some time, but I'm sure he'll remember me. My name is Yozerf. If he doesn't remember it, describe me to him."

In truth, Yozerf wasn't at all certain that Gevannin *would* remember him. They'd had little to do with one another, save for one night when they had gone with two others to break into a warehouse near the docks and steal a precious cargo meant for Lord Igen. Gevannin's nerve had failed him right before they reached the warehouse, and he had left the group. Which was perhaps just as well for him, considering that their other two cohorts had not left the warehouse alive.

They waited in silence for the doorkeeper to return. At last, Yozerf heard a grinding squeal as a rusty bolt was pulled back. The man on the other side of the door was small, his body stunted by malnutrition, but the muscles of his arms looked strong as ropes. An ugly scar marred his throat, as if someone had unsuccessfully tried to slit it, and Yozerf guessed it explained the rough quality of his voice.

"Follow me," the man said shortly. Gesturing for Suchen to follow, as she did not understand Aclytese, Yozerf did as requested. They went down a short corridor, then passed through small room filled with men, both Aclytese and human. The air stank of sweat, blood, and cheap liquor. Most of the men were stripped to the waist, their skin shining in the dim light of the tallow candles. Many smelled of fear and nervousness. From the other side of the wall, there came the muffled sound of cheering. A moment later, a door opened, and two men dragged in a third, who was clutching his stomach. Blood poured from between his hands, and Yozerf caught the scent of a punctured intestine. No doubt the man would die—after a few days of agony, anyway.

"This is where the fighters for the blood pit wait between bouts," he whispered to Suchen. Her blue eyes widened slightly, but she carefully kept her expression neutral.

They passed through the room and continued down another short corridor. This one ended in a door that let out into a small room. The room had no other exit, but a small window looked discreetly out into the main room of the building, allowing anyone within to keep an eye on the proceedings. A group of Aclytes were seated around a simple table covered with dice, rune stones, and other gambling paraphernalia. All of them were young, rough-looking, and heavily-armed.

A lone man stood peering out the window with the air of a petty lord surveying his ugly little demesne. His long hair was dyed black, and contrasted sharply with the luminous jade-green of his eyes. Although he was close to the same age as Yozerf, his pure blood had kept him young, and he had not changed much since they had last seen one another.

"Gevannin," Yozerf said with a slight nod of his head.

Gevannin turned from the window, took a sip from the wine glass he held, and set it aside. "Yozerf. It has been a long time." His gaze went to Suchen. "Who is the human?"

"A business associate. No one for you to be concerned with," Yozerf said sharply. He did *not* want anyone thinking her a way to get to him.

Gevannin let it pass—no doubt, in his line of work, he was used to observers who wanted their identities kept hidden. "I couldn't believe it when I heard you were here. I thought you were dead."

"So many do. You've risen far since I left."

Gevannin smiled and nodded, his black-dyed hair rustling against a tunic of green silk. "Indeed. I own several establishments such as this one around the Old Quarter."

Yozerf doubted that. More likely, Gevannin merely oversaw a few blood pits, brothels, and smuggling rings for more powerful men who were never seen in the Old Quarter themselves. But he was in a position to know a great deal about illicit trade and the like, which was what Yozerf wanted. "I'm impressed," Yozerf lied, accepting a wooden cup of wine from one of the servant-bodyguards.

"And you, old friend? What brings you back to Segg?"

"Business, of course." Yozerf took a casual sip of the wine, rolling it across his tongue and tasting for poison. Not that poison was likely—Gevannin had no reason to want him dead—but it never hurt to be careful in Segg. "I need to transport some cargo out of the city as soon as possible."

"Ah." Gevannin smiled slightly. "And you would just as soon not have the port authorities poking their noses into it?"

"Yes. I'm told you might be able to help me."

"I might. Can this cargo take itself to the dock, or does it need help?"

In other words: is it people or goods?

"It can get to the docks well enough on its own. And I will be traveling with it, to make certain that it doesn't get broken before it reaches its destination."

"Where does it need to go?"

"North. Any fishing village will do."

Gevannin nodded sagely, but Yozerf saw the questions in his eyes. "And how do I know that you aren't working for the guards?"

Yozerf went very still, his heart beating fast. The young toughs at the table had set aside their rune game and were now watch him and Suchen with flat, suspicious eyes. If there was a fight within this enclosed space, with the odds so unbalanced, they might not win. "*Me* work for the guards?" he asked dryly, letting none of his fear show. "Surely you jest, Gevannin."

Gevannin shrugged casually. "One can't be too careful. If not the guards, then you might be working for a competitor. The fact is, I don't know you anymore, Yozerf."

"What will it take to convince you?"

Gevannin's green eyes wandered to the window. "How urgent is this matter to you? Is it worth...fighting for?"

No. Damn you to Hel's domain, Gevannin.

He shoved down all his fear, all his doubts, to that tiny, dark place deep in his soul where he hid all the ugliness he had ever seen or known. Keeping his face an expressionless mask, he said, "A bet, then? If I win, then you will agree to do what I want."

A faint, calculating smile touched Gevannin's lips. "Agreed."

Mentally, Yozerf cursed. He had hoped that his willingness to do what Gevannin wanted would be all that was required; surely no one working for the guard would risk his life just to set a trap. But apparently Gevannin was not going to be satisfied with anything short of blood. He wondered briefly if Gevannin thought there was an old score between them that needed settling, one that Yozerf had either forgotten or never even knew existed. It would not surprise him.

"Come with me," said Gevannin, heading for the door. His bodyguards left off their game altogether to straggle along behind him.

Suchen grabbed Yozerf's arm, and he could feel the strength in her fingers as they dug into his muscles. "What have you agreed to?" she demanded in a low voice.

"I'm going to fight in the pit."

"No!"

He pulled away from her. "We don't have a choice!"

"Yes, we do. We'll find another way, damn it!"

The fear in her voice and eyes almost cracked through the façade that he needed desperately to keep in place. "And I tell you there is no other way," he snarled and saw her take a sudden step back, as if she had inadvertently drawn too close to a wild animal. He cursed silently and took a deep, calming breath. "I must do this. Don't worry. I've fought in the pits before and come out victorious."

Gevannin had stopped in the hall and was looking back impa-

tiently. Yozerf touched Suchen's shoulder lightly, then headed out
of the room. They went back through the corridors until they came
to the chamber where the fighters waited their turns.

"Wait here," Gevannin said. He left, his bodyguards trailing
after.

The other fighters stared at them. Ignoring the men, Yozerf
turned to Suchen. "Go up to the main room and watch from there."

"I want to stay here with you."

"I know." Yozerf touched her face lightly with his fingers. Her
strong jaw and nose gave her face a stubborn cast that he loved.
"But I will feel better with you out of harm's reach. If I'm worried
about you, I won't be able to concentrate on the fight."

She hesitated, but couldn't argue. "All right."

He gave her a quick kiss, then bent to whisper in her ear. "And
if I lose, leave this place as quickly as you can."

She started to protest, but he silenced her with another kiss,
then gently pushed her towards the door. She shot him an angry
glare, and he knew that she didn't like the risk he was taking at all.
Hel, he didn't like it either.

After she was gone, Yozerf calmly stripped off his shirt, ignoring the looks the other fighters gave the multitude of scars that
covered both his forearms. The knife in his boot was razor-sharp;
he pulled it out of its hidden sheath and held it loosely in his
hand.

He could feel the eyes of the other fighters on him, could hear
their whispers. None of them were old enough to remember him,
and he wondered suddenly how many of those he had known in
his youth stilled lived. Gevannin, obviously, but how many others
had managed the struggle of simply surviving?

His wait was not long. The man with the scarred throat came
back in and silently beckoned to him. Ignoring the stares of the
others, he went through the door and into the light and heat of the
pit.

The fighting arena that he emerged into was sunk below the
level of the main area where the spectators stood. The large room
was packed with humans of all descriptions, from rough-bearded
sailors to wealthy merchants surrounded by their bodyguards. Eyes
gleamed in the light of torches, wild and hungry for blood. Their
voices melded into a low roar, and Yozerf suddenly felt as if he had
inadvertently stumbled into the lair of some great beast that would
fall on him and rend him to pieces. A growl struggled to erupt
from his throat, and he felt the hair of his neck try to stand on end.

"You could kill them all," Telmonra whispered suddenly, catching him off guard.

For an instant, he could *see* it as clearly as a vision from the gods. He could sweep the room with flame, turn the humans calling for his blood into living torches. The stink of burning hair and roasting flesh would be sweet, and their screams would be like music. A laugh welled up in him, light and cruel and without mercy.

No. He shoved the vision away, blinking rapidly. *That isn't why I'm here.*

"*Vengeance,*" she snarled, and he felt her frustration. "*Why torment yourself with this when there is no need? Burn the city to the ground, my pretty boy. I know that you want to. Burn it. Burn it all.*"

He swallowed thickly, heart hammering. Fifteen years ago, the last time he had stood here, he might have done it if he'd had the power. Everything had seemed so simple then. Humans were the enemy. They were cruel, careless of other lives, capable of no emotions other than hatred or disdain. The only exception to that rule had died at the hands of her own kind, because he had failed to be there to protect her from them.

Now...nothing was simple at all.

His opponent was already in the pit, a grizzled human with ugly scars puckering his skin in a dozen places. As Yozerf calmly stepped out to face him, the other man smiled gleefully, as if he would take pleasure in the fight ahead.

Weakness, Yozerf thought. *Fighting for anything other than survival is weakness. It will make him want to prolong the battle.*

Of course, any good knife-fighter tried to prolong the battle in order to make the crowds happier, the betting heavier. But Yozerf was not here to please the crowds or anyone else. His eyes surveyed the crowd near the pit briefly, and he saw Gevannin watching him intently. On the other side of the circular pit, he caught a glimpse of Suchen's golden hair, and his heart contracted sharply.

A blonde human had just finished announcing the fight. No names were given for the fighters—none were needed in this place, where blood and lust of the crowd were all that mattered. As soon as the announcer was done, Yozerf dropped into a ready crouch, his sharp knife gleaming red in the torchlight.

As he had expected, his opponent immediately charged him with a bellow. Yozerf slid gracefully aside, feeling the keen edge of his knife touch flesh. The crowd howled as a line of blood showed across the human man's side, mixing with sweat to run down to his breeks.

The man was no novice, however. He ignored the shallow wound, instead spinning around and bringing his knife down in an arc. Yozerf tried to sidestep, but his opponent grabbed Yozerf's

knife hand with his free one. Swearing silently, Yozerf tried the
same move, managed to avoid the slicing blade and close his fingers around flesh. The instant he arrested the knife's forward
momentum, he brought up his right knee hard, cracking it into
the side of his opponent's knee. The man yelled as his leg started
to give, releasing Yozerf and jumping back.

They circled one another warily, the human now limping. The
screams and shouts of the crowd had become nothing to them, all
their attention focused on each other. Fear and aggression tainted
the human's scent, and Yozerf gave him a cold smile that revealed
small, sharp teeth. With a snarl, the human charged again.

The knives met, blade catching on blade, and this time the
human drove his other fist at Yozerf's groin. Yozerf leapt back nimbly, leaving a trail of blood on his opponent's arm. For the first
time in years, he found himself facing someone else who obeyed
no rules, conformed to no expectations. In other words, someone
else who had learned to fight on the streets of Segg, where honor
and pride were without meaning, and only survival mattered.

They closed again, and for a moment Yozerf thought that the
fight was his. But he had underestimated his opponent. The human distracted him by slicing at his eyes with his knife. Yozerf
jerked back instinctively—and felt a fist connect hard with his side.

Caught off balance, Yozerf fell to the sandy floor. The overwhelming stink of blood rose up from the brownish grains beneath him, and nausea clawed at his throat. Yozerf tried to roll
aside, but a booted foot kicked his chin, snapping his head back
so hard that he saw specks of light flare in front of his eyes. The
taste of blood filled his mouth, and he collapsed back, dazed.

Vaguely, he was aware of someone screaming his name. Then
the dark shape of the human came between him and the light.
Blinking to clear his vision, Yozerf looked up, and saw the knife
descending.

Terror jolted through him, and he scrambled back, at the same
time lashing out blindly, instinctively—

With magic.

Tight and focused, the wind struck the other fighter's injured
knee, shoving him off balance as surely as a blow would have. The
human screamed and fell to the ground, clutching wildly at his leg.
Blinking sand out of his eyes, Yozerf searched the faces of the
crowd and realized that no one suspected anything more sinister
had happened than the fighter had over-used his hurt leg.

I didn't mean to do it, he thought, coldness washing over him.
*I didn't even think about it, I just reacted, and the magic an-
swered.*

I don't know if I can control it.

"Fool," said Telmonra. And he realized that she was right.

Without the magic, he would no doubt have been killed, or at least injured. A feeling of power rushed through him, and he rose to his feet and stared down at the writhing human who would have slain him. It seemed suddenly that the other fighter was something far away, some sort of evil worm that deserved nothing better.

"Yes. It begins here, my pretty one. Feel it."

With a sudden, frenzied grin, Yozerf grabbed the moaning man by the hair, yanked his head back, and slit his throat.

The crowd screamed its approval as he let the dead man fall limply to the floor. With a smile of approbation, Gevannin reached into his tunic, pulled out the winning purse, and tossed it to him. "Two nights," he called, and Yozerf nodded his understanding. But as he turned to go back through the exit from the pit, he caught a glimpse of Suchen. She stood against the rail ringing the pit, her hands clenched so tightly around it that her knuckles showed white. And the look on her face was one of horror.

⁓⁓

Suchen waited in the shadows of the alley for Yozerf to return, unwilling to go back into the building with its stench of blood and sweat. The cries of the crowd still seemed to ring in her ears, like a pack of maddened dogs that wanted nothing more than to rend whoever they saw to pieces. The final scene of the fight, with its sudden reversal, replayed itself again and again, accompanied by those moments of terror when she had thought that Yozerf was going to die. And then she saw his face again, the terrifying smile as he slit his opponent's throat.

She had seen battlefields, had fought and killed men herself. A long scar on her side showed where she had almost met her own end on an enemy sword. But this...this was different. This was killing for the sake of killing. Killing not for survival, not even for the joy of battle, but for the pleasure of strangers unwilling to risk themselves.

The door opened and Yozerf emerged, his crimson hair catching the light of a far-off torch like a flame. He had put his shirt back on, and even in the dimness she saw that he had washed off the blood that had spattered his face when his opponent writhed in his death-throes.

"We come back two nights from now," Yozerf said as she fell into pace beside him. "Gevannin does not have a direct connection to any of the smuggling rings, but he knows someone who does."

"Fine."

There was a little hitch in Yozerf's step. "You're angry."

"No." She folded her arms across her chest, as if to ward off a chill. "Sickened. Disgusted."

To her surprise, Yozerf laughed coldly. "If you think the blood pits are bad, then you know little of human nature. There are much worse things in Segg."

"I find that hard to believe."

"Really? Did you know that you can buy a person with the express purpose of killing her? Him? Child or adult, whatever your preference."

Suchen stopped in the street, swallowing hard against the bile rising in her throat. Yozerf paused also; his face was terribly calm, as if they were discussing nothing more serious than the weather. "Tell me that isn't true," she whispered.

A faint, mocking smile touched one corner of his mouth. "You are all so naïve, it will be a wonder if I can keep any of you alive long enough to reach the docks. Haven't you ever heard the saying that anything can be bought or sold in Segg? It is a common practice with some panders, although I'll admit the majority of them don't indulge in it. But it is an easy method of disposal if one's 'stock' becomes too old, or too troublesome, or too worn-out. Some of the panders even provide rooms where the clients can play without interruption. After all, it is so unsatisfying to have to worry that someone might come in answer to the screams."

Oh, gods. It was horrible. And there was something in his tone that terrified her even more, a peculiar flatness that she had come to associate with tales that came too close to his own experience. Tears filled her eyes suddenly, and she turned away with a muffled sob.

"Suchen?" She didn't hear him draw close, but suddenly his arms went around her, pulling her against the wiry strength of his body. "I'm sorry." His long fingers began stroking her hair rhythmically, soothingly. "I'm sorry."

"No." She pulled back from him a little, wiping her eyes angrily. "I'm sorry. Gods, I'm not the one who should be crying."

"Shh." He brushed a last tear from her cheek, then tilted her chin up, giving her a little smile. "There's no use in weeping over old pains long done with."

But you're wrong, she thought, and knew that it was true. Not that he was likely to listen to her. "I love you," she said instead, tightening her grip on his hands.

For an instant, she thought she saw something flash through his eyes. Doubt, perhaps. But then it was gone, and she wasn't really certain that it had not been a trick of her imagination after all.

⌘

Londah sat at a table in a small Aclyte-owned tavern just on the edge of the Old Quarter. She had stopped at one of her bolt-holes on the way and changed into the clothing appropriate to a servant of a well-to-do merchant house. The dress and apron were loose, the thick folds of cloth concealing all the weapons beneath.

The woman across from her was a contact she had made many years ago. It never hurt in her line of business to cultivate friend-ships with people from all walks of life, even if the value of their knowledge wasn't immediately apparent. You never knew when you suddenly might need a particular piece of information, and old friends were far less suspicious than new acquaintances.

"I'm worried," Londah said, taking a sip of her ale. This was one of the better taverns in the Old Quarter, and the drink was dark and bitter. "There were guards everywhere in the streets to-day."

The other woman, Samilana, nodded emphatically. Her hands were rough and chapped from years spent scrubbing Lord Igen's floors, and a web work of wrinkles was beginning to spread out from the corners of her eyes and mouth. She believed that Londah was the handmaiden of a spoiled merchant lady, and the two of them had frequently commiserated on the vagaries of their mas-ters.

"Something's afoot," she agreed, shaking her head. "You know the lord took me with him when he moved into the palace last winter?"

Londah nodded. Samilana had been very proud of the move, as if she had arranged it personally. It occurred to Londah, not for the first time, that she didn't like Samilana very much.

"Well, there's strange goings-on. Up until yesterday, we were all in a frenzy, getting things ready for the Conclave, all the floors spotless and the beds made. Today, we're ordered to stay out of an entire wing of the palace, the very one that Lord Fellrant and Lord Auglar were quartered in! And there were guards running about all over the place, and a dinner cancelled, and the cook said no food was sent for from either of their suites." She shook her head, as if wondering at the madness of it all.

Londah pretended to be puzzled by this news. "Did they bring their own servants, then? But where would they be cooking, if not in the kitchen?"

"That's what I mean. It's very strange."

"Do you think..." Londah hesitated, then leaned forward, lowering her voice and widening her eyes into a look of worried innocence. "You don't imagine something's happened to them, do you?"

Samilana adopted the same conspiratorial air. "I don't know. Lord Igen was very angry about something, though—he threw his breakfast at poor Mendach's head! None of the rest seemed happy, either, and poor Lord Jehnav was downright distraught. His daughter was quartered with Auglar's steward—a woman, if you can believe it!—in the same wing as Lord Auglar. So you see, if something happened that involved the steward...well."

Well, that was something at least. Lord Jehnav would not bother to act distraught if Cybelen had been a deliberate plant. Or would he? If she had not been intended to accompany them, if this had been some last-minute plan of the girl's, he would have every reason to be worried.

"The poor man," Londah said. "Did he seem upset with anyone in particular?"

Samilana thought for a moment. "I don't know. I do know that he was demanding to see Lord Igen all day—yelled at every servant who came to attend him that he *had* to see the lord—but Igen never called for him that I know of."

Not allies, then, most likely. Or at least not close ones.

Long after Samilana had left, Londah sat and sipped her drink. It seemed unlikely that Cybelen would betray them, but better to stay on guard than to receive a nasty surprise.

Although, if she had to lay wagers on who was most likely to give them that sort of surprise, all her money would be on Lord Fellrant. That man was dangerous, and Auglar had been a fool to save his life, let alone take him into hiding.

A damned mess, that's what it is. If it had been anyone but Yozerf who asked her to do this, she would have walked away last night and washed her hands of the whole affair. Too dangerous, too messy, too likely to end in disaster.

But it was Yozerf. And that was the most shocking thing of all.

Chapter Seven

Yozerf spent most of the next day asleep, curled up beneath the tattered blankets in one corner of the room. The bitter scent of winter invaded his dreams, carried on a wind that had blown itself out centuries ago...

Telmonra walked quickly through the opulent corridors of Cade Kwil, her riding boots tapping out a harsh tattoo on the stone floor. Servants scattered from her path, but she ignored them, so used to their presence that they might as well have been mobile pieces of furniture. The summons had come to her in the stables, not even giving her time to change after a long ride. Her personal guards followed her, rushing to keep up with her quick pace.

The throne room was on the highest level of Cade Kwil. Elite guards, whose helms bore dragon wings to mark their status, opened a pair of solid gold doors as she approached. Sunlight skittered over the ornate shapes cast in the doors, making the hundreds of dragons and Aclytes depicted there seem to move.

The marble hall beyond was vast and open to the sky. Although rows of pillars carved in the shapes of ancient trees supported a far-away roof, there were no walls on three sides to keep out the elements or the wind. Power alone did that, the blood magic of the king, which came and went at his whim alone. In the deeps of winter, you might find the room warm and snug...or a frigid ordeal, scoured by wind.

Today it was cold, no attempt to blunt the last chill left behind by winter as it reluctantly gave way to spring. The wind that eternally whipped across the mountain's peak howled unfettered, moaning as it touched the pillars. Thousands of chimes jingled and jangled, filling the room with the sound of a wild music.

It was an indicator of her father's mood, she knew. But that was fine—it matched hers as well.

She marched the familiar distance until reaching the foot of the Dragon Throne. The throne was as ancient as the citadel, carved from the living rock of the mountain itself. A stone dragon coiled around the seat, its wings forming a canopy, its head glaring from over the shoulder of whomever sat in its cold embrace.

King Osha XIV stared down at his youngest daughter, his face as inscrutable as that of the dragon. As usual, he did not look particularly pleased to see her.

"You summoned me, Father," she said formally.

"I did. Hours ago."

"I was out riding." She did not add that she had spent half the morning dancing alone on a peak, with only the cold wind to clothe her. There was no need to do so—madness ran in their blood, it was said. At any rate, the clan was used to strange acts from its members, and overlooked them when it could.

"Your cousin has been found. Or, rather, made himself known to us."

She frowned, uncertain. "Jahcgroth?"

"Have any others gone missing as of late?"

She bowed her head slightly, hiding her expression at his biting retort. It had been a foolish question. "I assumed that he was dead."

"Far from it. There has been war in Argannon, as you know. Rumor has said that the rebels were led by a sorcerer. The sorcerer won and has been raised to Emperor. Jahcgroth."

She looked up, caught the expression of anger and cold disdain on her father's face. "Jahcgroth. A sorcerer."

But not one of theirs. Not one who drew on the blood magic of the clan, or else they would have known. He had gotten his power, his training, somewhere else.

Which made him a rival.

But her father had not called her here simply to give her news. "And what do you wish from me? Shall I lead an army against him?"

"No. Not yet. I would know more first…would know what his powers are, what he hopes to gain from his ascent. So I am sending you to visit him. A family visit, of course, to congratulate him on his unexpected rise."

And to spy on him. "But I was never close to him—never even knew him. Surely someone else…"

Osha frowned in displeasure. "Why do you think he left in the first place? That is why I have chosen you—he does not hate you, at least not personally. You have the best chance of gaining admittance to his presence."

It was not a task she would have chosen. But…at least the

trip would be something different. She could get away from Cade Kwii for a while, no doubt to the relief of the man the clan had chosen to be her husband, who did not understand her moods or her strangeness.

"Very well," she said, bowing slightly. "I will leave at dawn."

～～

Yozerf opened his eyes to the sight of the small, squalid room at the top of the tenement. For a moment, it made no sense, his mind still half-enmeshed in the dream, expecting to see the cold grandeur of a throne room.

A throne room that had been destroyed by human hands generations before he was ever born.

And yet...and yet he could still feel the marble floor under his feet, could still smell the scent of ice on the wind, still hear the ringing tones of King Osha's voice.

So real.

Almost, it seemed for a moment, more real than this: the stench of the privies out back, the stale tang of old blood, Cybelen's soft voice whispering to Peddock in a human language.

Suchen lay asleep beside him, her face drawn and pale even in her dreams. *So beautiful,* he thought, and ached to touch her. If only he could wipe away that look of concern and replace it with one of contentment.

And I will. I'll get us out of here...somehow. Gevannin will come through; he must. And...perhaps there are other things that can be done in the meantime.

He rose stealthily, so as not to wake her. A quick look around the room showed him that Londah was gone, and everyone else was asleep except for Peddock, who sat watch at one of the windows, and Cybelen, who kept him company. They both glanced at him; he merely nodded, saying nothing as he slid out the door. No doubt they assumed that he was simply going downstairs to use the privy. Well, they would realize their mistake when he didn't return soon, but by then it would be too late.

Instead of taking the streets, he found a low wall that let him climb up to the roof of a shed, and thence to a ledge surrounding an old stone building. The crumbling stonework offered plenty of hand and footholds, and he quickly found himself on the rooftop with Segg spread out beneath him.

Far below, the first torches bloomed in the night, beckoning the desperate, the bored, and the damned to their nightly rituals. The moon was rising over the sea, spreading its silvery blanket over the rooftops and pooling deep shadows beneath. Up here, it seemed that he was in some way removed from Segg, beyond its ability to touch him, out of sight of its ugliness.

He sighed, knowing that the feeling was just an illusion. Eventually, he would have to come down, after all.

Using the road that the roofs provided, he traveled quickly west, moving gradually up the hill towards the better parts of the city. No one saw him; he was nothing more than a shadow flashing briefly over the gap between buildings, then gone again. At times he ran, his feet pounding over lead or ceramic tiles, startling those beneath. Running was foolhardy, because he had been gone far too long to know the condition of the any of the roofs with certainty. But it felt good, exhilarating, to run and jump and climb without worry of what lay below.

Eventually, he found himself close to the palace. The buildings grew farther apart, and at last he was forced to descend to the ground once again. For a while, he considered trying to actually infiltrate Nava Nar, but his skills were simply not on Londah's level, and he would most likely be caught. No, he would have to sit and watch, and trust to luck. In truth, he had little hope that his quarry would even show himself outside of the palace.

But for once it seemed that luck was with him. As he watched from a hiding place deep in the shadows, a familiar figure emerged through the palace gates. His gait, scent, and face were all branded forever in Yozerf's mind, and the Aclyte felt a lupine growl start in the back of his throat. Forcing it down, he waited until his quarry was almost out of sight, then began to follow.

The man walked with his head down and his shoulders hunched, as if something shamed him. He did not look back or around, only stared fixedly at the cobbles before him, occasionally moving aside to make way for a larger group of walkers. He made straight for a tavern near the Old Quarter—not *The Wyvern*, thank the gods—and went inside. Yozerf found a semi-comfortable place to hide in the alley across the way, and settled in to watch.

The hours passed by slowly. Drunken revelers stumbled out, and others went inside to take their place. A gaggle of whores passed by, laughing, chatting, and calling invitations to the men loitering near the tavern entrance. Later, three young toughs robbed a man who'd imbibed too much to fight back, leaving him in a pool of blood and vomit. Yozerf idly wondered if he was dead or merely unconscious. If the latter, he'd best recover before the carts came around in the morning to collect the night's casualties for burial in the pauper's field, else he might find himself interred alive. The drivers of the carts were not known to be the most conscientious souls when it came to their work.

Finally, Yozerf's prey emerged. The smell of bad ale was strong on him, and his steps were a little unsteady as he made his way over the filth-slicked cobblestones. Yozerf smiled thinly, and a little thrill of pleasure went through him. The wolf hunted the lame, the injured, the sick, and seeing the poor condition of his human quarry called up much the same feeling.

Yozerf detached himself from the shadows and casually followed the human man down the street. No immediate opportunities for attack presented themselves, but he was patient, knowing that it would only be a matter of time. Eventually, they passed away from the more brightly-lit streets and the revelers that thronged them, and entered into a more residential area. The townhouses looked like they might belong to poor artisans or well-to-do laborers; at any rate, unlike the dwellings in the slums, they were closed tight for the night and no lights shone from any windows.

Now.

Yozerf closed the distance in a few long strides. Before the other man could react, Yozerf clamped one hand about his wrist, twisting it cruelly up behind his back. Shoving him hard into the nearest wall, Yozerf braced his other arm across the back of the human's neck, pinning him in place.

"Hello, Dara," Yozerf snarled in his ear.

Dara-Don jerked, his big, open face going white with fear. "Y-Yozerf?" he managed to gasp out.

"Don't cry out. Don't give me any excuse at all to kill you, because you know I'll take it," Yozerf warned softly. "You should be grateful that I'm the one who found you, traitor. If any of the Sworn had discovered you in my place, you'd already be dead." Yozerf gave a short jerk on Dara's arm, eliciting a gasp of pain. "You still might die if you don't tell me what I want to know."

So close, Dara-Don's breath reeked of fear and ale. "I didn't mean for things to turn out the way they did! Oh, gods, you have to believe me!"

"Of course I believe you. You meant for your masters, the Council, to triumph. You meant for Rozah to be locked away for the rest of her life, or else married off to Jahcgroth of Argannon. You meant to take your reward. Of course things did not go as you wished them to." Yozerf paused, then smiled. "Tell me, did you mean to share your reward with your wife? Or are you just as glad that Auglar hung her as a traitor?"

Dara-Don moaned, a low, animal sound. "No. Oh, gods, no, please."

"What? Have you been telling yourself that maybe Auglar let

her live? What a stupid fantasy, human."

Dara-Don said nothing, only closed his eyes. Even in the darkness, Yozerf could see the wetness of tears on his cheeks.

"She's dead," Yozerf repeated harshly. "But you might still live. I might be generous. After all, if I hadn't caught sight of you in the garden at Nava Nar, I wouldn't have realized the danger that Auglar was in, and he and Fellrant wouldn't have escaped. That must not have made your masters very happy. So I will give you the chance to keep your life if you answer me truthfully."

Dara-Don tried to shake his head, but was unable to move it very far. "Please. I-I can't breathe."

"What a shame."

His struggles became more frantic. "I'll tell you anything you want to know! Just let me go so I can breathe!"

"You promise not to run?"

"Yes!"

Telmonra laughed softly. *"He thinks you are a fool."*

Yes.

With a malevolent smile, Yozerf released his grip on the other man and stepped back.

As he had predicted, Dara-Don instantly shoved himself away from the wall and tried to flee. With a single, negligent gesture, Yozerf pulled fire from his mind and spread a wall of flames across the narrow street, only a few feet in front of Dara-Don.

"Yesss. Let it burn."

With a sharp cry of terror, the human staggered to a halt, barely saving himself from a bad burning, then turned and tried to run back the other way. A second barrier of fire stopped him, sent him reeling back to where Yozerf stood waiting.

The flames reflected hellishly off of Yozerf's white skin, and the terror in Dara-Don's eyes brought a feral grin to his lips. "You aren't the only one with secrets, you see," he said.

"Yes. Show him. Make him fear you. Do it!"

Yozerf called the wind, lifted Dara-Don into the air and slammed him against the wall. Dara crumpled from the impact, collapsing into a little heap on the filthy cobblestones. He lay still for a moment, then stirred feebly, bracing himself on his elbows. The sounds of soft sobs filled the street, audible even over the crackle of dying flames. "Don't kill me," Dara-Don whimpered. "Please."

Disgust filled Yozerf at the sight of the cringing, weeping man. Taking two steps forward, he grabbed Dara-Don around the throat, jerking his head up so that their eyes met. The human struggled feebly, clawing at Yozerf's fingers.

"How's your breathing now?" Yozerf asked. He narrowed his eyes balefully, saw terror bloom in Dara-Don's face. A wet stain spread across the front of the other man's breeks. "You are a coward and a liar. Perhaps you were once something more, but if so, I cannot see it. Now answer my question: who are your masters? Or are all of the southern lords traitors?"

"I don't know," Dara-Don wheezed. His skin was beginning to take on a bluish tinge, so Yozerf let go of his throat. The traitor collapsed to the ground, gasping and massaging his neck.

"That's not an answer," Yozerf said, crouching down by him. "You have one more opportunity to tell me what I want to know, or else I'll kill you as worthless."

"I'm telling the truth! I *don't* know, not exactly. It's not like they let me go around interviewing the lords! I'm just a foot soldier, that's all. I just do as I'm told, and I don't ask questions."

"Such a shame. I suppose I'll have to kill you, then."

"Wait!" Dara-Don's eyes all but bulged out of his skull. "Lord Igen! He's in on it. I came here after…after what happened at Nava Yek. I knew that Lord Igen had been a friend of the Council's, that he knew everything they were doing."

"Is this some plot of Argannon's, then?"

"No! Not that I know of, anyway. I'm not Lord Igen's confidante, for the gods' sakes!"

Yozerf smiled sardonically. "I wonder why they don't trust you more."

The misery in Dara-Don's eyes almost made Yozerf feel some pity for the man. "I know. Don't think that I don't. I wish every moment of every day that I hadn't listened to the Council. I wish that Rozah was still alive. I wish that I was still Sworn."

"But you did, she isn't, and you aren't."

More tears welled up in Dara-Don's brown eyes, and he wiped his nose on his sleeve. "I know. Lord Igen gave me a place in his guard. I don't like it, but what else can I do? I don't have anywhere else to go."

"And whose fault is that?" Yozerf sat back on his heels, eyes narrowed. Whatever pity he might have felt was gone now. Dara-Don had made his choices with full knowledge of their possible outcomes, and yet didn't want to bear the consequences of those choices. To Yozerf's eyes, those consequences were not even particularly bad. Did Dara-Don not have a roof over his head, a full belly, a place in his chosen company? "I'm not here to listen to your whining. Who else is in the conspiracy besides Lord Igen?"

"I don't know! I'm just a guard. I hear things from my superiors, sometimes, but half the time it's just rumor." Dara-Don hesitated, eyes darting around nervously. "He...he knows that Auglar and Fellrant are still in the city somewhere. He called me in to meet with him. But there weren't any other lords present at the time, so I don't know who his allies are."

"What did he want from you?"

"He wanted me to help find Auglar. After all, I know him and the Sworn better than anyone, don't I?" Dara-Don laughed, but it was a bitter sound devoid of all humor. "Igen seemed to think I'd have an idea where Auglar might go, that I'd have a chance of spotting him. So that's what I'm doing down here."

"It looks to me as though you were visiting the taverns, not looking for Auglar. Unless you truly believe that's where you'll find him."

"I don't *want* to find him!" Dara-Don shouted suddenly, then bowed his head and covered his eyes with his hands. "Oh, gods, I just want all of this to be over with. I don't think I could stand seeing him again, or any of the rest. They all hate me."

"Yes, they do," Yozerf said without pity.

"Are you going to kill me?"

"Not yet." Yozerf seized Dara-Don's hair, forcing his head back so that their eyes met. "At least not until after I've gotten some use out of you."

"What?"

"You're going to become more involved with your superiors, Dara. You're going to find things out and tell them to me. Like which other lords might be traitors. Like who might be willing to fight on Auglar's side and overthrow Igen's coup."

"I can't—they don't trust me—"

Yozerf let go of Dara-Don's hair and closed his hand tight around the human's throat. "I don't care," he said softly. Heat flowed through him, and he saw with some surprise that the soft skin under his fingers was beginning to redden. Startled, he let go. An ugly burn mark the same size and shape as his hand encircled half of Dara-Don's neck.

"I don't care," he repeated, trying not to look shaken. "You will find a way. Understand?"

"I don't know how—"

"Then find out. Or I will hunt you down and kill you very, very slowly. Do you understand me?"

Clearly terrified, Dara-Don nodded frantically. "You...what *are* you? You weren't like this before."

Yozerf's eyes narrowed. "That is none of your concern, human. You will tell no one else of this conversation. Nor of anything that you have seen here. Or else the pain you're feeling now will be as nothing." He rose to his feet and stared down at the huddled figure before him. "Remember, Dara—unlike you, I always keep my promises."

※※

Yozerf returned to the tenement, his heart beating madly in his throat and his veins full of molten fire. The farther he went from the place where he had confronted Dara-Don, the less worrisome his final lapse became, and euphoria took its place. He felt wild, strong, invincible.

The memory of the human's fear was unexpectedly sweet. All his life, Yozerf had been the one threatened, the one broken to the will of others. Now the tide had turned, though, and he almost laughed aloud at the feeling of well being that filled him.

Curious eyes greeted him when he returned to the small tenement room. "Where is Suchen?" he asked, ignoring the obvious questions of the men.

Buudi directed his eyes towards the ceiling. "On the roof, to get a breath of air, I think. Londah hasn't come back yet."

Yozerf nodded and left without giving them any answers. He felt so light within that he might have flown up the rickety ladder. Pushing aside the trap door, he emerged back into the warmth of a spring night in Segg.

Suchen was sitting cross-legged near the edge of the roof, staring wistfully at the stars. She had turned at the sound of the trap door opening, and an annoyed look touched her face when she saw that it was him.

"You might have told me that you were going out," she accused, the edge of her voice sharp.

"Sorry, my love. I wanted to look into some things on my own, and a human would not have been welcome," he lied. He smiled at her, putting the heat and the energy that thrummed through him into the expression.

Her face softened slightly. "Want to tell me about it, then?"

"Later." He crossed the intervening space between them, dropped down beside her, and bent for a kiss. Her mouth was soft and pliant under his, and the wildness and sense of power that the magic had given him melded with desire.

"Someone might come up," she objected softly, when she had her breath back. He nipped at her neck, running his fingers over her breasts beneath her baggy shirt, and the words died away into a soft moan.

"They won't." He pulled her breeks off the rest of the way, felt her hands scrabble at his belt. She bit her lip hard when he entered her, as if to hold in any sound that might be heard by those in the room below, so he sealed his mouth over hers, stifling her groans. Her short nails dug into his hips, and the rush of ecstasy that filled him was like a faint shadow of the fire he had wielded.

⁓⁓

"You did well, my pretty boy," Telmonra whispered.

Yozerf sat near the edge of the roof, idly watching Suchen dress. The wind had dried the sweat off their skin, but Brenwulf would not doubt smell their scents on each other as soon as they went down. Not that Yozerf cared.

What do you mean? he asked the ghost.

"You used your strength against the human man. You did not hesitate. You are beginning to learn what I have to teach you."

And what is that?

"You will see."

Yozerf smiled at Suchen when she came over to him. Their lips met again. *Dara-Don could easily betray me,* he thought, even as Suchen kissed him. *What I did was a risk—he could be at Lord Igen's feet now, telling him everything that I said. Telling everyone about the fire and the wind.*

"And why would he do that? Does he want his masters to learn that he spoke to you? Does he want them to wonder what he might have told you out of fear? I think his life would not be worth much then. He will tell no one. He is a coward and a traitor, like all humans, and cares only for himself."

Perhaps.

Alien images flashed through his mind: a tall castle with spires like knives, piercing the belly of the sky. Dragons. Snow on stone, and men marching, marching. The snow turned red from blood.

"They are all traitors, my pretty, mad boy," Telmonra whispered as Suchen's kissed deepened suddenly into one of returning desire. *"All of them."*

Chapter Eight

When Yozerf and Suchen at last returned to the small room below, it was to discover that Londah had just arrived before them. Her evening had been successful, in that she had contacted what she euphemistically called a 'songbird'—someone willing to sell information to the highest bidder. In this case, the bird was an Aclytese chambermaid with a bitter grudge against her human employers, one whom Londah said had been of help to her before. How, she did not elaborate, but no doubt the question occurred in human minds. She had agreed to meet Londah an hour before sundown the next day.

"You shouldn't go alone," Suchen said to Londah—but she cast Yozerf a hard look as she spoke. Yozerf winced slightly—clearly their lovemaking had not entirely distracted Suchen from her annoyance with him.

But what else could I have done? None of them can ever learn about this magic in me, no matter how badly I might want to tell them.

"Who then?" Londah asked in her cool, steady voice. "Will you come out, Lord Auglar? Lord Fellrant?"

"I will," Buudi answered, before anyone else could speak. "The lords should stay here, where it is relatively safe."

Auglar sighed. He looked as though he had aged years in the last few days. His long black hair straggled limp around his face, and hollows showed beneath his eyes. The smell of old fear and frustration clung to his skin. "This confinement wears on me," he admitted.

"The confinement of a grave would be even worse," Fellrant pointed out with a vulpine smile. Unlike the rest of the humans, he seemed calm, composed, and utterly unaffected by the stress of days of hiding.

Auglar gave him an unfriendly look. "That's why I will agree to stay here. A small group will have a better chance of going unnoticed."

"And his skin will be safe if it is a trap," Telmonra hissed in amusement.

The servant is an Aclyte. A trap seems unlikely.

Telmonra responded in memories rather than words. For one disorienting moment, Yozerf was no longer seated in the tenement, but instead lay in a bed. A familiar face, flushed with passion, hung above him, and he recognized Jahcgroth, the Emperor of Argannon. Telmonra's lover. Telmonra's cousin.

He blinked back to reality, pushing the foreign memory aside. He understood her meaning well enough: if Jahcgroth had betrayed Caden and Telmonra, then how could a stranger be trusted?

The faint tramp of boots came to him, and for a moment he thought it was the memory of the massacre at Cade Kwii; Jenelese soldiers marching through the streets, killing everyone in sight. But then he saw Brenwulf's head snap up, followed shortly by Londah's. She was on her feet in an instant, gliding to the eastern window to look out.

"Soldiers," she said quietly.

Yozerf joined her, motioning for everyone else to stay back. A small troop of guardsmen from the city watch were making their way down the street, banging on doors and peering into alleyways. Even as he watched, dread slowly forming a lump in his stomach, they came to the door of the tenement.

How could they know? Do they know? Or is it just bad luck?

"To the roof," he ordered sharply, moving away from the window.

Peddock took a threatening step towards him. "Why? So we can be trapped? Was that it? Have you betrayed us—"

Yozerf narrowed his eyes, and for a brief moment considered heaving Peddock out the window as a distraction. But to his surprise, Cybelen rounded on Peddock. "That's insane," she snapped, gathering her skirts in her hand prefatory to flight. "If Yozerf had wanted to betray us, he could have done it in Nava Nar and saved himself this trouble."

"While you argue, the guards are coming," Londah warned from the doorway.

With a final glare at Peddock, Yozerf moved to follow.

꙳꙳

Fear made Suchen's heart pound against her ribs like a caged animal as she followed Yozerf up the rickety ladder leading to the roof. He took her hand, helping her up and guiding her away from the trapdoor. The moon had set while they were downstairs, and the darkness was almost total, relieved only by starlight and the distant flicker of torches from other parts of the city. Nevertheless, he moved as if it was noon on a bright day.

Everyone moved as quietly as possible away from the trap-door, until they were bunched up near the edge of the flat roof. Striving not even to breathe, Suchen strained to hear any whisper from the tenement below. Distant voices floated up…then the sound of doors being shoved open, a few faint curses, and the heavy tread of more boots on the stair.

"Damn," Yozerf breathed, his deep voice little more than a whisper on the wind. She could feel the tension in his body, sensed more than saw the slump of his shoulders.

A moment later, fingers touched her hair, tugging at the headcloth she still wore. "I need to borrow this," he murmured in her ear. "Just in case any of them remember seeing a red-haired Aclyte in Lord Auglar's retinue."

Someone made an abrupt motion on his other side, quickly aborted. The faint starlight outlined Fellrant's thin, beautiful face; Suchen caught a glimpse of mingled surprise and uneasiness before he looked away.

What by Hel…?

But there was no time to wonder. Yozerf knotted the scarf quickly around his head, and moved towards the edge of the roof. Suchen reached for him, but he evaded her touch. "Don't worry," he whispered…then disappeared over the side.

Don't worry, she thought grimly, and put her hand on her sword. *Of course. Why should I worry?* She didn't know what he had in mind, but whatever it was, it couldn't be safe.

But there was nothing she could do about it—she doubted that she could have taken his route over the side of the building even in broad daylight, let alone in the dark. There was nothing to do but sit and wait, listening to the steps on the stairs below as the guards drew closer and closer…

They were in the room below, now, where only a few minutes before the two lords had sat in an illusion of safety. Faint murmurs floated up: "No one here now."

"Maybe not," said another, "but it looks like someone was here not long ago. The candle wax is still soft, see?"

Damn.

More steps, the scrape of hard boot soles on rotting wood. Then a rattle…as of someone testing the ladder beneath.

"What's this?"

She shifted her weight, ready to grab her sword and fight, knowing that there was no way they could escape detection now. It was dark on the roof, yes, but not that dark; they would be spotted the instant someone came through the trap door.

"Hey!" yelled a voice that sounded as though it was blurred with alcohol. "That's my stuff! What're ya doing, robbin' me—"

Yozerf's voice.

Gods—

"A drunk," one of the guards muttered in disgust.

"Man can't go down to the privy without somebody breaking in, messing around with his things—" Yozerf continued to rant.

"Shut up!" The smack of a fist on flesh was followed by the thud of a body hitting the wall below.

No! Without thought, Suchen started to get to her feet, knowing only that Yozerf was in trouble, that she had to help.

Someone grabbed her wrist, jerking her back down. The scent of lavender washed over her a moment before Fellrant's voice whispered in her ear. "Don't. He planned it this way, to distract them. Don't throw away his sacrifice."

She froze, knowing he was right but hating the fact. There came a few more muffled thumps from below, then one of the guards said, "By the gods, there's nothing in this damn hole but a bunch of drunken Aclytes."

"Damn wild goose chase," another opined.

Boots thumped on the stair, going down. Even though every instinct screamed at Suchen to get down the ladder and help Yozerf, she forced herself to listen until the door at the bottom of the stair had closed. Then, shaking off Fellrant's grip, she rushed to the trapdoor.

Yozerf was climbing to his feet as she came down. He moved stiffly, and even in the dim light she could see that one of his eyes was rapidly swelling shut.

"Damn them," she muttered, touching his face. "Are you badly hurt?"

"No." His voice was tight, clipped, as if he fought against anger.

"We cannot stay here," Londah said, materializing beside them. "It is no longer safe."

Fellrant laughed hoarsely. "And you know anywhere that is?"

"Not entirely, of course. But safer, yes. Just not as...comfortable as this."

This was comfortable? Suchen cast a dismayed glance at Auglar, read the despair in his eyes as well. But he nodded.

"Take us there, then," he said.

❧❧

"You are a fool!" Telmonra railed at him. *"A fool, a fool, a fool!"*

Yozerf walked behind his pack, fighting to control his temper, fighting to keep any expression off his face. A face that ached from the guard's blow, the bruise throbbing in time to his heartbeat. The bruises on his side where they had kicked him—they hadn't been interested enough to break any ribs, thank the gods—hurt with every jarring step he took.

"Why do this to yourself?" the ghost went on, her rage eating like acid at the edges of his mind. *"Why suffer, why become a martyr? You could have destroyed them all, burned them to ashes, but instead you allowed them to beat you!"*

I had no choice, he snapped back, finally provoked into argument. *I had to distract the guards. And I couldn't let anyone else know about the magic.*

"Because you cannot trust them. Because they will turn against you. Because your so-called friends would rather see you beaten by others of their kind than know you have the power to defend yourself."

It isn't like that.

"Then what?"

He couldn't answer. His thoughts felt jumbled, incoherent. Scattered by her rage, her certainty.

One of the figures in front of him dropped back, and he caught the scent of lavender and human. *What now?* he wondered tiredly.

"Mayhap Lord Auglar does not value you," Fellrant murmured, too low for anyone else to hear, "but I do. That was an extraordinarily brave act. Such loyalty should be rewarded. If you desire land, a place in my demesne, you have but to ask it."

A trap. Fellrant only looked to sow dissension among them.

Perhaps.

Londah, who led the little group, came to an abrupt halt, which fortunately saved Yozerf from having to reply. They had crossed most of the Old Quarter, all the way to the southernmost edge of the city. Not far beyond them lay the city wall, and on the other side of that nothing but trackless swamp.

A low wall rose up in front of them; tall trees hoary with moss towered over it. An iron gate barred their passage, but Londah picked its lock within moments, shoving the rusty gate open with an ease that suggested she had been keeping the hinges oiled in case the need to lay low brought her here.

Pale stone gleamed in the shadows beyond. They started in—and then Auglar stopped, staring about in horror.

"Where are we?" he asked faintly.

Yozerf swung the gate shut behind them. The air was heavy with the scent of the swamp, but even that couldn't mask the all-pervasive stench of decay that shrouded this place. Row upon row of what looked like miniature stone houses stretched out before them, interrupted here and there by a few much larger structures. Stone angels and gods lifted their hands heavenward, their eyes blinded by moss and bird droppings.

"It's a cemetery, of course," he said.

"Not one in use now," Londah added mildly. "But at one time, I assure you this was the most sought-after place in Segg to be buried. Only the wealthy could have their bones molder here. But the city grew and moved on, and their descendents turned out to be forgetful, and so it has been abandoned for the most part. It is said to be quite haunted, by the way."

"But what are we *doing* here?" Peddock demanded, his eyes darting about, as if he expected ghosts to leap out from behind every tree.

Londah cast him a withering look before turned and heading off into the maze of crumbling monuments. "Hiding, of course. Water lies close to the surface of the ground here in Segg—dig a hole for a body, and it quickly fills up. The rich couldn't allow their precious remains to get wet, so they built these houses for the dead where they could stay nice and dry. Some of them built for entire families, and so the crypts are quite large. And the trees provide something of a vantage, as well, if one is willing to climb high enough."

No one said anything in response. Possibly they didn't quite believe she was serious, or were simply too overwhelmed.

Londah led them to a spacious crypt tucked away near the back of the cemetery. A truly enormous oak overhung it; dead limbs lay strewn all about, adding to the general air of decrepitude. There was a rusty lock on the heavy stone door leading into the crypt; Londah opened it easily, and Yozerf suspected that she had used this place as a hideout more than once before.

As he passed inside, he caught sight of an ancient family crest carved above the door. Not one he recognized, and he wondered if those who slept here had left any descendents to carry it on, or if their line had been lost to time. Within, the structure was a simple, single room. The two longest walls were lined with stone shelves that bore the rotted remnants of caskets, now reduced to nothing more than dust and fragments of mice-gnawed bone. The third wall boasted a plaque depicting the seven gods, with a wall sconce beneath for a votive. Two large sarcophagi dominated the floor space, their lids carved into the effigies of a man and a woman. Other than that, there was nothing save dust.

"Make yourselves comfortable," Londah advised. She went to

one of the wall shelves, pulled out a tallow candle from its hiding place amidst the bones, and lit it.

The humans stood in a nervous group to one side, murmuring amongst themselves. Feeling stifled in the windowless building, Yozerf slid out the door and stood in the humid night beyond. Lights flickered here and there beneath the trees, as if unseen hands bore ghostly candles to and fro.

Are there ghosts here? he asked Telmonra.

"No. It takes power to make a ghost. Or great hate. Or both."

Which is what made you.

"Vengeance. Power. Yes. So few understand these things, so few have them, or else the world would be full of shades. You are my vessel."

He didn't understand what she meant and certainly didn't like the sound of it.

The door behind him opened and closed softly. Londah paused beside him, a shadow in shadows. "They are not happy."

Yozerf sighed. "No. I don't suppose they are."

"The meeting tomorrow, with the songbird. It will be at *The Wyvern.*"

It felt as if a fist had suddenly squeezed his heart and lungs until he could no longer breathe. *No. Not there.*

A memory, of blood and searing pain, rose up despite all he could do. And, on its heels, Telmonra's memories, a flood of them: *Little Gesidah, her throat slit, Calaevrion's manhood cut off before the soldiers killed him, the bodies of her cousins hanging from the pillars of the throne room, their blood dripping sluggishly onto the white marble floor.*

"It is not required of you to go, my son," Londah said.

And he was not sure if there was guilt in her voice or not. They had never spoken of the incident that had taken Ginny's life—and, indirectly, almost claimed his as well. Never, because Londah was so convinced that it had been her failure that had put him on the path that had led to Ginny, and to all the grief he and Ginny had brought one another over the years.

For a moment, he almost told her that it bothered him. That he didn't want to go. That it still hurt, after all this time. But the weight of his mother's guilt had been a terrible thing to bear in the aftermath of his attempt to end his own life, had almost been beyond his strength to handle. And now...it was too late to do anything differently.

"Of course I'll go," he said lightly. And people dead for three-hundred years continued to scream in his head.

Chapter Nine

This time, the dream was disjointed, fragments and glimpses only, like a tapestry rotted through by the long accumulation of years.

The wind in Argannon smelled of stone and ice, and if it was not quite the stone and ice of Caden, it was at least similar enough to make the mountain fastness feel like home. The fortress Jahcgroth had chosen had been carved out of the heart of the mountain itself. Torchlight glinted off veins of silver in the walls, found hidden jewels half-cut from columns. The air was cool and dry, kept fresh by windows and cleverly-crafted shafts. During the day, sunlight streamed down some of these shafts, bringing unexpected brightness to rooms otherwise cut off from the sky.

Telmonra sat at one end of the small table, Jahcgroth at the other. Although their dinner was formal that night, the setting was far more intimate than a meal in the great hall would have been. Servants moved here and there, while two of his Sworn waited quietly against one wall.

Shape-changers they were, she knew that much. Kk'ithii'kk. Red Guard.

"I'm impressed," she said, and was.

Her cousin smiled slightly from his end of the table. He looked very regal, she thought—beautiful, really, with his hair the color of gold and butter. His father's shame, he'd been called—a half-breed, unanticipated by-blow from an affair with a human servant. It didn't show, though, as far as she could see.

"Thank you," he said.

The dream shifted a little; some threads were lost. "...how?" she was asking when it righted itself.

He smiled again. Beautiful. "I can't tell you that—forgive me, but I have taken oaths. I can say that I was fortunate enough to meet a wizard and study with him. He told me that, even though I would never lie on the Dragon Stone and bleed my life out into the land, the potential for magic nevertheless existed in me. Exists in all of us, I suppose, but it needs something to wake it up, make it more than mere potential. The ritual that our kings and queens undergo is but one path to awaken it. I took another. After, my master taught me a great many things, ways of gaining more power, of using it, that have nothing to do with Jonaglir blood magic."

"Is there a way for you to get an heir?" she asked curiously. As a half-breed, he was sterile, unless some magic existed to counter that.

But he only shook his head. "No. No, I will have no heir of my body. But...there are other things. Ways of extending one's life, shall we say, that will at least put off that question for a very long time."

"How?"

Again that gentle smile. "As you might guess, not to reveal that is one of my oaths. Youth cannot be regained once it is lost— I had a fellow apprentice, in fact, who came late to the magic and will live out the long years as an old man. But it can be prolonged."

The dream twisted, slid. Flashes: visiting a waterfall with Jahcgroth and his guard. Riding horses across the mountain. Laughing. Singing.

Falling in love.

Screaming in passion as they made love in his great chamber with its vaulted ceiling.

And then they were in the throne room, and Jahcgroth's expression was grave. A messenger dressed in Caden's colors stood before Telmonra, bowing low. "I have ill news, Your Majesty," he said to her.

And she wondered why he would call her that, when she was a younger child, not in line for the throne.

"There has been a plague. Your parents...your siblings...all are dead. You are Queen now. You must return to Caden as soon as possible."

And she turned towards her lover with a cry of despair...

⌇⌇

Yozerf lay wakeful for a long time, remembering the dream. The crypt was dark as night even during the day, but he could sense the slow decline of the sun outside. Those whose bones lay here had not even been born when Telmonra had come to the throne of Caden; no doubt her sorrows would have been as meaningless to them as theirs were to him.

"All are dead." That had been the beginning of the end, in a way. She had gone home, borne her husband an heir as was needed...and spent every evening looking North out the window. Wondering if she would ever see Jahcgroth again. Wondering if he thought of her with as much longing as she thought of him.

"Until he betrayed me," she whispered. *"As you fear your lover will betray you, if she learns the power you wield."*

Suchen is different.

"So was Jahcgroth."

Yozerf sighed, climbed to his feet, and went outside. The evening breeze was rising from the ocean even as the sun sank, and the leaves on the great oak above his head whispered anxiously to one another. He shared their dread.

Why did it have to be The Wyvern? But of all questions, "why" was the one that was most seldom answered.

As it grew darker, he heard movement from inside the tomb. Soon Londah, Buudi, and Suchen came out as well. Suchen came to his side, and he forced himself to smile and take her hand.

"It is time," Londah said.

❧❧

"You don't have to do this," Suchen said urgently as they walked down the street. She and Buudi were disguised as well as they might be with their old clothes, dirty faces, and covered hair. Even so, Yozerf found himself scanning the crowd intensely, certain that at any moment he would hear soldiers shouting for them to halt.

"Of course I do," he said tightly.

"Then tell me why. Tell me what this place is to you. Damn it, Yozerf, don't shut me out like this!"

Buudi glanced back from ahead of them, and Suchen winced and made an apologetic motion. But her blue eyes returned to Yozerf's face; he could feel her gaze like a pressure against his skin, demanding answers. She was already angry with him for slipping away the day before without word. What would she feel if he remained silent on this as well?

I need you, he thought desperately, risking a glance at her. Her sapphire eyes were so beautiful and so deep, he felt as though his soul had gotten lost in them forever. Which would be worse—her anger at his silence, or her disgust at the truth?

"Someone I was close to died there," he said finally, numbly. The scars on his arms ached, and he rubbed them absently. "Her name was Ginny. Sweet Gin—that was what they called her on the street, but she never would say what name she'd been born with. Her father had given it to her, and I suppose it says something that she would prefer a name from our pander over a name from him. Ginny was the older one, the experienced one, when we met. She was ten then, and she'd been in the game for three years already." He stopped, on the edge of anything safe. "She was like a sister to me," he finished, hearing the bitter irony of the words even though Suchen was unaware of it.

"I'm sorry," Suchen said softly. A stray bit of her hair had straggled out from beneath her head cloth, and she tucked it behind her ear absently. "I understand how hard it would be to revisit the scene of a tragedy like that. You don't have to go with us."

"Yes, I do. I failed her, and she died. I won't let that happen to you."

Her head came up, an expression of consternation on her face. "Yozerf, no, that won't happen. I don't know what went on here before, but I can take care of myself."

"So could Ginny. She took care of both of us." He shook his head savagely. "I won't abandon you."

She sighed, and he realized that his words probably sounded irrational. "Whatever happened here, I can't believe that her death was your fault."

"Then you don't know me as well as you think."

Hurt bloomed in her eyes, and he immediately regretted his words. "And whose fault is that?" she snapped.

"Suchen—" he started, hoping to apologize. But she deliberately quickened her pace and went to walk beside Buudi, her back straight and her chin up. Despair touched him—he had hurt her, as he had hurt Ginny, as he had hurt everyone that he had ever cared about. Even Londah was not immune. In his mind, he could still see her sitting there in the chair beside his bed after he had cut his wrists to ribbons, her back straight and her eyes remote. *I blame myself,*" she had said, effectively killing any attempts he might have made to share his pain with her.

I should have known better than to try and tell Suchen anything. I should have hidden it all away, should not have let her realize that something was wrong. Gods, what if she found out the whole of it? What if...what if she finds out what I really am.

He ached to talk to her, to try and heal over the wounds his words had made, but there was no time. As it was, he had not been concentrating enough on their surroundings, and he cursed himself, knowing that there was no quicker way to get killed in Segg.

Although more of the city guard than usual were out, none of them appeared to pay any more attention to their small group than normal. *And what about yesterday? How did they find us then? Have we been betrayed?*

"*Vengeance.*"

Such thoughts distracted him until they at last they reached *The Wyvern*. *The Wyvern* still stood on its little corner between Piety Lane and Gibbet Street, and for an instant Yozerf felt his feet slow, certain that he would hear Ginny's voice floating out from the open windows. But the years had taken their toll, he realized as he approached, and the tavern was not quite a duplicate of the one he held in memory. The walls were more weathered, and the roof sagged lower. The paint on the board hanging outside was sun-faded and peeling. He remembered the day he and Ginny had drawn the red wyvern on a blue field. She had dabbed paint on his nose, then laughed at his indignation, as though nothing in life could possibly ever be taken seriously. That had been her way of holding the world at a distance, and it had worked so well that most people believed it was her true nature.

Inside, *The Wyvern* was a clean but plain place. For the most part, its clientele consisted of laborers such as stone masons, barrel makers, or bakers. Their clothing was simple but serviceable, their hands scarred and callused from the work of long days. Two small symbols painted discreetly on the door indicated that the establishment was open to both humans and Aclytes, and indeed the crowd inside was composed of both. No one paid much attention to the small group that entered, although one of the servers gave a nod and a smile to Londah.

Yozerf's eyes went to the bar automatically, but it was a moment before he realized that he was looking for Ginny. With a silent curse, he instead sought out the tavern keeper. Jarvin stood behind the bar, wiping clean a well-used but still serviceable mug. The years had taken their toll on him, and it was something of a shock to see that his dark skin was now contrasted with white hair.

"She's in the back, in one of the private rooms," Jarvin said to Londah as they approached. Then his eyes went to Yozerf, and he nodded guardedly. "Your mother told me you weren't dead. Good thing we didn't wager money on it, because I wouldn't have believed it if you weren't standing here in front of me."

Suchen frowned. "Why is that?"

Jarvin shrugged carelessly. "Man's been chasing death for as long as I've known him. Normally it isn't that hard to find."

Yozerf glared at Jarvin, who appeared undisturbed to his look. No doubt working with Londah had given the tavern keeper a certain immunity to such things. With an angry flick of his cloak, Yozerf followed his companions through a door at the back of the bar. The smells of beer and food poured out from the kitchen to the left, and he caught a glimpse of the cook, a thin human woman wiping sweat from her brow with the back of one wrist. To the right was the pantry, and Yozerf glanced inside automatically—

And, for an instant, he *saw* her, just as clearly as he could see Jarvin or the cook. She lay on her back in the center of the room, her curly black hair fanned out around her head. Her skirt was shoved up to her waist, her thighs parted wide. A ring of bruises blackened the dark skin of her slender throat, and blood no longer seeped from the dozens of knife wounds lacerating her breasts.

He jerked back with a gasp, closing his eyes in denial.

"Yozerf?"

He could *smell* it, even with his eyes closed, the stink of blood and semen. His heart pounded wildly, dinning in his ears, dampening out every sound.

"Yozerf!"

Startled, he opened his eyes and found Suchen staring up at him in concern. He risked a glance into the pantry, but it was just a room once again, with no sign of the abattoir that it had once been. The stains on the floor might have been from Ginny's blood, or they might have been from spilled food and the accumulated grime of fifteen years.

Londah grabbed the door of the pantry and slammed it forcefully closed. "Go outside and watch for soldiers," she said harshly.

He nodded dimly. It wasn't even a bad suggestion, could have been made for reasons other than the fact that he was seeing things that weren't there. Without speaking to either woman, he turned and made his way back outside. The customers in the common room stepped quickly away as he approached, and he realized that he must look like a madman.

The cool air of evening was a relief after the stuffiness within the tavern. He breathed deep gulps of it, his body sagging against the wall of the building as if he could not stand up alone. A sob tried to tear itself free of his chest, but he forced it back frantically. He had a job to do, he reminded himself. Everyone, his pack, was depending on him. He could not fail them.

For an instant, he saw the scene again, only this time it was Suchen lying raped and butchered on the floor. With a snarl of fury, he pushed away from the wall and went back to the alley. In moments, he had clambered up to a nearby roof, which gave him an unobstructed view of the area around *The Wyvern*. He turned all his attention to scanning the streets for soldiers, for anyone who might be coming to close a trap. But every few moments, his heart began to race again, and memories flooded back into his mind. To make matters worse, his own memories served to provoke Telmonra's, death and blood and screams mixed in together until he was no longer sure what had happened to him and what to her, or if there was any difference.

By the time his companions emerged back into the street, his hands were shaking badly. He rejoined them, startling Buudi when he dropped down from above.

"Success," Londah said succinctly.

Yozerf stared blankly for a moment, before his scattered thoughts returned the reason for their visit in the first place. "Oh. Good."

"Based on what she's seen, the chambermaid thinks that only a few of the lords were in on this. Unfortunately, they were all the most powerful." Buudi smiled without mirth. "I suppose that makes sense—they have the least motive to want things to change, after all. But Cybelen's father is cleared. We can trust him."

"Peddock will be glad to hear that," Yozerf said absently.

No one said anything after that. Yozerf walked like a ghost, lost in his own thoughts, unresponsive to anything outside of himself. When they were only a few streets away from their hiding place, however, Londah made an unexpected turn.

"Where are we going?" Suchen asked. "This isn't the way."

"It is now," Londah said without looking back. "We're being followed."

Damn it! Pulled back to reality, Yozerf realized that he could hear the measured tread of following footsteps and catch the faint scent of oil and metal on the wind. He had been so lost within himself that he had not even noticed danger when it practically screamed its name in his ear.

"What now?" he asked quietly. His sword was back at the graveyard, so he slid a dagger from its sheath at his belt. He had many other weapons, but most of them were better concealed, and he hated to reveal their presence before he had to do so.

"We'll take to the rooftops," said Londah, making another turn that took them farther from the cemetery. "If they're members of the city watch, or the guards of some nobleman, then they won't know to look up." Her tone implied that such a shortcoming could only belong to fools of the first order.

Londah quickened her pace, but subtly, so that the distance between them and their pursuers increased only gradually. As they turned down one alley, momentarily disappearing from the sight of anyone following, she suddenly broke into a run. As they charged after her, Yozerf winced at the din the two humans made, and sincerely hoped that it wasn't truly as loud as it seemed to him.

A line of drying laundry hung from one side of the alley to the other, high above. Londah paused and drew a piece of metal from her belt. It had started as a thin circle of steel, but its edges had been cut away and sharpened into a lethal starburst. With a flick of her wrist, it vanished into the night; a moment later, one end of the laundry rope dropped down to hang at eye level.

Without pausing to admire her work, Londah grabbed the rope, braced her feet against the side of the building, and hauled herself up into the shadows above. Buudi went next. Suchen was the shortest of them all, and Yozerf had to boost her up so that she could reached the laundry-entangled line. As she began to work her way slowly upwards, the sound of footsteps grew louder, and he heard a man's curse.

Silently hoping that the men didn't notice the swaying end of the rope, Yozerf grabbed hold and began to haul himself up after Suchen. The line didn't go all the way to the top of the building, of course, but within reach above it were cornices and rainspouts that offered handholds for climbing. The other two had already vanished above, but Suchen paused at the top of the rope, a look of uncertainty on her face.

Wanting to encourage her, Yozerf gave her leg a squeeze, wishing that he could offer her some verbal advice but knowing that it was too dangerous. Suchen cast a glance down into the alley, and her face paled slightly. Looking down himself, Yozerf saw that their pursuers had come into the alley below. All of them were dressed in the livery of Igen's personal guard.

Damn it.

The glimpse of the soldiers apparently solidified Suchen's resolve, because she hurriedly edged a foot off onto a cornice, then transferred her weight when it held. But as she reached for the rainspout, a fragment of the old masonry broke away beneath her foot, first striking the side of the building, then the ground below.

At the sound, the heads of the guards whipped around, then up. "There they are!" one of them shouted.

Suchen swore furiously and hauled herself up and over the rainspout so quickly that Yozerf found his heart in his mouth. Someone reached down from the roof and helped her the rest of the way up. "Go!" he called after. "I'll be right there!"

But as he reached for the first handhold, an arrow shattered against the stone beside his head. Twisting about, he saw the archer take careful aim and loose a second shot, this one straight for his chest.

It took no thought. Acting on instinct, he flung out his hand and saw the arrow suddenly go wild, blown off course by a gust of wind. The archer below cursed in surprise, and another man yelled at him for being a poor shot. Yozerf took advantage of their momentary confusion to swing himself free of the rope, standing balanced lightly on the ancient cornice.

The rope beside him went taut as a guard grabbed it and began to climb up. Yozerf swore, drew his knife, and severed the thick cord. The man let out a shriek as he hit the ground, but the fall had not been far enough to hurt him. "Take the stairs, you idiots!" shouted their commander, aiming an angry kick at the fallen man.

With a soft oath, Yozerf hurriedly scrambled the rest of the way up. Another arrow whizzed past as he fell over the low parapet onto the roof. The rest of his companions were already on the far side of the flat roof, although Suchen was looking back anxiously. Rolling to his feet, Yozerf sprinted to them. "Hurry! They're coming up the stairs."

Londah didn't hesitate, but ran to the edge and leapt the gap to the steeply-slanted roof of the next building. But neither of the humans had experience doing such a thing, and both hesitated too long before making the jump. Even as Yozerf braced himself to follow, a trap door was flung open, and a host of angry guards boiled out.

Yozerf swore and flung himself over the gap, landing precariously on the slick, red tiles. A moment later, the archer loosed another arrow, barely missing him. Even as he regained his footing and started to run, the building shook from the weight of the guards landing behind him.

Londah let out a wild war cry and met the first of the guards with her own charge, flinging him off his footing and down into the alley below. A moment later, Buudi and Suchen also closed, their swords drawn. Feet slipped on the slick tiles, and opponents on both sides struggled to keep from falling.

Yozerf snarled and stabbed a guard in the neck with his knife, wresting his sword out of his lifeless hand. "Keep them from crossing!" he shouted, and stabbed at the latest man who had landed on their side of the gap. A moment later, an arrow fell near him, almost striking another guard, who began yelling abuse at the archer.

"There are too many of them," Suchen said falling back by him. And indeed, almost all of the guards had already made it across and were quickly finding their footing on the treacherous roof tiles.

"Then run," he replied, fending off one of the guards with a few swipes of his stolen blade.

"What about you?"

"I'll be right behind you." He cast a desperate glance at Londah. "Go! Get them out of here!"

She nodded and started off, Buudi and Suchen following as quickly as they could. Yozerf threw himself at the guards, startling several badly enough that they fell and scoring a wound in another's arm that caused him to drop his sword. It clattered off the roof tiles and bounced away into the alley below, making a hellish din.

Yozerf took advantage of the distraction, turned, and ran after his fleeing companions. The next building had another peaked roof, this one broken up by several gables of varying height. The structure had recently burned, and although it was still standing, it looked to have been largely gutted by the fire.

His companions had made their way safely to the other side of the charred building, so he started after. As he did so, Londah turned towards him one hand lifted in warning. "Yozerf! Be careful—it isn't stable—"

His foot came down on soot-covered tiles, and he felt something give beneath his weight. He tried to leap back, arms flailing wildly, but the burned building had taken too much abuse. With the shriek of nails ripping loose, the entire section of roof gave way under him.

And he fell.

Suchen's scream rang in his ears, and for a moment he was back at Kellsjard, falling from the top of a tower with his enemy. Terror jolted through him, and he might have cried out himself, the sound lost in the crash of falling tile and fire-weakened beams. There was nothing between him and the lowest floor, everything else gone in the fire, and he saw a flagstone floor covered in soot and ash rushing up at him.

He flung his arms out, shoving wildly with the wind, as if he could somehow push the floor away from him. And then, to his shock, he felt his fall slow.

Tiles and roof beams crashed down like hail, passing him to shatter on the floor below. But like a seed pod broken loose from a dandelion, he drifted slower and slower, until he came to a complete halt with his palms only a few inches above the grimy floor. A whirlwind of ash spread out around him as the force of the wind against the flagstones scattered it to all sides. Then, when he did nothing to halt the wind, he began to drift slowly upwards.

Gods.

He let go of the wind and dropped the last few inches like a stone. More ash puffed up around him, and he blinked it out of his eyes.

How did I do that?

Before, he had always used the wind to push other things away from him. It had never occurred to him to wonder what might happen if he directed it against something that he couldn't hope to move: a building, or the earth itself. He had never thought that it might then be used to move *him* instead.

From far above, he heard Suchen shouting his name. He drew in a deep breath to answer her, then found himself coughing violently as soot filled his throat. Spitting ash from his mouth, he staggered to his feet and picked his way as carefully as he could to the nearest exit. The darkened building was treacherous, filled with jagged ends of burned and broken timber, but at least its stone walls seemed unlikely to come down on his head.

He paused in the shadows just inside the gaping hole where the door had been, but there were no guards outside. With any luck, they had been thwarted by the collapse of his section of the roof. As he started out, he heard running footsteps; a moment later, Suchen, Londah, and Buudi rounded the corner and almost collided with him.

"You're alive!" Suchen flung her arms around him tightly. Startled, he returned her embrace, felt her body shuddering against his own. "Oh, gods, I thought it was the tower all over again."

"So did I," Yozerf said with a wry grin. "But I was lucky. Something broke my fall—a beam that was about ready to give anyway, I think. It broke under me, but it slowed my fall enough to keep me from getting hurt."

"Amazing," Buudi said. But Yozerf thought he saw puzzlement in the Sworn's eyes.

He can't suspect. There's no reason for him to think it was anything other than luck, he told himself frantically, even as his heart hammered in his chest.

Telmonra moved, like snake uncoiling in his gut. *"And if he does suspect?"* she asked, and there was something malevolent in her tone. *"What will you do to keep your secret?"*

Yozerf ignored her. "We must get out of here before the guards find a way down to us," he said.

Londah nodded. "Come, then. We'll head back to the cemetery the quickest way. And then you will tell me all about this 'tower' and what happened on it."

⁓⁓

"So do you believe that the meeting was a trap?" Auglar asked when they had finished telling him everything that had happened.

They were all seated within the crypt, in varying positions of restlessness. Yozerf was still trying, with limited success, to remove the soot and ash of the burned building from his hair. Suchen sat beside him, occasionally brushing futilely at her tunic; their embrace had left quite a bit of ash on her as well. Given the increasing state of everyone's filthiness after being confined to a single set of clothes for days, Suchen supposed that a little more grime didn't make much of a difference.

"I don't know," she said honestly when no one else volunteered an answer. "Wouldn't it have been easier to trap us while we were in the tavern, in that case?"

Yozerf paused, a comb in one hand and a lock of hair in the other. "Not if they intended to follow us to Auglar and Fellrant."

"True." Suchen took the comb from him, wiped it on a rag, and began to work the tangles and soot out of his long hair. Yozerf went still at her touch, his eyes half-closing, and she was reminded of nothing so much as a wolf enjoying being petted.

Fellrant stirred from where he sat like a shadow near one wall. The dim light from a tallow candle touched his face obliquely, leaving it half in darkness. "That seems most likely. In which case, nothing the girl said can be taken as truth."

"Not quite." Londah looked up from where she was busy polishing her vast array of knives. Her gray eyes gleamed feral. "The soldiers who followed us were in Igen's livery. He is most certainly a part of the conspiracy."

"And I do not believe that my father is," Cybelen added staunchly. Peddock, who sat beside her, nodded his head in vigorous agreement.

Fellrant smiled thinly. "So you say."

Chapter Ten

This time, Yozerf did not argue when Suchen came with him to meet with Gevannin. After the excitement earlier in the evening, Suchen would have preferred to stay at the crypt and sleep, but she couldn't in good conscience let Yozerf go alone to a place like the blood pit.

And your presence kept him so safe before, didn't it? she asked herself bitterly. *To Hel with it. I'll kill anyone who even suggests that he ever fight there again.*

She kept her hand on her sword as they walked, alert for any sign of the soldiers who had chased them earlier. None appeared, thankfully, and she wondered if it was just luck on their part, or if Igen's men had returned to Nava Nar to report their failure.

This time, they were immediately ushered in to Gevannin's small observation room. The Aclyte was standing at his ease before the small window, watching intently as two humans tried to gut one another in the pit outside. A small cone of incense burned on the table, no doubt meant to mask the stench of blood.

Gevannin turned slightly as they entered, the light from a lamp painting his features in gold. His skin was pale, although not nearly as white as Yozerf's, and he lacked Yozerf's height. But he had those high, sharp cheekbones that all Aclytes shared, and his large, canted eyes were so green they almost glowed. By any measure, he was a striking man.

"Welcome." Gevannin sat down in one of the chairs, tucking his black hair back behind one ear. His accent was not quite so pronounced as Yozerf's, but it still flavored his words like an exotic spice. "May I offer you wine?"

"No," Yozerf said shortly. He remained standing, like the dark ghost of some long-dead fighter. "Have you found us a ship?"

Jade-green eyes glanced up piercingly, and Suchen saw the hint of a malevolent smile begin to form. "I have. You will have to make the final arrangements, including price and place, with my contact."

Yozerf drew out a small sack from his beneath his cloak, and Suchen saw that it was the pouch his winnings from the other night. He tossed it negligently onto the table. "You will see that more has been added," he said obliquely.

Gevannin picked up the sack, weighed it in his hand, then nodded. "Very well. There is a man who is willing to see you safely out of the city. His name is Cleistus."

Yozerf froze. Feeling the sudden tension in him, Suchen glanced up and saw that what little color he had was gone from his face.

"I see you remember him," Gevannin said, and there was a mocking tone in his voice that Suchen did not understand. "He certainly remembers you. I believe that he is anxious to renew your acquaintance."

"Where?" Yozerf asked. If a stone statue had come to life and spoken, it would have sounded as he did: flat, dead, and utterly without emotion.

"He is currently ensconced in the third warehouse south of *The Toothless Whore* on Sinker Lane, one street back from the docks."

"Very well." Yozerf turned and walked away without further comment, his movements jerky and abrupt rather than his usual fluid grace. Now deeply worried, Suchen hurried after him but did not speak until they were safely back out on the street.

"Who is this Cleistus person?"

"It is none of your concern."

The cold answer startled her, and it was a moment before she could find her voice. "I rather think it is."

"Leave it!" He turned on her abruptly, lip curled into a snarl, and she saw the flash of wolf fangs in the torchlight.

"No." She glared at him, blue eyes meeting gray and refusing to back down. "If nothing else, *all* of our lives depend on this person's ability to get us safely out of this accursed city." Her tone softened, and she reached out to put a hand on his arm. "And I am worried for you."

He flinched away from her touch. "Don't be. I can handle Cleistus."

Frustration made her clench her hands into fists. "Damn it, Yozerf, *talk to me!* How can I help you if I don't know what's wrong?"

"I don't need your help!"

They stared at one another, anger and desperation in a silent war between them. Then, suddenly, Yozerf looked away. "What I mean," he went on in a calmer tone, "is that I'm capable of walking down to the docks and back by myself tomorrow night. It will be safer that way." He hesitated, then reached out and put his hands on her arms, drawing her closer. "I will negotiate with Cleistus if that's what is needed." One hand lifted, stroked hair tenderly off her face. "I will get us out of this city, I swear it. I won't fail you. I won't let you die."

Although his touch and his words were gentle, his eyes were frenzied, the pupils dilated until there was only a narrow silver ring around each. Suchen reached up and gripped his hand. "Is this because of that woman who died at *The Wyvern*? Ginny?" she asked, feeling as though she groped her way through a darkened room.

"No!" He jerked away from her, and the moment between them shattered beyond repair. His shoulders set in a straight, angry line, Yozerf turned and stalked away from her. For a moment, she considered remaining where she was so that he would be forced to turn around and come back for her. Then, deciding that the impulse was childish, she followed.

Neither of them spoke during the walk back. A mixture of hurt and frustration boiled in Suchen's gut. Ever since they had come to Segg, Yozerf had been gradually shutting himself away from her, building a wall of silence to stand between them. If he would only open himself to her, if he would only tell her what demons preyed on him, she could at least give him her support, perhaps lend him some of her strength.

But he would not. Gods, he was so stubborn that she wanted to strangle him sometimes. No matter what she tried, he would not go that final distance, would not open up that dark part of his heart to her. Instead, he would go on bearing his burdens alone until they broke him.

And there wasn't a damned thing she could do about it.

❧ ❧

Yozerf was turning to ice.

The cold had started to grow in him when Gevannin gleefully told him that Cleistus, of all people, held the keys to life and death for Yozerf's pack. The other man's mockery had been meant to cut, meant to indicate that Gevannin had no illusions as to what sort of relationship Cleistus had with Yozerf, but the edge of the words had blunted against the glacial stillness that was even now spreading out from Yozerf's core.

All of his life, his choices had been desperate ones, made to ensure his survival no matter what else it cost. But that had started to change. The ice he used to keep the world at bay had started to melt, and he had begun to believe that he had left such desperation behind.

Gods, what a fool he had been.

"What do you think the price will be?" Auglar asked when Yozerf numbly reported the arrangements he had made with Gevannin.

"High," Yozerf said, half-surprised that his words didn't steam in the warm air, like snow brought before a fire. "We'll sell everything we can—the clothing you brought from the palace, any weapons we can afford to be rid of, any jewelry."

Cybelen put her hand to the pendant at her throat. "I can't—I mean, my mother gave me this on her deathbed. I...I don't want to part with it."

Yozerf stared at her as if from a great distance. It seemed laughable to him that Cybelen should be so pained over the loss of a trinket. After all, he was giving up his soul.

Again.

"You don't have to," Peddock said quickly, putting his hand to her shoulder. Cybelen looked up at him with a grateful smile. From his new distance, Yozerf dimly observed that they had somehow fallen in love. How incredibly foolish.

Suchen tried again to talk to him after, but he couldn't sustain it for long. He had to encourage the ice, of course, and every word she spoke chipped away at it.

I'm doing this for your sake! he thought when she turned away at last in anger. *Why must you make this even harder than it is?*

There was one other thing that needed to be done before they left the city, though...and it would keep Londah occupied and distract her from questions that he couldn't answer. The next morning, after a troubled sleep that gave him nothing but nightmares, he signaled her to follow him outside the crypt.

"I have a favor to ask you," he said once they were alone. They stood a little ways apart from the crypt, in the shadows of the old oaks. Heat shimmers danced on top of the sunlit walls surrounding the cemetery, but here it was cool and damp. The smell of growing things, of wet earth, blotted out the stink of decay, soothing him a little.

She nodded, her dragon-gray eyes grave. If she had noticed any change in him from the day before, she gave no indication, and it occurred to him that he probably seemed normal to her for the first time since his return. Probably his other self, the one that touched Suchen and smiled at jokes, had seemed a puzzling aberration.

"There is a man...one of Igen's now...by the name of Dara-Don." Briefly, he told her of the human man's treachery and of their earlier encounter. He omitted how he had forced Dara-Don into giving him information, although he supposed he could have done so. She would never tell anyone else, would never judge him when he told her he had used the magic to kill the Council. Hel, Londah would not judge him if he had killed Rozah with his own hand, instead of just having her die for him.

"Watch for him near the gates. I won't ask you to go into the palace after him, but if he comes out, demand answers from him. And if he refuses to give them to you—kill him."

Londah nodded, unperturbed. "I shall."

≈≈

That afternoon, once Londah was gone, Yozerf went out with only a vague excuse of needing to prepare for the meeting with Cleistus. Which was true enough. Alone, encased in a cold that deadened the heart and the mind, he went to the marketplace and spent some of their precious coin on the things that would be necessary to make the smuggler look on their cause favorably. Once he was done, he went to a tavern that rented the rooms on its second floor by the hour.

The little chamber he found himself in was squalid, but it had a cheap brass mirror, and so fit his purpose well enough. He took off his old clothes and laid them carefully aside before pulling on a form-fitting pair of leather breeks dyed in his habitual black. The shirt was a dark green, cut so that the two sides didn't join until they reached the waist, exposing the hairless, white expanse of his narrow chest, the pale pink nubs of his nipples.

Once dressed, he brushed out his hair carefully, then applied perfume to his throat. Kohl outlined his large eyes, making them even more exotic, and very pale rouge highlighted his sharp cheekbones. The paint that went on his lips was red as blood.

"*Good,*" said Ginny's ten-year-old voice in his memory. "*Like that around your eyes. And hold yourself like this. And whatever you do...don't let them see you're afraid.*"

The face that stared back at him out of the brass mirror with dead eyes was like an old friend, long forgotten. It had been a long, long time since he had seen this part of himself. They had called him Frost on the streets, for his coldness, the ice in his eyes. "*Like a spring flower opened too early and caught by winter,*" Daryn had said when he was still a little child. And Frost could do this, could do anything. Bear anything.

Ginny had died because Yozerf failed her, and Rozah had died because he had been unable to protect his pack from his enemies. But he would not fail those who had survived. He would not fail

Suchen.

No matter what it cost.

It could be worse, Yozerf told himself. At least Cleistus was not sadistic, at least not as Yozerf's experience judged it, who had been sold in order to die. Cleistus' taste ran to pretty sixteen-year-olds, and he didn't like to deal with panders, preferring those who had at least a nominal choice.

Something deep inside him sobbed like a lost child, but he clamped down hard on it, smothered it in ice. He stood there, still, looking into the mirror until the ice had covered everything, until his heart was dead and his mind was focused only on what he had to do in the next few moments, nothing more or less.

And then, once he was ready, he turned and went out to keep his appointment.

～～

"I don't like this." Suchen paced restlessly, her arms folded across her chest. The walls of the crypt seemed more confining than ever, the musty smell of the ancient bones more cloying. She had stared at the carved faces on the sarcophagi so often by now that she was beginning to hate their long-dead owners.

"None of us do," Brenwulf said. He had been looking more and more pale and drawn over the last few days, as if some vital substance was gradually draining out of him. Hollows showed beneath his dark eyes, which darted about nervously, like those of an animal in a cage.

Buudi had cracked open the door to the crypt once the sun had set, trusting that no casual visitors would come to such a place after nightfall. The breeze that sighed in the oak above failed to enter the crypt, although the mosquitoes invaded by the thousands.

"Is something wrong, Suchen?" Cybelen asked.

Suchen glanced at the other woman and had to suppress a surge of annoyance. *She* didn't have so much as a single mosquito bite to mar her flawless skin. Although Cybelen was as dirty and tired as the rest of them, somehow she still managed to convey a noble air, wearing her ragged clothes as if they were the finest silks.

Don't be such a harridan, Suchen told herself with a mental sigh. She pressed her fingers against her temples, aware of a growing headache. *Just because she's beautiful and poised doesn't mean you should be mad at her. Although it would be nice if she was just a little less perceptive.* "I'm worried about Yozerf."

Peddock frowned, as if the mere mention of Yozerf's name

was an irritant greater than an entire army of mosquitoes. "What-ever for?"

"He's been acting odd lately, for one thing."

"He *is* odd," Peddock pointed out tartly. "Surely it didn't take you this long to notice."

Suchen glared at her brother. "That isn't what I meant. He's hiding something about this meeting with Cleistus—something he doesn't want to know."

"Do you think he means to betray us?" Fellrant asked, and Suchen jumped slightly. He had been so quiet that she had forgotten he was there at all.

"What? No!" she answered. "But he is keeping back some-thing. He was...afraid, I think. I asked him what was wrong, but he wouldn't tell me."

"Well, then." Fellrant rose lithely to his feet. "Do you know where this meeting was?"

She nodded. "I remember what Gevannin told Yozerf. It didn't sound too hard to find."

"Then perhaps we should go ourselves and discover just what it is our Aclytese friend doesn't want us to know."

Suchen hesitated, torn. Would Yozerf take her sudden appear-ance as a sign of distrust? Was she over-reacting? Would going endanger whatever negotiations he might be engaged in?

To Hel with it. Better that than whatever frightened him so badly.

"You're right," she said, and started for the entrance.

Buudi took a quick step forward and caught her elbow. Weari-ness had given his eyes a bruised look, and like them all he was in dire need of a bath. "Are you sure this is a good idea?"

She hesitated, then nodded. "Call it instinct, if you will. But something tells me that Yozerf is in some sort of danger."

"Then you shouldn't go alone. I'm coming with you."

"And I," said Fellrant.

They both looked at him in surprise, but his blue-violet eyes remained impassive. "If there is a danger to us all, then I want to see it. And my eyes will not be blinded by friendship or...other considerations...if the Aclyte is indeed a traitor."

Suchen clenched her fists, wanting to smash one into Fellrant's sensuous mouth. "Yozerf wouldn't betray us."

"Then you have no reason to object to me coming with you. Or are you so concerned for my safety, steward?"

His mocking smile said clearly that he had not missed her antipathy towards him, and that he did not consider it worth his while. Suchen gave him a look of pure venom. "You have a point.

Come with us, then."

She brushed past Buudi went outside. The night was several degrees cooler than the stuffy confines of the crypt, and she took several deep breaths of free air. Eerie lights flickered under some of the trees, and she shivered, telling herself not to be superstitious. Whatever the lights were—ghosts or sprites or some natural occurrence—there was no reason to think they heralded ill fortune for her. Or Yozerf.

Sinker Lane ran parallel to the docks and appeared to be a favorite of sailors and dock workers. Warehouses where cargo was unloaded and stored clustered at one end of the street. The taverns, brothels, and gambling dens that provided the nightly entertainment for the workers were conveniently located at the other end. Light from fish oil lamps poured out of these, augmenting the flickering torches set outside every building. The sounds of laughter, curses, and badly-played instruments filled the air. Rough-looking men dressed in sailors' togs staggered down the street or lay in the doorways, while whores called from windows or stood outside, making lewd invitations to everyone who passed. To Suchen's surprise, a band of dark-skinned women dressed like men and armed with long knives passed by.

The Toothless Whore was a particularly disreputable-looking brothel just at the boundary where the warehouses began. They passed it by quickly, ignoring the pander outside, who looked more as though he might be more inclined to murder and rob his clients than take them to a woman. The warehouses beyond were enormous buildings made all of brick, with a few windows high up to let in light. The first two they passed had guards at the entrances, who gave them hard, warning looks, and Suchen guessed that the cargo stored within must prove a tempting target for thieves.

When they came to the third warehouse, however, no guard stood outside the main entrance. Suchen exchanged looks with Buudi and Fellrant, then shrugged and knocked on the unpainted door.

The door was opened almost immediately. Two men stood on the other side. The first was the heavily-armed thug whom Suchen had expected. But the other was a tall, slender Aclytese man. Butter-gold hair framed a delicate, beautiful face set with a pair of eyes like topazes. His clothing matched him in pallor, all shades of cream and light yellow, and was both form-fitting and revealing. He looked young, but his true age was impossible to guess: it could have been anywhere from twenty to forty. When he saw them, he gave a haughty little sniff and took a sip from the goblet held loosely in one hand. "What do *you* want?"

Suchen glanced at her companions, wondering what to tell him and cursing herself for not having thought up a plausible story to begin with. The truth, or at least some of it, seemed safest. "We're looking for Yozerf."

The Aclyte gave her a condescending look. "There's no one here by that name. Now off with you if you don't have any business here."

"He might not be here yet," Suchen said hastily, blocking the door with her body before they could shut it. The guard gave her a wary look, and she prayed that he wouldn't just decide to attack. "He is supposed to meet with Cleistus on our behalf. He's an Aclyte like you. Tall. Red hair."

"Oh." The Aclyte rolled his eyes. "Frost. You practically walked in on his heels. I just took him back. But I thought this was a private meeting."

"We wanted to make certain that everything went smoothly."

The Aclyte gave them a look that clearly said they were amateurs in this business of smuggling. "Hmph. I'm not surprised. Come in, then. But I don't want to upset Cleistus—you'll have to wait until they're...done."

He took a step back, and the guard opened the door. "Stay here," the Aclyte told the guard—clearly, he didn't think the three humans were much of a threat.

"Yes, Adrylin."

Adrylin led them back through a darkened hall, the walls of which were covered in expensive tapestries. Perfume scented the air, covering even the pervasive stink of fish from the docks. From the luxury Suchen guessed that Cleistus must live here as well as do business.

"Really, you didn't even have to worry," Adrylin went on as they walked. "You types should trust your agents more. Frost was always one of Cleistus' favorites. I thought he would wet himself when Gevannin said he was back."

Suchen exchanged a confused look with Buudi. "I don't understand."

"I've been with Cleistus for a long time," Adrylin said, taking another healthy swallow from his goblet. Suchen suspected that he might be more than a little drunk. "He saw my potential early, and I'm his personal assistant now, taking care of the books, looking out for his interests. I even remember when he brought Frost in. Oh, yes, he did favor that boy." Adrylin's eyes narrowed at the memory, and Suchen realized with a little shock that he was jealous. But of what?

"Here." Adrylin stopped and opened a discreet door. "We can

watch through here. Cleistus likes to have me keep an eye on the proceedings, you know. I have such a good memory, he says, and I record things for him to review later on."

The door opened onto a small room that reminded Suchen of the one Gevannin had used to observe his own little domain in the blood pit, save that this one was far more sumptuous. Lavish hangings covered the walls, and a mahogany desk sank carved feet deep into Undish carpets. Although she could make out a silver candelabrum on the desk, the only light for now came in through the small window that looked out onto a larger room. A second door also let out into the room, and Adrylin gestured negligently towards it. "You can use that if you decide he's really making a mess of things," he said, as if nothing would please him more. Going to a decanter on the desk, he poured another large measure of wine into his goblet.

An old enemy, Suchen realized. Whatever the source of contention between the two Aclytes, it was clear that Adrylin had let them in with the expectation that they would somehow sabotage the agreement Yozerf was trying to make.

Feeling more confused than ever, Suchen and her companions moved closer to the little window. It looked out onto a large chamber that reminded her irresistibly of a throne room, as if its owner was some petty tyrant who enjoyed lording it over those who had to come to him for help. The same expensive hangings and carpets decorated it, along with a single chair, elaborately carved and gilded.

The man who sat in the chair could easily have been any merchant she had ever known. His body beneath the velvet doublet and hosen was quickly going to fat, and the line of his short gray hair was receding towards his ears. Rings glittered on his plump fingers, and a heavy chain of gold hung about his neck. But rather than the shrewd, calculating expression that she had expected on his plain face, he looked oddly wistful as he gazed at the second figure in the room.

It was all she could do to stifle as gasp at the sight of Yozerf. He looked...magnificent. His hair had been brushed so that it hung about his face and shoulders in a glorious mane, begging her to run her hands through it or rub it against her skin. Paint decorated his face, but in such a way that it didn't seem obvious in and of itself, but only brought out the hidden sensuality in his large eyes, his sculpted lips, his feral cheekbones. The clothing he wore made no secret of the temptations of the body beneath.

Suchen's heart quickened in an involuntary rush of desire. She cast a glance quickly at the two men with her, saw that they were staring at Yozerf as well. Buudi's lips were parted slightly, and he had a slightly glazed look to his eyes.

"You've aged, my boy," said the man who could only be Cleistus, drawing Suchen's attention back to the other room.

Yozerf smiled seductively. His eyes were half-lidded, the lashes long against his pale skin. "Have I?" He moved closer, but the way he carried himself, the way he moved, was the gait of a stranger. It was a sensual prowl, an invitation, a walk designed to get an instant reaction from anyone who could appreciate his beauty.

And then he turned his face to the side, very slightly, and she saw the look in his eyes. They were flat, dead, as if the living flesh had been replaced by gray ice. It was as if Yozerf had stepped out of his own body, leaving behind...nothing at all.

Adrylin snorted at Suchen's shoulder. "Damned eunuch," he muttered in a whisper, glaring out the window as if he wished he could hurl daggers at Yozerf.

"What?" she asked, confused. Her heart raced, but with fear now rather than desire. The way Yozerf was dressed, the way he acted...there seemed to be only one explanation. But that wasn't possible. He wouldn't do something like that.

But he used to. You know that.

When he was a child, though. Oh, gods, I don't understand. What by Hel does he think he's doing?

Adrylin's mouth twitched contemptuously. "That's why they called him Frost, you know. Because he was supposed to be so talented, but ever get a rise out of *him*, oh no. Impervious to pleasure or pain, do anything you want to him, and he acts it doesn't matter at all." He took another large gulp of wine. "That was the allure, you see. Cleistus—all of them—thought that *they* would be the ones to break through that indifference. It usually started with pleasure—'I'll make you writhe, I'll make you moan'—and then when that didn't work, the frustration would set in, the anger, and then they'd turn to pain just to make him acknowledge that they were even there at all. He's lucky no one killed him, the stupid chook."

Any words she might have said died on Suchen's tongue, overwhelmed by the slow roil of nausea in her belly. But Buudi had no such problem. "What are you implying?" he whispered hoarsely, his face oddly pale. "Are you trying to say that Yozerf...."

"I believe the words you are so unsuccessfully looking for are 'was a whore,'" Fellrant murmured, looking utterly unperturbed by the situation.

Adrylin stared at them as if they had utterly lost their minds. "Of course. What did you think he was?"

"He was only a child," Suchen whispered, struggling with the urge to strike out at someone, anyone. Starting with Adrylin, as he was conveniently at hand, then moving on to the monster in the room outside.

Adrylin rolled his eyes. "Cleistus doesn't do children, silly girl. I'm sure Frost got his start when he was young—most of us do. But he was sixteen when Cleistus took him in. At least he was on his own and not working through a pander." The Aclyte spoke as if this dubious qualification was the only good thing he could say about Yozerf. "But he would have been better off working the street, if you ask me. Not good for a long-term thing. He was always getting into fights, running off for days on end, wasting time with some stupid bar maid. Finally Cleistus realized what a mistake he'd made and threw the bastard out."

The smugness in his tone made Suchen want to gut Adrylin on the spot, but somehow she held back her urge, instead turning back to the window, a sense of desperation growing in her. They had to get Yozerf out of here. What had he been thinking, to come here at all?

While Adrylin had distracted her, Yozerf and Cleistus had apparently been discussing terms. Yozerf had drawn nearer to the smuggler, standing only a few feet from him, one hand on his hip and every line of his body a temptation. "Will that be enough?" Yozerf asked, and Suchen knew that it wouldn't be. Yozerf must have known it as well, even before he came here.

"That depends." Cleistus set aside the bag of coins that Yozerf had given him. His small eyes ran hungrily over the Aclyte's body, and he moistened his lips with his tongue. "I might be persuaded to settle for such a small amount."

Yozerf smiled. To Suchen, who knew him, it was utterly false, but Cleistus either didn't know or didn't care. He walked slowly over and knelt down in front of Cleistus' chair, every motion a study in seduction. Cleistus reached out and knotted his fingers in Yozerf's long hair. "I can't wait to find out what you've learned in your time away," he whispered, then leaned over and kissed Yozerf hungrily on the mouth.

Suchen didn't even realize that she had started for the door until Fellrant's hands locked around her upper arms, jerking her back. "Let go of me!" she snarled, wrenching at his surprisingly-strong grip. Then she felt the kiss of cold steel on her throat.

"No." Fellrant's fingers dug into her arms as he jerked her back against him. "All of our lives depend on this," he said, his mouth almost pressed against her ear. "Your lover knew what was going to be asked of him. Obviously, he thought it was worth it. I'm not going to let you get us all killed to prevent something that he went to willingly. Even if I have to cut your throat."

And he would do it, she knew. "If Yozerf goes through with this, it will destroy him," she said.

"Destroy him, or destroy your relationship with him?" Fellrant countered.

"Him." She laughed bitterly. "I may have learned a few things tonight, but I already knew the truth at the center of them. Yozerf is doing this because he thinks there is no other choice, and I won't love him any less if he does. But he will. Now let me go, or cut my throat, because I swear that I will kill you if you hinder me."

To her vast surprise, she felt him pause, even though she had never expected her pleas to reach him. Then, suddenly, he let go of her—and walked out through the door himself.

Cleistus' head jerked up and he glowered at Fellrant. "Who by Hel are you?" he snarled. "Adrylin!"

"This is one of the people Frost is representing," Adrylin called back, his drunken state clear in the way he slurred half the sentence together. Cleistus scowled, obviously put out with his assistant.

Yozerf, on the other hand, didn't seem surprised by Fellrant's sudden appearance—indeed, he didn't seem to feel anything at all. He sat unmoving on the floor, his head tilted back passively against Cleistus' hand, his eyes terrifyingly blank.

"I'm very sorry to interrupt," Fellrant said with a sinister smile. "But I fear my pet has not been entirely honest with me." He reached out and brushed a lock of hair from Yozerf's face, the casualness of the gesture making it seem like one oft-repeated. "Isn't that right, pretty one?"

Cleistus' eyes narrowed. "In what way?"

"He knows that I'm a jealous man, but he thought that he could get away without telling me. Such a bad boy."

Cleistus leaned back and folded his hands over his ample belly. "One night with him in addition to the coin you've already paid will be enough to complete our agreement. Surely he isn't worth that much to you."

"Ah, but that isn't the point, is it? The point is that what is *mine* remains *mine*." Fellrant suddenly slipped his hand around the back of Yozerf's head, gripped his hair tightly, and pulled him close. "Kiss me."

Like an automaton with no will of its own, Yozerf obeyed. Fellrant wrapped his arms around Yozerf and returned the kiss with a passion that was too deep to be faked. Then, with a sudden, convulsive movement, he shoved Yozerf away.

"See? He's well-trained," Fellrant said, his voice not quite steady. "But a hound only answers the call of one master. Take this instead."

Fellrant drew out the silver fillet that he had worn up until their flight from Nava Nar and tossed it negligently to Cleistus. Cleistus missed, and it fell to the carpets, deep blue gems shining sultry in the candlelight. The smuggler stared at it for a long moment, probably weighing its value, then finally gave a sharp nod. "Very well."

Suchen sighed in relief and closed her eyes. She felt as weary as if she had run a long race. Buudi put a hand to her shoulder, and she touched his fingers, glad for the comfort.

Fellrant pulled Yozerf up, and they both walked to the door, neither looking back at Cleistus. "You owe me, Aclyte," Fellrant said when they entered the little room.

"I—" Yozerf began, then stopped when he saw Suchen and Buudi. His eyes widened slightly, and Suchen saw the beginnings of something like panic in their depths.

"An interesting drama," Adrylin slurred, pouring more wine into his cup.

Fellrant shot him a withering glance, then headed towards the way out. "We're leaving. Don't bother showing us the door."

As soon as they were outside, Yozerf broke away from them, walking fast down the street. His head was bowed and his arms were wrapped tightly about his chest, as if he held in a scream.

"Yozerf!" Suchen jogged after him, feeling sick and desperate. "Stop. Slow down."

When he made no response, she grabbed his arm, intending to force him to stop. As soon as her fingers closed around him, he wrenched away violently, spinning around and staring at her as if he had never seen her before in his life.

"Don't touch me!"

Suchen froze, her hands held out towards him. His eyes were wild and half-mad, and the look on his face was one of such utter desperation that it broke her heart. With a soft cry, he turned away from her, going to the side of one of the warehouses and leaning against it, his back to them. Then, suddenly, he cracked his forehead as hard as he could into the brick wall.

"Yozerf, no!" she shouted. She grabbed one of his arms and Buudi the other, intending to pull him away from the warehouse.

He fought them, like a wild thing that has been cornered. Suchen hung on to his arm determinedly. "Yozerf, stop it! It's us! Please don't hurt yourself!"

After a few moments, he settled, defeated by their tenacity. He stood very still, head bowed, his breathing on the ragged edge of hysteria. Blood gathered in the shallow scrape the bricks had left on his forehead.

"I told you not to come," he said at last, his voice rough, as if he had swallowed broken glass.

"You should have known that I wouldn't just let you go alone, especially when it was clear that you were upset. Gods, Yozerf, what were you thinking? Finding a smuggler's ship out of Segg wasn't worth *this*!"

"Yes it was!" he shouted, making her flinch. "I couldn't fail you! Anything would be worth it to keep you from being hurt, from dying." He closed his eyes, as if his outburst had taken the last of his strength. "Let go of me. Please."

Exchanging a wary glance with Buudi, Suchen reluctantly released Yozerf's arm. He didn't run, though, as she had half-expected him to.

"Yozerf," she said softly, hoping to get through to him, "we love you. We're your friends. We would never ask you to do something like this. Not for any reason."

He didn't look at her. "What did Adrylin tell you?"

The defeated tone in his voice made her wince. "That you had a...a history with Cleistus. That they called you Frost."

He flinched, as if she had slapped him. "Did he tell you why?"

"Yes."

"That was how I failed Ginny. But I wasn't going to fail you. I wasn't." He put his hands over his eyes, as if to block out some terrible sight.

Suchen hesitated, not certain if she should ask. "How did you fail Ginny?"

"She was like a sister to me. We looked out for one another. She taught me everything I needed to know, when we were little. And then later, after she got a job at *The Wyvern*, on the nights when she would stay late to take stock of the pantry, or count the mugs, or do whatever else she could to earn a few more jentarrii, I would go and stay with her and walk her home after. I wanted to protect her."

"But you couldn't," Suchen guessed.

"She didn't want to be my sister," Yozerf whispered. He had wrapped his arms defensively around himself once again, and rocked slightly back and forth as he spoke. "One of her customers wanted to marry her. She didn't love him, but he was kind enough, and he had steady pay as a barrel maker. But she said that before she got married, she wanted just once to be touched by someone who loved her, who she loved too." He shook his head miserably. "I didn't love her that way, but I wanted to make her happy and...I don't know. She'd be angry if I said no, so I didn't." He paused to wipe his eyes. "But when the time came I just...I just *couldn't*. Oh, gods, I was so humiliated, and she was so angry."

Suchen felt as though pain had eaten a hollow place in her heart. *Oh, gods. Gods, no.*

"I couldn't stand to face her," Yozerf went on raggedly. "I was such a coward. So I stayed away. I didn't visit her, I didn't walk her home like I should have. And finally one night, I decided that enough time had passed that she might have forgiven me, so I went to *The Wyvern*. Only I was still too embarrassed to see her, so I had to work my courage up and didn't go until it was late, until she had already been alone there for hours.

"I found her in the pantry. I don't know who they were or how many of them there might have been. They'd forced their way in through the back door, stolen what they could, but they'd been gone for a while by the time I got there. She was already cold." He pressed the heels of his hands hard against his eyes. "I should have been there. If I hadn't been such a failure, she would still be alive."

"It wasn't your fault," Suchen cried. The urge to hold him was overpowering, but she didn't know if he could accept her touch yet, so she forced her hands down by her sides. "You didn't kill her."

"I might as well have!"

"That isn't true!"

He shook his head, denying her words. "I failed her and she died. But I wasn't going to fail you. Not even if you hated me for it."

With an abruptness that startled her, he spun about and raced away down the dirty street. She and Buudi both ran after him, shouting his name and ignoring the looks they drew, but he was too fast. By the time they reached the end of the street, he was gone without a trace.

Chapter Eleven

Patience did not come naturally to Londah; it was something she had learned in the long years of her trade. Waiting for the perfect moment to strike was the key to the assassin's art, and those who did not learn it died on the gallows. So she waited and watched the streets outside of Nava Nar, comparing every man who walked past with the description of Dara-Don that Yozerf had given her.

Normally, she would have expected it to take days to find the right man, but Yozerf had said that Lord Igen had Dara-Don scouring the streets for Auglar. And indeed, shortly after sundown, she caught sight of the tall, brown-haired human slouching away from the palace gates.

She followed him like a shadow, waiting until they had reached an area with plenty of dark alleyways in easy reach. Modulating her voice, she called out from the shadows: "Good evening, handsome."

He stopped and peered in her direction. He had haunted eyes, and his face might have belonged to someone twice his years. Even from a distance, she could smell the wine on his breath. She had seen many others like him over the years, men—and women—desperate to escape their own memories.

"You look troubled," she called. "But I'll make you forget all your worries."

Dara-Don took a hesitant step closer, still trying to penetrate the gloom of the alley and get a glimpse of her. "I don't know…"

Too late, fool.

She was on him, too fast for him to react. Grabbing his wrist with one hand, she pulled him off-balance, so that he staggered into the alley. Before he could even attempt to fight her off, she had his face pressed against one damp brick wall, his arm twisted up behind his back and a knife at his throat.

"Don't cry out," she warned softly.

"If you want money—"

"Unfortunately for you, that isn't what I'm after. Yozerf sent me to see if you were keeping your part of the bargain." She tightened her hold on his arm, making him whimper. "Tell me what you know."

"Gods! I told him, I'm not Lord Igen's confidante!" Dara-Don's breathing was ragged, and she could hear a mixture of anger and fear in his voice. "He's keeping a heavy guard on some of the minor lords, like Lord Jehnav, but that's all I know!"

"And the ambush that almost took us outside *The Wyvern*? Whose doing was that?"

"The maid's! I overheard them talking about it after it had already failed. They said someone had been asking questions, that they might know where Auglar was, but that the plan had gone wrong. That's all I know!"

She weighed whether or not it was enough to spare his life. Under normal circumstances, she would have killed him rather than let such a danger walk loose, but Yozerf had seemed to think that Dara-Don was a resource they could use.

"Let me go, please," he whispered, as if aware of her thoughts. "I haven't told anyone I saw Yozerf. I don't even know who you are, so I couldn't tell them about you if I wanted to. If you're a sorcerer like he is, you know I can't fight you."

"A what?" she asked, puzzled.

"A sorcerer, like Yozerf. He called down fire—wind—he burned my throat."

She reached out and jerked down the edge of his tunic. Although the light was dim, she could still make out an area of reddened skin that looked eerily like a hand.

"So...I'm not the only one who kept secrets," Dara-Don said nastily.

She shoved him away. "Go. Run, before I change my mind."

After he was gone, she took to the roofs, hurrying back in the direction of the cemetery as quickly as she could travel. But the entire time, her mind raced in confusion. Was it possible that Dara-Don was telling the truth, that Yozerf had somehow acquired some strange magic that he had not told her about?

That he had not, perhaps, told anyone about?

What has befallen you, my son?

❧

As they walked back through the tangle of streets to the cemetary Suchen's grief and despair began to gradually transmute to rage. What had happened to Yozerf was not fair, by the gods, and she wanted desperately to slaughter everyone who had ever dared to lay a hand on him. Other than Cleistus, though, she could not even guess who they might have been, or if they still lived. But there was one person within her reach whom she could blame.

As soon as they were back inside the graveyard, she began to run, threading her way in between half-seen monuments. When she burst into the crypt, everyone jumped, and both Peddock and Brenwulf drew their swords. "Where's Londah?" she demanded furiously.

Cybelen frowned at her, puzzled. "She returned a short while ago—I think she went to keep watch somewhere."

"What happened?" Auglar asked worriedly, climbing to his feet. "Where is Yozerf?"

"Ask Buudi," Suchen snapped. The first among the Sworn and Fellrant had just come in the door; she shoved them both aside rudely, too furious to care.

"Londah!" she called when she was outside. "Where are you, damn it?"

Something moved in the periphery of her vision; turning, she saw that the other woman was crouched on top of a crypt halfway across the cemetery. No doubt the height gave her a vantage to observe all the comings and goings, and the distance gave her some privacy from the humans.

Suchen stalked across the graveyard, barking her shins once on an unseen bench placed in front of one of the tombs. Londah crouched like a gargoyle atop the crypt, her long, black hair blowing like a silk curtain in the window. She looked down as Suchen approached, and the moonlight illuminated her face: remote, serene, and beautiful.

"How could you have let that happen to him?" Suchen snarled. She stopped a few paces away from Londah, her rage making her hands shake. "You, who fight like one of the old war goddesses out of legend. You were supposed to protect him! He's your son, for the gods' sakes!"

For a moment, she thought that Londah would not answer her. Then the serene mask crumbled, and a mixture of grief and despair bloomed in Londah's eyes. "What happened?"

"This damned smuggler paid your son to sleep with him, and to be abused, and the gods alone only know what! And tonight Yozerf was going to be part of the price to get us out of this accursed city."

Londah's eyes went cold as the dark spaces between the stars. "Ah. I never learned about that one. Otherwise, he would not still be alive." She paused. "Is Yozerf safe?"

"We put a stop to it, if that's what you're asking."

"Good. Now, if you'll excuse me, I have a smuggler to kill."
Londah rose lithely from her crouch and jumped down from her
perch, every movement a study in deadly grace. Only a madwoman
would have wanted to get in her way.

Suchen blocked her path, saw cold anger flare briefly in
Londah's remote eyes. "No. Not until you give me some answers.
What was your part in all this?"

Londah's mouth became a taut, flat line. "Very well, then. What
was my part? It was to abandon my son when he needed me most."

The two women stared at one another in silence. When it became clear that Londah was not going to say more, Suchen asked,
"What do you mean?"

Londah turned away and went to stand near a stone angel,
leaning one shoulder against it for support. The wind tumbled
back her hair, twisting it into a dark storm. "I am sure that Yozerf
mentioned that he never knew his father," she began obliquely. "I
was young and foolish when I came to this city, human woman. I
was born in a hamlet on the Kellsmarch so small that it didn't even
have a name, and I thought that coming here would give me opportunities that didn't exist at home. What a fool I was.

"I met and fell in love with a man I thought was human. His
name was Llynir, and I do not know what became of him. He disappeared even before I realized that I was pregnant. I didn't even
know that he was Wolfkin, not until Yozerf discovered it himself,
shortly before his twentieth birthday. That was the happiest day of
my life aside from the day he was born, because I knew that he
could use it to escape this place forever, even though at the time I
thought it meant I would never see him again."

She shook her head, sending her long hair floating about her.
"But that is beside the point. When Yozerf was young, I worked
very hard to keep us both fed and clothed. It was not easy. There
are few opportunities for Aclytese women save for servitude or
prostitution. Often they are one in the same; few rich masters see
any need to keep their hands off a female servant, whether she
welcomes the attention or not. I would not have that for myself, so
I hired out as a caravan guard. There were few who would hire an
Aclyte, let alone a woman, even after I demonstrated my skills to
them, but I had a few reliable employers. Of course, traveling as a
guard meant that I was often away from Yozerf, but it seemed worth
it at the time.

"One winter, when Yozerf was eight, I was wounded during a
bandit attack in Undah. It was almost a year before I made it back
to Segg, only to find that the tenement we had lived in had burned
down. The Aclytese family he had been staying with was gone—I

expect they all died in the fire, as I never saw any of them again.

"As you can imagine, I was desperate. I searched everywhere, asked everyone if they had seen him, to no avail. I will not go into the painful details, but, just as I had given up hope, I finally found him. At that time, there was a small enclave of Kyarthan nuns here in Segg. Apparently, they believed that their gods commanded them to minister to the poor, so they were acting as healers in the Old Quarter, living on donations from the converted and taking in anyone who was sick or injured. Someone thought she had seen my son in their infirmary.

"I went there, and they took me to see the child. There was a beautiful little girl sitting beside his bed; she was the one who had brought him in. They had belonged to the same pander, and she was afraid of going back because of her act of kindness. The child in the bed had been badly beaten, raped, and bitten. Tortured, really. His face was so swollen that he didn't bear any resemblance to my son, and I remember being thankful that it wasn't Yozerf after all. Then he opened his eyes and I knew that I had been mistaken.

"The girl was Sweet Gin—Ginny, she liked to be called. She told me that she and Yozerf had worked the streets together, that she had tried to take care of him. But then their pander decided to sell Yozerf to some n'ykar men with the understanding that he would not be returning alive. When they were done, they dumped what they no doubt thought was his lifeless body in the river and left. Ginny fished him out and took him to the healers. She stayed with him, even though she knew that by not going back to their pander she was probably dooming herself.

"Ginny told me all of this, because Yozerf never spoke of it. In fact, he didn't speak to me at all for the first six months after he had healed enough to leave the nuns' care. We moved back into the tenements, and I arranged for Ginny to stay with Jarvin with the understanding that she would work at *The Wyvern,* at least until she was old enough to be on her own.

"And then, using the information Ginny gave me, I hunted down everyone I could find who had abused my son, and I killed them. I killed them, and I cut out their hearts, and we ate them raw."

Londah fell silent. Suchen stared at the other woman. "It wasn't your fault," she said at last. "You did the best you could."

"It was my fault, human woman. As you said, it was my responsibility to protect Yozerf, and I did not. There is no accusation you could make that I have not already made myself long ago."

"But it didn't end there?"

The Aclytese woman sighed and stirred. "Of course not. You

cannot imagine what it was like. There was nothing left of the sweet little boy that Yozerf had been. Nothing. My child had been replaced by a stranger who blamed me for what had happened.

"Of course I could not think of leaving again. But we still needed to eat. In the course of my vengeance, I had discovered something about myself—that I am very good at killing in silence, in darkness, and without leaving a trace behind. So I became an assassin, and I killed again and again and again. I became so good that they began to call me the Crow Queen, because the carrion birds of Segg had surely grown fat on all the corpses I left in my wake." Londah smiled, but it was bitter and without humor. "None of it did me any good. I tried very hard to make Yozerf happy, but it was beyond my means. As he grew older, we began to fight more often. Finally, when he was sixteen, he left and rented a space on the floor of another tenement. We did stay in contact, but I did not always know what he was doing, although I guessed that when times were desperate he had resorted to selling himself once again. I killed anyone I could find who had used him, but as you know, I could not discover them all."

"You did as best as you could," Suchen said again, when it became clear that Londah's narrative was over. "I'm sorry for what I said to you. I was angry, and I wanted someone to take it out on."

Londah shrugged off the apology; no doubt, as she had said before, anyone else's accusations were meaningless beside her own. "Is Yozerf in the crypt?"

"No." Suchen bit her lip, feeling miserable. "He ran off. Buudi and I tried to restrain him, but he got away from us. I don't know where he went."

Londah's mouth tightened slightly. "The mind fears to consider. Hopefully, he will return soon, but if not then I will look for him. In the meantime, though, I have business elsewhere." She started purposefully towards the gate leading into the graveyard, and Suchen realized what she meant.

"Wait!" she called. "You can't kill the smuggler!"

Londah stopped but did not turn around. "I can and I will."

Suchen took in a deep breath, trying to calm herself and think clearly. "And I want you to. Hel, I want to help you. But Yozerf risked himself so that we can get out of the city tomorrow. If you kill Cleistus tonight, I seriously doubt that his ship will be disposed to aid us. At the least, we would probably have to work out another agreement. Don't throw away Yozerf's sacrifice when one day more or less won't make any difference."

"I had thought to come with you," Londah said unexpectedly. A faint, wry smile touched her lips. "After all, you lot do seem to need some looking after. But you are right, my daughter."

The breath caught painfully in Suchen's throat at that. Her own mother had not had much interest in her after she had proved utterly inadequate at all the things considered proper for a young woman of her class: needlework, dancing, and generally cultivating the appearance of being beautiful and useless.

"Thank you," Suchen said uncertainly. But she spoke to the wind; the Crow Queen had vanished into the shadows, as if she had never been there at all.

～～

Yozerf took a deep, sobbing breath and tried to calm his racing pulse. He had run and run, until he had no running left in him, until his side ached and his lungs burned. But when he finally staggered to a halt in some nameless alley near the docks, he knew that he had not run far enough. After all, he could never outrun himself.

Shame flared in him, made him double over with its intensity. Gods, Suchen had been there, she had seen everything, heard everything. His limbs trembled so violently that he had to drop to a crouch. Memories flooded his mind: the taste of Cleistus' mouth, the faint pain of a hand knotted in his hair, the scent of sweat and lust.

Yozerf took a deep breath, smelled it on his skin, still. He had to get to a bathhouse, he thought dimly, had to get it *off* of him, even though he suspected he would still smell it even if he scrubbed his flesh to the bone.

"Why do you let them do these things to you?" Telmonra demanded.

Yozerf flinched. But there was no outrunning her, either. *I had to. I had to get them out of the city. Away from the lords.*

"Why do you want to flee this city, when you could burn it to the ground instead?"

I can't do that.

"Because you are weak. Because you are a victim. If that is so, then perhaps you deserve everything that has happened to you."

He shivered violently, afraid that she was right. Her hiss of disgust dragged across his nerves like the edge of a knife.

"You do not need to suffer this. Go back and burn Cleistus. Watch him scream. Have your revenge. And then find the others—the wealthy, the noble, the bourgeoisie—and add their bodies to the pyre. I see your mind—you are afraid to go back because your so-called friends know what you are. But you don't

have to be afraid. Wipe away all the shame, all the pain. You can do it. You can take it away forever."

He wanted to. Gods, he wanted to never feel this way again, not ever. Memories beat at him with relentless fists: his own, hers. The destruction of Caden, and the destruction of Yozerf. At least with Caden things had come to an end, not dragged on and on, years of slow decay.

"The human woman does not understand why everyone is so surprised to see you still alive. They cannot understand why anyone who hates himself so much would struggle to continue so fiercely."

It was true. He was defiled, unclean, dirty. Undeserving. He closed his eyes and rocked back and forth on his heels, moaning softly.

"You don't have to feel this way. Never again. I offered you vengeance, and you took my hand. Don't refuse my offer now, my darling. The humans are strong—they have trampled you into the dust. But you are stronger, because you survived. Because now they are the ones who will be trampled. You can do it, Yozerf. You can. Remember the power in you and take it."

He took a deep breath and closed his eyes. His head ached and his thoughts scattered wildly. For a moment, he pictured it, imagined Cleistus' warehouse going up in flames. Then the flames swept over the city and everything in it—no, over all of Jenel, wiping out this abominable kingdom of humans.

No. His eyes flicked open. *No. I do not have a quarrel with the entire kingdom.*

"Of course you do. How can you not see it? It was Jenel that brought down Caden, after all. If not for the Jenelese and their treachery, you would have grown up safe and cherished in Cade Kwii. You would have had food, pleasure, riches. You would have been a prince and a sorcerer, and the world would have trembled in fear at your slightest displeasure."

That may be. Slowly, like an old man, Yozerf forced himself to his feet. *But nothing can undo the past.*

"But we can change the future."

"No," he said aloud. "The best we can do is hope to survive it."

Telmonra fell silent, although he could still feel her watching him. Still shaking, he stumbled away from the alley and went in search of something to make him feel clean again.

ॐॐ

The rest of the night passed in uneasy silence in the crypt. Buudi had told Auglar that the deal with Cleistus had been completed, but had been vague about the details of what had actually passed with the smuggler. It was not, Suchen supposed, anyone else's business, really, and telling Yozerf's secrets to all would not be to anyone's advantage. Fellrant said nothing at all, except to confirm that he had given away his last valuable possession to seal the agreement. But all night, he sat and watched Suchen, a slight smile on his lips and his eyes full of secret thoughts.

Angry and unnerved by his gaze, Suchen had to suppress the desire to walk across the room and pummel him senseless. But he had helped them, she reminded herself, when he had no clear advantage in doing so.

Or did he?

She remembered the unfeigned passion with which he had kissed Yozerf and felt jealousy like acid in her veins. It was foolish, she told herself angrily—even if the young lord was attracted to Yozerf, there was nothing mutual about it. Yozerf loved *her*. One kiss, especially when it was contrived to extract Yozerf from a far worse situation, was nothing to be envious of.

That might have been easier to accept, of course, if Yozerf hadn't been planning on sleeping with Cleistus to get them away from Segg. And she didn't know what to feel about that. On the one hand, she could understand his reasoning. He was so certain that he would somehow fail and get them all killed, as he believed he had done with Ginny, that he was ready to do any mad thing to keep that from happening. And she grieved for him, that he felt that way, that he believed he had been pushed into such an untenable position.

But I'm his lover, damn him! How can he say he loves me, then decide to sleep with someone else? Even if he didn't want to do it, even if he thought it would keep me safe, surely I still had some say in the matter. But instead, he lied to me—said that it was none of my concern.

How could he do that? How could he say that?

He had known that she would be furious if she found out, had said as much before running off and avoiding any confrontation. But that hadn't stopped him—no doubt he had told himself that he would rather have her angry than dead.

The blankness in his eyes returned to her, and she shivered, grief changing places with anger yet again. If she had not seen that, it might have been hard to believe the things that Adrylin had said about him. It was hard to reconcile the image of Frost with the Yozerf she had known, who had always been so open, so generous, in bed. The Yozerf who laughed when she tickled him, joined her in pillow fights, whispered her name in moments of passion.

Maybe Londah's sweet child hadn't died after all.

Gods. Suchen closed her eyes against sudden tears. *He must truly love me.*

The object of her inner turmoil did not return that night, however. As the day wore on, Suchen began to grow more and more nervous. What if something had happened to him? What if someone had taken advantage of his distracted state and hurt him—or what if he had hurt himself? What if the soldiers had recognized him, taken him back to Nava Nar, and were even now torturing him to learn Auglar's location?

Londah did not come back either, although Suchen couldn't say what that signified. In a way she was glad, for the more she thought about their conversation of the previous night, the more it disturbed her. Yozerf's mother, the woman who had taught Suchen the first rudiments of swordplay, the woman whom Ax had asked to protect Auglar...was a hired killer.

What was she doing in Iddi all those years ago? Suchen wondered uneasily. Hadn't one of the neighbors taken ill and died suddenly around the same time? *Coincidence...or poison?*

By the time the sun began to set, Suchen was growing seriously worried, as was everyone else. But just as she was beginning to consider suggesting the rest take the two lords to the docks while she remained behind and looked for Yozerf, the door opened. Yozerf stood on the other side, his eyes reflecting the candlelight like a pair of green coals. He had changed back into his normal clothing, the paint was gone from his face, and his hair had resumed its normal straggling appearance. Weariness and stress had left dark circles under both eyes, giving him a haggard look. But when he spoke, his voice was calm and cold.

"It's time," he said.

Chapter Twelve

Yozerf led his human pack through the slums down towards the docks, his every nerve on edge. Although it should have felt good to have his sword at his side once again, tonight it gave him little comfort against the thoughts plaguing his mind. Returning to the crypt to face his friends had not been easy, and it had taken all his courage to even look at them again. Shame burned like fire in his blood, and he realized that he feared to see the expression on Suchen's face. So he had lingered until the last possible moment before going back, so that there would be no time for any condemning words to be exchanged. Still, he knew in his heart that it would make no difference. Soon they would be aboard ship, in close quarters, and there would be no escape. What if Suchen despised him for what he had done, or almost done? What if everyone else knew as well?

The moon had waned to a narrow sliver, so the streets were steeped in shadow in between the isolated pools of torchlight. Most of the taverns and brothels were back from the docks by a few streets, so the night felt unnaturally quiet as they drew closer to their goal. For the most part, the humans smelled of nervousness and fear, with the sole exception of Cybelen, who seemed almost preternaturally calm and accepting of her fate. Peddock had taken her hand, ostensibly to help her through the darkened streets, although in truth she seemed more sure-footed in the gloom than anyone save for Yozerf and Brenwulf.

Londah was waiting for them near the docks. Yozerf caught her scent long before he saw her, for even to his eyes she was nothing more than a shadow in a shadow. Most of the humans jumped when she appeared, and Buudi and Peddock drew their swords before realizing who it was. Londah gave them a chill smile, then fell in beside Yozerf.

They went slowly, carefully, all their senses searching for any hint of guards or soldiers. The docks remained quiet, without even a wandering whore to break the silence. The ships creaked at their moorings, and rats chittered softly as they ran about on the stout lines. The smells of pitch, rotting fish, and brine filled every breath of air.

At last, they came to the berth of *The Wayward*, a Jenelese ship owned by Cleistus that supposedly carried a hull full of raw wool, but in actuality carried far more profitable cargo from Undah: spices, coffee, incense, and exotic perfumes. Even on the docks, Yozerf could scent the contents of the hull, and he wondered how he would endure several days' confinement below decks with such a mix. Behind him, Brenwulf sneezed explosively.

A gang of surly-looking sailors ran the plank down when Yozerf called out the password that Cleistus had given him. He went up first, giving the sailors hard looks and making certain that they got a glimpse of his sword. When dealing with smugglers, there was always the possibility that they would decide simply to cut the throats of any passengers and dump the bodies overboard. Given that their party was large and well-armed, Yozerf doubted that they would have such troubles, but it never hurt to make sure.

Everyone else followed, with Peddock solicitously helping Cybelen up the swaying plank. Auglar looked green at the slight movement of the ship at dock, and Yozerf guessed that he would be truly miserable once they put out to sea. The captain, a short, grizzled man with a face tanned to leather by wind and sun, awaited them on deck. As they approached, he idly leaned over and spat into the bay with great accuracy.

"You'll be staying below decks," he said gruffly, gesturing towards a hatch.

"Thank you," Auglar said graciously.

The captain grinned, exposing a gap in his front teeth. "No need to thank me. Your coin is doing enough of that."

The Sworn made their way over to the hatch, no doubt intending to check the hold before calling Auglar down. But even as Buudi reached to pull it open, the hatch was flung violently back from within. Soldiers dressed in Igen's livery and that of the city watch surged out, their swords drawn and at the ready.

Buudi yelled a warning and fell back, barely drawing his blade in time to block a heavy-handed strike from the lead guard. Brenwulf charged into the fray, while Peddock fell back, nearly tripping over a coil of rope.

Rage snapped through Yozerf. Cleistus had taken their coin— would have taken more—and then betrayed them. Letting out a howl of fury, he leapt onto an unsecured crate and ran one soldier through from behind, then slashed the throat of another who rushed to his comrade's aid. More soldiers were coming up from below;

Yozerf sprang from the crate to come down on the hatch, knocking it closed on them. Someone screamed, and he guessed that he had probably crushed fingers and knocked at least one man off the ladder.

A sword swished by too close for comfort. Yozerf jumped back, sheathed his sword, and leapt as high as he could into the air. His hands closed around a web of rigging and he swung, kicking his attacker full in the face with both booted feet.

A guard with a long pike spotted him and rushed over. Yozerf swung again, this time far enough so that he could loop his feet through the rigging higher up. Letting go with his hands, he swung free, the pike passing just underneath him. He yanked it free from the guard's grip, and bashed him in the head with it.

The Sworn and Suchen had fallen back to make a small circle around Auglar, Fellrant, and Cybelen. Londah had also taken to the rigging, and bodies were rapidly accumulating around her. Even so, there were too many enemies for them to have any real hope of winning.

"Run!" Yozerf shouted, dropping free of the rigging and heading towards the plank himself. One of the sailors ran to remove it, and was rewarded for his efforts by a kick to the head that sent him flying overboard. Yozerf stood by the plank, guarding it fiercely while the humans fought their way closer. As soon as they were within distance, they all broke and ran, boots thudding wildly on the board and making it jump. A moment later, Londah joined him, and they both also ran down the plank. Yozerf paused long enough to kick it aside, even though the dock was within easy jumping distance of the ship, and his gesture wouldn't stop their pursuers for more than a few moments.

"We should split up," Yozerf panted as they ran. "Confuse the trail."

Auglar managed a nod, despite the fact that he was already winded. "Agreed. We'll meet back at the crypt."

Arrows clattered into their midst, and they swerved wildly to avoid them. Peddock grabbed Cybelen's hand and sprinted off down an alleyway with her, while Buudi and Auglar went in another direction. Fellrant and Brenwulf headed away at the next intersection.

Suchen ran to one side of Yozerf and Londah to the other. He risked a look back and saw to his dismay that the soldiers were gaining on them rapidly. "Protect her!" he shouted, shoving Suchen in Londah's direction. "I'll act as bait!"

"No!" Suchen protested.

"As soon as they lose sight of me, I'll become the wolf. I'll hide;

and even if they do find me, they'll think I'm just a dog. I have a better chance of losing them than any of the rest of you. Now go!"

Certain that Londah would protect Suchen, Yozerf didn't watch them go. Instead, he spun on his heels to face his pursuers for a moment, shouting a stream of Aclytese invective at them. Even though they didn't know what the words meant, his tone must have made their intent clear enough, for the guards charged at him en masse with a yell.

Now I only have to lose them for a moment, Yozerf thought. Easier said than done when you were exhausted from too little sleep and too much stress. *Perhaps this wasn't such a good idea.*

He pounded around a corner and into an alley between two warehouses, intending to take a short cut to another side street. But for once, his memories of Segg failed him. At some point in the last fifteen years, someone had decided to build high wooden wall in between the two buildings, perhaps to discourage thieves. Yozerf stumbled to a halt and found himself staring up at it in despair.

I stopped my fall from the roof, he thought desperately. *Perhaps I can use my powers to leap over the wall?*

"Surrender yourself!" shouted a guard behind him.

Out of options, Yozerf spun and put his back to the wall. The clot of human guards seemed to fill the entire alley before him, and he felt his heart beginning to race with fear.

"*Yes, fear,*" said Telmonra. Her presence rose in his mind, until it was as though she stood beside him. "*Because that is all you know, isn't it? You let them make you a victim. Instead of taking what you need, you crawl to Cleistus on your belly, all but beg him to abuse you, just so that he can hand you over to your enemies without a second thought. Maybe you should do the same thing now—put down your sword and lick the soldiers' boots, ask them to take you back to their dungeons so they can rape and torture you.*"

His anger over Cleistus' betrayal came back stronger than before. *No.*

"*Why not? You're not a predator, you're prey. You're a victim—you always have been, ever since you were a child. Nothing has changed.*"

"No," he said out loud. His hand tightened on his sword hilt until his knuckles showed white.

"Do as I say or else things will go even worse for you," the guard warned, mistakenly believing that Yozerf had answered him. "Do it! Now!"

Very slowly, Yozerf straightened. He felt the power rise in him like heady wine. Telmonra was right—had always *been* right. He had been behaving as if he was still a weak, powerless child instead of what he truly was: the descendant of kings whose blood magic had shaken the Northern world for three-thousand years.

No more. No more!

A baleful smile spread over Yozerf's face. "No," he said firmly, clearly.

The lead soldier started forward, no doubt intending to force Yozerf into submission. With a negligent gesture, Yozerf pulled fire from the air and sent it streaming forward, igniting clothing and hair in an instant. The soldier screamed in unbelievable agony, flailing madly in his pain and stumbling into his cohorts. They shrieked and fell back in confusion.

"Surely you aren't giving up that easily?" Yozerf asked. He flung out his arm, and a wall of fire burst forth, roasting half the contingent even as they stood.

Again and again he tore fire from the core of his being, until the night air shimmered and the cobblestones cracked from the heat. A blast of hot air filled the alley, blowing his hair back from his face, and he heard himself laughing.

"Yes! Kill them!" Telmonra cried jubilantly, and he felt her euphoria as if it was his own.

The screams of the soldiers didn't last long. Yozerf allowed the flames to die away. Pools of molten metal that must have once been swords glowed hotly amidst the darkness of charred bone and ash. A sense of his own power flooded through him. He felt unstoppable—invincible.

"Vengeance," whispered Telmonra.

Yes. These soldiers had only been an annoyance. Next he would—

A scream broke the stillness of the night. Startled, Yozerf spun about and stared up at the warehouse roof above him. The dim moonlight outlined two figures. One was a soldier, a bow dangling loosely from his hand, and with a chill Yozerf realized how close he had come to being killed through his own inattention.

And the other figure…was nothing human.

Humans called them Red Guard for their dull, ruddy skin and crimson eyes; in his own language they were *kk'ithit'kk*. Shape-changers with the ability to take on human form, they were the minions of Jahcgroth, Emperor of Argannon.

Bat wings rose up against the night sky, and a gargoyle-like head armed with rows of wicked teeth swung about to consider him. From one clawed hand dangled the archer, who still struggled feebly. With a casual gesture, the Red Guard curved its head around and bit out his throat.

Hatred slammed through Yozerf, and he heard Telmonra howling with agreement. Almost without thought, he summoned the wind, launching himself upward in a gentle arc so that his boots came down on the warehouse roof.

The Red Guard narrowed crimson eyes. "So. You gain more control of your power with every day that passes," it said in a low, grating voice.

Yozerf snarled. Pain bloomed in his face as his jaws and teeth elongated and his eyes shifted to the wolf's golden orbs. He would kill this monstrosity, would rend it to pieces...

"I am not your enemy," the Red Guard said, breath hissing between its razor fangs. It shook the guard's limp body in his direction. "This one would have slain you had I not interceded. The Emperor does not want you dead."

Yozerf lunged, growling furiously. With a snarl of its own, the Red Guard flung away the archer's body and leapt into the air. Leathery wings snapped open as the hot wind from the alley caught them, sending the creature skimming rapidly away over the city. Snarling, Yozerf reached for the wind, intending to smash the creature back to earth. But there was a blankness inside him where the magic had been, and not so much as a zephyr responded to his call.

Shocked, he drew in a sharp breath, automatically shifting back to fully-Aclytese form. The wind rose instantly, and he felt the power come flooding back, but by that time the Red Guard was out of reach.

What happened?

Telmonra hissed impatiently. *"It is your mixed blood. The wolf is inimical to the magic. Do not shape-shift again."*

Yozerf swore softly and scanned the night sky, as if the Red Guard might come back. He had fought Red Guard thrice before, and each time they had done their best to kill him. But this one...this one wanted to save him?

It made no sense.

"Jahcgroth is our enemy, as are all his minions," Telmonra reminded him. *"He was of our clan, yet he betrayed us and destroyed the dragons, leaving us vulnerable to Jenel's army. What does it matter if this one spared your life? We will make it regret the act."*

"Yes," Yozerf murmured out loud, but even he could hear the lack of conviction in the word.

❧❧

Yozerf hurried through the shadowy graveyard, anxiety for his friends filling him. He wrenched open the door to the crypt, only to have Suchen throw her arms around him before he could step inside.

"You're all right!" she cried, clutching him tightly.

Feeling a bit weak with relief, Yozerf returned the embrace. "I told you I would be," he said, as if there had never been any doubt.

Peddock's pale face appeared over Suchen's shoulder, his eyes wild. "Have you seen Cybelen?"

"I thought she went with you," Yozerf said as Suchen disengaged and stepped back. A quick glance around the crypt revealed that everyone else had made it back. Buudi had a rag wrapped around his head to staunch the bleeding from a cut above his eye, and Auglar's wrist was tightly bound, as if he had sprained it, but for the most part they looked to be unharmed.

"She was!" Peddock replied, as if Yozerf had accused him of murdering her in an alley. "But we were separated in the dark! I only let go of her for a moment, but when I turned around, she was gone. I couldn't find her anywhere, so I came here, hoping that she had found her way back."

Yozerf frowned as he considered all of the things that could befall a beautiful, unarmed woman such as Cybelen. She would be as a sheep set before the wolves. "I'll go out and look for her. She might still be safe if—"

At that moment, footsteps sounded outside. Drawing his sword, Yozerf dropped into a crouch, until a slender figure emerged in the doorway.

"Cybelen!" Peddock shouted in relief. He pushed Yozerf roughly aside, ran to her, and swept the young noblewoman into a tight embrace. "Thanks the gods! I thought I had lost you!"

She smiled up at him. Although her long hair had come half-undone from its pins, and her dress had a torn sleeve, she looked unharmed. No, more, Yozerf thought. She looked radiant.

"I'm not that easy to lose," she said, touching Peddock's face gently with her fingers. For a moment Yozerf thought they would forget themselves utterly and kiss in front of everyone. But instead Cybelen dropped her hand and took a step back, breaking the moment. "I'm fine, really. I got confused for a while, but once I had my sense of direction back I didn't have any problems finding the cemetery."

Yozerf ran his hand through his hair, feeling vaguely annoyed. "You're fortunate you didn't find any trouble," he said harshly. "If humans don't frighten you enough, there are Red Guard about."

Several people gasped, and Brenwulf came to his feet with a

growl. "What?"

"You heard me." Yozerf sheathed his sword and looked grimly at his pack. "After I lost the guards, I encountered a Red Guard. I would have fought it, but for some reason it left."

Cybelen frowned, clearly perplexed. "What is a Red Guard?"

"They are unholy servants of Jahcgroth," Peddock said, a look of disgust on his face. "Demons. They killed Uzco—he was another of Auglar's Sworn. They would have killed us all, given half the chance."

There was more bravado than truth in the last statement, but Yozerf let it pass. "If Jahcgroth's spies are in Segg, then he may have other allies here."

"Lord Igen?" Auglar suggested. "It might explain why he wanted to kill Fellrant and me."

Somehow, the reasoning didn't sound quite right to Yozerf, although why he couldn't say. "Perhaps," he agreed neutrally.

Suchen sighed. She looked tired in the soft light of the tallow candle, but also very beautiful. Her golden hair hung loose about her face; she had pulled off the headcloth he had given her. A smear of dirt marked one cheek, and her sapphire eyes were troubled. "So...what now?" she asked softly. "What more can we do? If Red Guard are hunting us as well as human soldiers, we can't stay here. But where will we go?"

The defeated sound of her voice cut straight to Yozerf's heart. His anger at Cleistus returned, burning like the fire he had loosed in the alley. If the smuggler had kept his word, they would all be safely away from Segg by now, instead of sitting here trapped, afraid of Red Guard and human soldiers alike. Had Cleistus gone to the rebel lords, or had they come to him? And how much had they paid the smuggler for the lives of Yozerf's pack?

Suchen's image seemed to almost blaze before his eyes. How cheaply had Cleistus sold *her* life?

"He betrayed you," Telmonra hissed, latching onto his rage like a parasite. *"He would hand you over to those who would kill you and despoil your mate."* A picture formed in his mind, though whether it came from her or from him he didn't know: Suchen weeping, her face bruised, struggling to cover her abused body with her torn clothing while the guards laughed aloud.

A blind wall of fury rose up in him, blanking thought. With a snarl of rage, he turned back and started out the door.

"Where are you going?" Suchen called after him in surprise.

"To find some answers for you," he replied, and then broke into a run.

Chapter Thirteen

Yozerf could feel the fire growing within him at every step as he paced along Sinker Lane. Unlike the night before, when he had approached sheathed in ice, he no longer felt afraid and powerless. He was done with being made a victim, he told himself. Tonight, others would cower at *his* approach.

"Yes," Telmonra whispered, a continuous murmur beneath his own thoughts. *"Vengeance. Destroy them. They would kill you, they would kill your mate, they would kill these humans you call your friends. Finally, finally, you see the truth of my words."*

As usual, the street was filled with carousing sailors and dock workers, but even the most drunken of them took one look at Yozerf's face and moved aside. Their fear brought a smile to his face—after so many years of keeping his head down, afraid to draw too much of the wrong sort of attention to himself, it felt good to watch others move out of *his* way.

Yozerf didn't bother to knock on the door to Cleistus' lair; he simply hit it as hard as he could with the wind, blasting it back off its hinges and shattering it to kindling. The blow caught the unlucky door guard as well, slamming him into the wall so that he collapsed into a bloody heap. Whether he was alive or dead Yozerf didn't know or care.

The carpets in the hall smoldered dangerously under his feet, but he held the magic back, not yet ready to give it free rein. The sound of running feet alerted him to another's presence, accompanied a moment later by a whiff of perfume. Then Adrylin appeared in the hall before him, a crossbow in his hands.

Adrylin's pale topaz eyes widened slightly at the sight of Yozerf and the shattered door. "What's going on here?" he demanded, pointing the crossbow at Yozerf's heart.

Yozerf smiled and had the satisfaction of seeing the other Aclyte pale even further. "Surprised to see me, Adrylin? I suppose that your master told you I would be dead by this time."

The hands holding the crossbow shook just a little. "I don't know what you're talking about."

"Liar." Yozerf slapped the crossbow aside with the wind, sending the bolt flying free into the nearest wall. Adrylin cried out in shock and fear, and tried to scramble back, although what sort of safety he thought it would buy him Yozerf didn't know. "Tell me where Cleistus is."

Adrylin shook his head dumbly, blindly groping behind him for a door. Yozerf clicked his tongue reprovingly. "A shame. I'll have to find him myself, then."

He left Adrylin's lifeless body on the floor behind him. A quick check of the sumptuous room where Cleistus conducted his meetings showed it to be empty. That left only one obvious place to look for the smuggler.

Cleistus had moved his lair over the years, perhaps for security, so the bedroom was not the same as the one where he'd had Yozerf. Nonetheless, the Aclyte felt a chill descending on him as the approached the closed door. The smell of sex wafted from within, and his sharp ears could hear the muffled groans through the thin door. He stopped for a moment, unable to take another step, his heart beating hard.

"*Weakling,*" Telmonra hissed, and suddenly she had crossed the empty space between them. Confused memories smote him, some hers, some his.

...Humans rampaged through the streets of Cade Kwil, killing men and babies, raping women and children, destroying everything that she had ever loved...

...Cleistus' meaty fingers twined in his hair, pulling his head closer, filling his mouth...

...Another man slapped him hard across the face, then shoved him back across the bed. "Look at me!" he screamed, and then when Yozerf did so, "Look at me as if I'm here!"...

...The flies had already come, crawling in and out of Ginny's dead lips and across her open eyes. Her expression was one of terror and pain, but to him it was also one of accusation, as if her ghost screamed "How could you have let this happen to me?"...

..."I love you, Telmonra," Jahcgroth whispered huskily, sliding into her, and she screamed in passion and ecstasy...*

..."You can stay here, if you want," Daryn said, his fingers tracing Yozerf's young cheek and mouth. "But if you do, you have to do some things for me." And Yozerf nodded, pathetically grateful, because it was so cold outside, and he knew with a dreadful certainty that he would die if he had to go back out there—that*

he had in fact been dying when Daryn found him, two weeks
after the apartment fire. He had already been raped twice in
alleys by strangers at that point, and even though he suspected
what Daryn had in mind, he could survive it, he knew that he
could...

Yozerf and Telmonra both screamed in rage and pain. The
door disintegrated, fiery debris flying outwards in a whirlwind that
rained ash and burning coals down on everything inside. Cleistus
let out a shriek of surprise and scrambled back across the bed,
his hand going under the mattress for whatever weapon he kept
concealed there. The Aclytese youth who had been servicing him
froze in place, like a rabbit in a thicket, his huge, terrified eyes
staring at the death that had come so unexpectedly through the
door.

Yozerf stared at the youth, but saw only his own face looking
back. "Get out of here," he snarled.

Few whores lived long without acquiring some sense of self-
preservation, and this youth was no exception. Without question-
ing, he snatched up his clothes and bolted from the room, the soft
sound of his bare feet on the carpets quickly receding. Satisfied,
Yozerf turned back to Cleistus, who now crouched naked on the
bed, a sword in his hand.

A feeling of revulsion rose up in Yozerf, and for an instant he
was sixteen again, sprawled out on that same bed with Cleistus on
top of him, distancing the pain and the humiliation with a shield
of ice.

"But you aren't, are you?" Telmonra asked.

"No," he replied aloud. "I'm not. I have the upper hand here."

Cleistus stared at him as though afraid Yozerf had taken leave
of his sanity. "My b-boy," he said with a pasty smile. "What are you
doing here? I thought you were going to take ship tonight."

"You thought I would be dead or in chains," Yozerf corrected
coldly. "But clearly, I am not. Now you will tell me which lord paid
for your betrayal."

Cleistus swallowed thickly. Fear-sweat ran over his naked body,
and it occurred to Yozerf that the smuggler had never thought that
his old catamite was dangerous in even the smallest way. A slow,
malevolent smile twitched Yozerf's lips. Cleistus had forgotten the
first law of Segg, which was never to trust, never to let your guard
down, and to treat everyone as a potential enemy.

And now he was going to pay the price.

"I don't know," Cleistus said, voice quavering.

"How unoriginal. Do you know how many people have said
that to me lately? Adrylin tried to same sad excuse, right before I

killed him."

"No," Cleistus gasped, as if he might have actually had feelings for his assistant. But of course that was impossible—humans such as him had no feelings at all.

"None of them do, pretty boy, none of them."

"You have one last chance," Yozerf said, taking a threatening step closer to the bed.

With a grunt of effort, Cleistus lunged at him with the sword. Yozerf had seen the blow coming, however, and used the wind to wrench the blade away. The smuggler screamed in pain, curling up over his hand, and Yozerf guessed that he had inadvertently broken several fingers when disarming the man.

"Fool, he is a fool to try you, make him pay, make them all pay, yes..."

Yozerf felt his mouth twitch into a smile. "Wrong choice," he said softly.

"No! Wait!" Cleistus screamed, his eyes going round in fear. "It was Gevannin's doing! He was the one in contact with the palace, not me! He was suspicious that your sudden reappearance coincided with the disappearance of two lords, especially when you said that you wanted passage out of Segg! He made a few discreet inquiries, found out that a man matching your description had been seen in Lord Auglar's retinue! He set it up so that we would get paid by you for passage, plus by someone in the palace for finding Auglar! But I don't know who it was!"

Yozerf lowered his hand and stepped back. "I believe you."

Cleistus closed his eyes in relief. "Thank you. I swear, I will make this up to you, just give me the chance."

Yozerf nodded and turned away, walking back towards the door. *"Shall we?"* Telmonra asked with an evil laugh.

"Yes," Yozerf said aloud.

The power rose in him, like a hot wind in his soul. Behind him, the bed erupted into flames, and Cleistus' sobs of relief turned into shrieks of agony. Without looking back, Yozerf left the building and its dead inhabitants behind. Most likely the fire would spread and destroy everything in the warehouse, but he did not particularly care so long as it obliterated the bed and the man in it.

The humid night air felt cool against his heated skin. He paused for a moment, smelling the scent of the ocean and the estuaries. An ache had started in his head, behind his eyes, and he rubbed absently at his temples.

Gevannin.

Somehow, he had not expected to be betrayed by an Aclyte.

"But he is no longer one of us," Telmonra hissed. *"Just as*

Jahcgroth betrayed Caden, so has Gevannin betrayed you. He is a lap dog of the humans, without honor, willing to betray his own kind to his human masters, when he should be bowing to you as his king. Adrylin was of the same ilk—and you had no question what to do with him."

"Yes," Yozerf whispered, feeling her absolute certainty within him. Suddenly, everything had become so clear, and he marveled that he had not seen it all before. With a soft, fell laugh he moved out into the street, watching those around him shrink back in fear. It was time to settle his score with Gevannin.

๛

The doorkeeper at the blood pit didn't seem terribly surprised to see him, clearly not realizing that Yozerf was supposed to be in chains somewhere. Which suited him well enough; fighting his way in would have been a waste of time and effort. As the doorkeeper led him back through the fighters' room, Yozerf paused for a moment, running his eyes over the hard-bitten, scarred men. Some of them were here because they enjoyed fighting and killing, but others were gambling their lives because they were desperate for the coin that winning would bring.

"I would advise all of you to leave here now," he said.

Several of the men, including his escort, gave him strange looks. He simply shrugged and went on; whether they listened to him or not was their choice. *Would I have done so, in their place?* he wondered. He believed that he would have; a bizarre stranger with an ominous warning would have been enough to make him put off the fighting until another day.

Maybe.

"Hello, Gevannin," Yozerf said as he stepped into the room.

Gevannin froze by the window overlooking the blood pit, his face going white. The familiar goblet of wine slipped from his fingers, falling to spill on the floor. For an instant, uncertainty flashed in the depths of his jade eyes, and Yozerf could all but see the questions forming: what had gone wrong, did Yozerf know about his betrayal...and if he did, what was he going to do about it?

"Kill him," Gevannin ordered sharply.

The ever-present bodyguards swarmed up from their table. Yozerf blew two of them into the wall, then transformed the third into a living torch. The last two bodyguards broke and fled, terror in their eyes.

Gevannin backed up to the wall, his expression one of horror and fear. A wet stain spread across the front of his breeks, and now the ammonia scent of urine underlay the smell of cooked flesh. "Y-Yozerf, w-wait," he stammered frantically, one hand flung out as if he could ward off the next attack. "I'll do whatever you want—anything, just name it, please!"

"Traitor," Telmonra said, and Yozerf felt his mouth echo her words. "Cleistus already told me that you were the one who sold us to the lords. Was it Igen, Gevannin?" Yozerf raised a hand wreathed in fire. "I hope he paid you well."

"It was Igen," Gevannin whimpered, huddling back against the wall. "I'm sorry, Yozerf! We can work something out—just tell me what you want!"

Yozerf smiled. "I want you to die, Gevannin."

His hand swept in a semi-circle, and flames bloomed everywhere in the little room, transforming it instantly into an inferno. Gevannin barely had time to scream before his body vanished into ash and charred bone.

Yozerf went back down the hall, fire trailing him like a cloak, igniting the old, wooden walls. By the time he reached the main room, panic had already arrived before him, like a herald. The humans who had come to watch others die for their pleasure were now stampeding over one another, struggling to escape as smoke and fire surrounded them. Yozerf watched for a moment in disgust, and he heard Telmonra whispering to him: *"See? They are nothing, lower than animals, creatures that will crawl over the fallen bodies of their fellows to save their own pathetic lives. But, oh, they were so eager to see others die for them, were they not?"*

Yozerf pulled fire from his mind and sent it streaming away from him on the wind, blasting the room and everything in it. Then he turned and walked back to the alley door, hurling aside anyone who crossed his path. As he left the burning building behind, the smell of smoke heavy in his hair and clothes, he heard the screams behind him. Someone had tried to start a water brigade, in an attempt to save the buildings around the blood pit, but even now the ancient wooden structures were going up along with it.

The euphoria that came with use of the magic gripped Yozerf still, making him feel as though his feet barely touched the ground as he walked. It sustained him until he was several blocks from the site of the fire. Then, gradually, the sensation of invincibility, of infallibility, began to slip away, leaving in its wake a terrible weariness. He stumbled against an uneven cobblestone, and the world swayed dangerously around him. Shivering took hold of his body, as if all the heat had been drained from him, and he staggered into an empty doorway and sank to the ground.

What's happening to me? Yozerf wondered, but the thought

had no urgency against the overwhelming desire to collapse into oblivion.

"All magic has a price to pay," Telmonra said, and he thought he caught a glimpse of gray eyes and a cruel face before realizing that she existed only in his own mind. *"You have started down the path of vengeance this night, but it has taken its toll. Give in to sleep—it is the only thing that can restore your strength."*

Yozerf struggled to regain his feet, but his body felt like lead. "Not safe...too exposed...," he mumbled through lips gone numb. Then the rough wood of the doorway was pressed against his cheek, and darkness took him.

꩜꩜

"The city burns," Londah said. She sat perched in the great oak, her legs dangling to either side of the enormous limb she straddled. On the horizon, she could see an angry red glow that silhouetted the taller buildings.

The humans had ventured outside of the crypt, perhaps needing the free air of the night and the feeling that at least they could die in the open instead of trapped inside. They clustered beneath her tree, talking in soft voices, and she could all but hear their despair. Things had not gone well for them, not at all, and she wondered at the betrayals that seemed to dog their steps.

"What do you think is happening?" asked Auglar worriedly.

Good questions, human lord. She narrowed her eyes and scanned the horizon. A huge column of smoke was making its way into the air, reflecting the flames below it.

"He called down fire," the human traitor had said.

There was no particular reason to think this blaze had anything to do with Yozerf. Most tenements were lit with candles or fish oil lamps, and fires were hardly unheard of. But Londah remembered his anger before he had rushed out. It was a familiar anger, a rage against the world that had burned in him far longer than any fire he now possessed. And knowing that, it seemed too great a coincidence to believe this blaze had nothing to do with him.

Not that she would say as much. "I do not know," she replied, half truthfully. "Let us hope that the fire does not spread far."

They all gathered silently near the eastern wall, watching the glow intensify. But as dawn approached, thunder began to rumble and rain moved in, spreading a gentle blanket across the city. The glow began to die away.

"Well, at least there's one piece of good luck," Peddock said from where he stood with one arm about Cybelen's shoulders. The pendant around her neck gleamed faintly in what little light struggled through the heavy cloud cover.

"Perhaps," said Londah softly.

Suchen frowned. "What do you mean?"

Londah shook her head, only half certain herself. "Only that I saw no sign of rain coming last night. I don't know. Perhaps I was mistaken."

"What other explanation is there?" Auglar asked uneasily.

"I don't know." But, like the fire, the rain felt wrong to her. There were wizards involved in this disaster, Ax foremost, and she would not take anything for granted until she knew more.

And sitting here speculating will get me nothing.

She leapt down from the tree, landing lightly on the soggy ground beneath. "Wait here. I want to see what burned."

And find out if Yozerf had anything to do with it.

❧❧

After Londah left, the light increased slowly, although the rain did not slacken. Suchen climbed into the lower branches of the tree herself and stared in the direction of the cemetery gates, desperate for the familiar flash of red hair. Yozerf had been gone for many hours now, and although she knew that he was the best able of all of them, save for Londah, to take care of himself in this city, she could not suppress her worry. The look in his eyes when he left had been more than half-crazed, as if he was in the grips of some powerful rage or sorrow.

They were all upset, of course. Glancing down at the small gathering outside the crypt, Suchen saw that for the most part her friends waited alone, their heads bowed in despair. Only Peddock and Cybelen sat beside one another, Cybelen talking softly to him, as if to cheer him up. Even Fellrant looked tired, his careful composure ragged at the edges.

What are we going to do? Suchen wondered. There seemed no hope of escape from Segg, and she remembered the words Yozerf had spoken in Kellsjard, before they had ever left. He had been so certain that the city would devour them, like some sort of sentient thing always hungry for new souls. At the time she had thought it groundless paranoia, but perhaps he had been right after all. Perhaps they had walked into the jaws of a beast that would never let them go.

Stop that, she told herself firmly. One hand wrapped around her sword hilt, drawing strength from its solidity. *Last night may have been a disaster, but it wasn't our final chance. Londah and Yozerf will find a way to get us out of here. Yozerf is working on it now. Don't despair over one setback, no matter how great it seems.*

Good advice, but hard to practice, particularly as the day wore on with no sign of either of the Aclytes. Finally, Peddock stood up and started off.

"Where are you going?" Auglar asked sharply.

"To find out what's happening," Peddock said. He turned around, and his face was flushed with anger and tension. "We can't just sit here and wait for the soldiers to find us, damn it!"

Buudi rose to his feet, locking his gaze with Peddock's. "It's too risky. You might be recognized."

"No more risky than the Aclytes leaving! For the gods' sakes, who is going to forget either one of them?"

"And maybe that's what happened, Peddock. Maybe Yozerf and Londah haven't come back because the soldiers found them."

"Then all the more reason to know for certain, before Lord Igen's men show up here to arrest us!"

Buudi shook his shaggy-haired head. "I know what you're feeling. I know, because we are all enduring it right now. Fear. Uncertainty. Wondering how we'll ever get out of this city, or *if* we'll get out. But charging off on your own won't help anything. Sit down." When Peddock made no move to obey, Buudi's eyes narrowed slightly. "That is an order, Sworn."

Peddock's lips pressed together, and there was a wild light in his eyes. For an instant, he glanced at Cybelen, as if he wanted to say something to her. But instead, he spun abruptly on his heel and ran.

"Peddock! Come back here!" Buudi shouted, rushing after him. Suchen jumped down from the tree, intending to join in the chase, but Peddock's form disappeared amidst the rows of tombstones too fast for either of them. A few moments later, they all heard the clang of the cemetery gate slamming shut.

Fellrant looked up, a thin smile on his pasty face. "Well, well, Auglar," he said softly, "it looks as if your little group is fragmenting."

"Shut up!" Brenwulf snarled threateningly.

Auglar met Fellrant's gaze squarely. "At least they're still alive, which is more than I can say for your Sworn."

Anger flashed in the depths of Fellrant's eyes, and Suchen realized uneasily how close to the edge he must be to let such emotion show. "My Sworn died to protect me, whereas yours are deserting you. If not for me, your little circle would have already fallen to pieces."

"What are you talking about?" Auglar demanded coldly, blue

eyes flashing in the shadow of his black hair.

"If not for me, your Aclytese whore would have been gone days ago."

Auglar put his hand to the dagger at his belt. "I will hear no insults from you."

"Then hear the truth, Auglar. You would have traded your safety for Yozerf's body, and don't think that he will not remember it."

Auglar's face was white. "I don't know what you're talking about."

"You don't want to know, Auglar. You're a fool. If one of my men was falling apart in front of me, you had best believe that I would find out why, because that sort of pain is what leads to a knife in the back. But you don't care. You can't see what's in front of your own face. You can't even see that your steward has him, but your first wants him."

Buudi pressed his lips together in a grim line, as if he wanted to attack Fellrant physically. "Ridiculous. You're only saying this because you know my history."

"Oh, I know your past indeed. But I also know your present, first among the Sworn. I *saw* what was in your eyes that night at Cleistus' warehouse. You want the Aclyte, and your jealousy burns your heart every time you see him with the steward."

"Liar! You're the one who wants him!"

Fellrant smiled malevolently. "Unlike you, I see no point in denying it. Maybe it is because he wants me, too."

Suchen snatched her sword out and held it point-first at the diminutive lord. "That isn't true."

Fellrant met her eyes, ignoring the length of steel pointed at his heart. "Are you so sure?"

"Put your sword down, Suchen," Auglar ordered harshly. When she hesitated, he took a step towards her. "I will have no blood shed in some petty quarrel, especially one instigated by a treacherous liar."

"I have not said anything save the truth," Fellrant argued. "If your retainers dislike it, that is their problem, not mine."

Auglar rounded on him, and something in his expression made Fellrant falter. "Be silent," Auglar said levelly, "or by the gods I will have you gagged and bound. I saved your worthless skin during the coup because I believed that it was the right thing to do. I see now that I was nothing but a fool."

Fellrant fell silent, but his blue-violet eyes burned with anger. Glaring acid at him, Suchen reluctantly sheathed her sword. How dare he drag Yozerf's private pain into the light? How dare he suggest that Yozerf could feel anything for him?

He's just trying to provoke us, Suchen told herself harshly.
*You're only giving him what he wants. Auglar may have hoped
that having mutual enemies made Fellrant a friend, but he was
wrong.*

Shaking and angry, she dropped into a crouch, wrapping her
arms around her knees. To Hel with Fellrant. And to Hel with
Peddock. And to Hel with this entire damned city.

Ah, Yozerf, my love, where are you?

When Yozerf finally awoke, the light was that of late afternoon.
Alarmed, he sat up gingerly, wincing as a fierce headache smote
him. His entire body hurt, but a careful check revealed that no one
had disturbed him while he lay unconscious, which was in itself
almost a miracle. Perhaps everyone had been too busy looting in
the wake of the fires to worry about one scraggly Aclyte.

Rain poured down only a few inches away from where he lay,
a continual stream of cold gray water from a cold gray sky. Pulling
up his hood, Yozerf made his way wearily into the street. He would
have to invent a good explanation for his prolonged absence, he
thought.

"Why?" Telmonra asked. "*Why should you explain anything
to them?*"

They will expect it of me.

"*So? They are humans. They are Jenelese. Their kind destroyed our kingdom and nearly obliterated our line. They made
slaves of us, and when that was not enough they did their best
to grind us into submission through poverty and despair. You
owe them nothing, but they owe you much.*"

Hatred scalded him, and he stilled, shocked at the intensity of
the emotion. An old man bumped into him with a curse, and with
a snarl of rage Yozerf turned, hand uplifted to strike. The man's
face paled and he flung down the smoke-stained bundle he carried, hobbling off into the crowd as fast as he could.

No. Yozerf forced himself to calm, drawing upon memories of
Suchen and the Sworn. They were not his enemies. They loved
him.

"*They love you so much that you must hide your power from
them, lest they turn on you.*"

"Be silent!" Yozerf snapped. A few passers-by gave him alarmed
looks, no doubt thinking that he was one of the mad who occasionally wandered the streets, talking only to the air.

He could still feel Telmonra's presence close to the surface,
but when she said nothing further, Yozerf decided that she had

chosen to obey. Shaking off his trepidation, he started back down the street, headed for the cemetery.

Several large buildings had burned around the blood pit, and ash still hung heavy in the air, but it seemed that the rain had kept the destruction from spreading. Yozerf walked past his handiwork quickly, shoulders hunched and hood drawn up. Faint memories of the fire that had destroyed the tenement where he had lived as a child sparked in the back of his mind, but were quickly smothered.

"Are you sure?" asked a familiar voice amidst the babble of the onlookers and looters who crowded the street and picked among the ruins.

Yozerf's step faltered, and he cast about in alarm. There, off to one side, stood Peddock's familiar figure. His back was turned to Yozerf, but there was no mistaking his scent. He appeared to be talking to a one-legged beggar who sat on a low stool in front of a wine shop.

"Oh, aye, my lord," the beggar said, nodding his head wisely. Most of his teeth were missing, and the skin of his face was red with some nameless rash. "I sit here most nights, including the last one. Well, I smelled smoke and saw some flames, so I shouted for a bucket brigade to get started. While the whole lads were lining up and trying to douse the flames, I saw him walking down the middle of the street, bold as you please. An Aclyte, he was, with hair like the blood on me stump. Terrifying, he looked, with his white skin and all those black clothes, his cloak blowing in the wind. Then a while later, after he had gone, a fellow stumbled past me. He was all burned up on his face. I asked him what had happened, and he started babbling about some Aclyte with fire shooting out of his hands! I asked him if it'd been the one I had seen earlier, but I couldn't get no more sense out of him."

"Thank you," Peddock said, passing a jentarrii to the old beggar. The tone of his voice was one of smug satisfaction. Then he turned and began to walk rapidly away, back in the direction of the cemetery.

Yozerf stood as if the sudden chill that gripped him had frozen his feet to the street. Peddock knew, or at least guessed. Peddock, who had never liked him, who had always disapproved of his relationship with Suchen. Peddock, who probably saw himself as being vindicated at last in all his prejudices and dislikes.

"You can't let him reach them," Telmonra whispered urgently. *"He hates you—he always hated you. He will tell them lies about you, turn them against you! Stop him!"*

It took Yozerf several minutes to catch up with the Sworn, but when at last he did, satisfaction thrummed in him. There was no one else on the street, and they were not yet within sight of the cemetery. *"Perfect."*

"Peddock," Yozerf called in a deceptively mild voice.

Peddock started and spun about, his face going pale. His sword was in his hand in a moment, but Yozerf noted with detached amusement that its tip wavered wildly.

"Why, Peddock, whatever is wrong?" he asked, cocking his head to one side. "You seem afraid."

"I know about you," Peddock spat through clenched teeth. "I don't know what you are, but I know that you've been lying to us. Cleistus' warehouse and the blood pit were both destroyed by fire last night. I wasn't surprised when I heard that you'd been seen near both places just as the fires started. But when I heard the first person say that you had started the fire in the blood pit by sorcery, I didn't believe it. I thought he was confused. But funny thing is, he wasn't the only one with such a tale."

Yozerf's heart pounded wildly. Damn Peddock!

He forced his demeanor to remain calm as he approached, even though he was not yet certain what he could do to salvage the situation. "Don't be foolish, Peddock. If I had these powers, why wouldn't I have used them before? Why wouldn't I have stopped Staafon with them instead of letting myself be tortured and almost killed, eh? Why wouldn't I have used them to kill the Council and save Rozah?"

Peddock backed away slowly, clearly not willing to take his eyes off Yozerf for even an instant. "I don't know," he admitted. "Unless you murdered Rozah yourself. You were the only one there— you were the only survivor! Explain to me how you came to live when everyone else in that room died!"

No. It was Yozerf's worst fears become terrible reality. He forced a smile onto his face. Peddock paled sharply, and he realized how ghastly his expression must look. "Peddock. We can talk of this rationally," he said, deliberately moving closer to his adversary. "Just put your sword away and come with me—"

At that moment, Peddock, who had continued to blindly back away, caught his heel on an uneven cobblestone. With a cry, he fell into a puddle full of slime. Telmonra let out a triumphant howl, and Yozerf found himself lunging forwards, hand upraised as if to fling fire.

Something heavy struck him from the side, sending him spinning to the ground and knocking the breath from his lungs. He rolled wildly and found himself staring up at the hulking figure of the Red Guard he had fought before. The creature let out a thunderous bellow that must have been heard by half the city, and then snapped a mouthful of fangs just inches from Yozerf's face.

Yozerf scrambled back. Peripherally, he was aware that Peddock had regained his feet and fled. "Curse you!" he shouted at the monster, even as Telmonra raged inside of him, demanding that he kill.

His hand shot out, fingers closing around the Red Guard's thick wrist, his touch burning its skin like hot coals. The monster roared, jerking its arm back so that Yozerf was hurled halfway across the road. The wind cushioned Yozerf's fall, though, and he sprang to his feet, ready to kill.

Claws raked at his eyes, making him jerk back instinctively. Then the creature launched into the sky, wings tearing frenziedly at the air. Telmonra screamed in frustrated rage, the cry emerging from Yozerf's throat.

They crouched in the alley, mutual rage flowing together, back and forth. Some memories rose, such as the sack of Caden, while others, ones of love and tenderness, sank into darkness. *"The creature protected him. Peddock must be one of Jahcgroth's allies, just like Dara-Don. He's going to tell everyone else about you. You have to kill him before he can do that. You have to kill him before he can betray Suchen. You have to kill him."*

"Yes," Yozerf snarled, then burst out of his crouch and into an all-out run on Peddock's heels.

Chapter Fourteen

"Here comes Peddock," Buudi said sharply. "And he's running."

The first among the Sworn had taken up the watch position high in the oak tree; now, he scrambled down fast enough to put his neck in jeopardy. Hardly had his feet touched the ground but he drew his sword and fell in beside Auglar, who had been sitting on a low monument.

Suchen and Brenwulf hurriedly followed suit. Even Fellrant stirred, looking as if he wished he had someone to wait by him. Casting about for Cybelen, Suchen remembered that the young noblewoman had slipped into the deeper recesses of the cemetery to visit the secluded spot they had designated a privy, and she cursed mentally at the poor timing.

The gate clanged as Peddock flung it open, and within seconds he came into view, dodging wildly around stone benches, statues, and monuments. Sweat plastered his hair to his head, and his face was deathly pale. His naked sword was clutched in one shaking hand.

"It's Yozerf!" Peddock gasped between breaths. "He's trying to kill me!"

Of all the things Suchen had expected him to say, that was not one of them. "What?"

"It's true!" Peddock's eyes darted frantically from one face to the next, begging them to believe him. "Those fires last night—they were at Cleistus' warehouse and the blood pit. He went there for revenge on them for turning us over to the lords and burned their buildings down. But that's not the whole of it—some people escaped the blood pit alive. It wasn't just arson. They said that he used sorcery to do it."

Suchen shook her head, bewildered. "Peddock, that's ridiculous. You know it is. Whatever people thought they saw, it wasn't Yozerf."

"It was!" Peddock insisted, hysteria edging his voice. "Gods,

Suchen, you have to listen to me! He found me somehow, just before I came back here! He tried to deny what I said, but he was lying! I think he meant to kill me, but before he could, a Red Guard appeared and distracted him! It must have been his ally!"

It was ridiculous, insane. Suchen sheathed her sword with an annoyed sigh. Buudi followed suit, then fixed Peddock with a hard glare. "I know that you've never liked Yozerf," he said coldly, "but this is beneath you. First you leave here against a direct order, but then you return with a wild tale like this? I wants some explanations from you, Peddock."

"No, I'm not lying! You have to believe me! I—" Peddock froze, his face going white as the sound of the gate swinging open sounded through the cemetery. "Oh, gods, he's here!"

Peddock dashed away from the crypt in a desperate bid to seek shelter somewhere else. Despite her own certainties, his very real terror made Suchen's stomach uneasy.

Like a shadow detached from the night, Yozerf came into view around the tall vaults. His white face was an expressionless mask, but his gray eyes seemed to burn from within. A wind that somehow failed to touch Suchen blew his hair back from his face and rippled his cloak wildly.

Auglar stepped into Yozerf's path. "Yozerf," he said, "I think you should stop where you are. Peddock has said that—"

Yozerf didn't even bother to look at Auglar, only made a negligent gesture with his hand. An invisible force punched into the lord's chest, flinging him backward into Buudi and knocking them both to the ground.

All of the warmth seemed to drain out of Suchen, replaced by a deep cold that turned her body to ice. She could not have seen what she had seen. It was not possible. Yozerf was no sorcerer—he would have told her.

He loved her. He would have told her.

He loved her.

"What's happening?" she demanded in a trembling voice.

Yozerf ignored her—it was as if he could neither hear nor see her. Pausing by the crypt, he tilted his head, as if listening for something. Then with a heartless smile, he turned in the direction that Peddock had fled—and literally *flew* over the monuments in his way.

Oh, gods...

"Stop him!" cried Auglar, breaking them from their paralysis. Brenwulf rushed after Yozerf, followed by Buudi. Shaking off her shock, Suchen ran on their heels.

꙳

Yozerf landed near the back of the cemetery. Frogs and other creatures called from the depths of the swamp that lay just beyond the low wall, and a humid, decayed smell filled the air. The rain had died away, but the rumble of thunder in the distance promised more. The heat of his body made wetness steam off of his clothes and hair, wreathing him in mist.

Peddock had run to the wall, but now he turned and put his back to it, an expression of defiance and despair on his face. "Come on, then, you demon!" he shouted, shaking his sword wildly in Yozerf's direction. "Come and kill me, if that's what you want! Murder me in front of Suchen, in front of everyone!"

For an instant, the mention of Suchen's name made him hesitate. But then Telmonra rose in him, blotting out all other thoughts with her rage and pain. *"He wants you weak—they all want you weak. But he is a traitor—you must destroy him!"*

Of course. His confidence restored, Yozerf funneled the wind, using it to slap the sword out of Peddock's hand. Peddock fell into a crouch, his lips pulled back from his teeth in a snarl worthy of a Wolfkin, and Yozerf took a step forwards to tower over him.

"Stop! What are you doing? Have you gone mad!"

Yozerf didn't spare a glance at Brenwulf. "He is a traitor," Yozerf said calmly. "The Red Guard protected him. He is in league with Jahcgroth."

"That's ridiculous!"

"Is it? You would have said the same thing about Dara-Don, wouldn't you?"

Peddock glared up, hate bright in his eyes. "You bastard. *You're* the traitor! The Red Guard is your ally! You killed Rozah, didn't you, sorcerer?"

"Be silent," Yozerf said, trembling with rage. "I am sick of your lies and your spite." He drew himself up, an aura of flame bursting into being around him. "I am the dragon's son. I am the lord of wind and fire. I am the wolf in the woods. Look upon me and despair."

"No!" Suddenly there was a body between him and his quarry. A woman, dirty and dressed in ragged clothes, her stringy air hanging down around her face, and it seemed to him for a moment that he should know her.

"A human, nothing more," Telmonra snarled. *"They are all against you, don't you see?"* Images of Caden's destruction poured through his head, fanning the flames around him higher, until he shone like a beacon of terror. *"They have all plotted against you,*

all of them. They would have given you to Cleistus, because he is one of them, after all. They let you be taken and tortured last winter. They have beaten you down for your entire life, and yet you crawl back to them, let them do it all to you again. No more! NO MORE! KILL THEM AND BE DONE WITH IT!"

Glorious images filled his mind: the palace in flames, the streets littered with dead humans and rejoicing Aclytes. Once they saw what he had done, his people would fall behind him, and he would march at the head of an army of free Aclytes, laying waste to Jenel, burning and destroying anything that humans had raised. And then, once that was done, Jahcgroth would be next, and Yozerf would sit on his throne, and all the fear and all the pain would be gone forever. Vengeance—no, *justice*—would finally have been served. And all he had to do to make it come true was to take this first step, to obliterate these cowering humans and free himself from all the deadly ties he had forged with them.

He lifted his hand, intending to incinerate them.

A dark, snarling shape cannoned into him, flinging him from his feet. Rolling, he locked his hands around its throat, trying to keep it away from him. His attacker was a black wolf, he saw, and a snarl of fury erupted out of him. Instinct that could not be denied surged to the fore—this male, with whom he had never had more than an uneasy peace, was depriving him of his kill.

Snarling, Yozerf let the wolf within take him, felt his face burn as his eyes turned golden and his teeth became fangs. He would show this other male that he was no easy target, he would…

…he would….

What am I doing?

With a convulsive move, he flung the black wolf from him and staggered to his feet, his body screaming in pain as it hung in a hybrid state, neither man nor wolf but something not meant to exist for long. He ignored the pain, forcing himself to look, to *see* without Telmonra clouding his vision.

Peddock still huddled against the wall. But the woman who protected him—whom Yozerf had been going to kill—no longer seemed a stranger.

"Suchen," he whispered, horror blooming in him.

The wolf howled, outraged. Violated instinct, not to harm his own pack, not to harm his own *mate*, tore at him, and with sudden, cold certainty he saw what had happened and what Telmonra had almost led him to do.

She had found the cracks in his armor, had found all the wounded places in his soul, and she had exploited them until he had begun to agree with her way of thinking—until he had given her just what she needed to finally take over his mind altogether. Only Brenwulf's attack and the waking of the wolf had suppressed her enough for him to think clearly once again.

But he had already fallen under her influence once—if he resumed Aclytese form fully, what was to stop him from doing so again?

The wolf in him knew only one way to prevent that. And so in his mind he dove deep, moving through the blank space where Telmonra had lived, reaching farther than he had ever reached, falling deep into himself.

In the graveyard, his body collapsed into a limp heap.

⋙⋘

The wolf found himself in a cold, cold place. The sky was black, and a freezing wind tore across a glacial plain where nothing would ever grow. His thick fur kept out most of the cold, but even it would not protect him for long.

Telmonra hung on the wind, her toes barely scraping the ice beneath her. Brown hair swirled in a storm around her narrow, pixie-like face. Gray eyes like dirty ice watched him, and a sneer of contempt distorted her beautiful mouth.

"You cannot rid yourself of me," she said disdainfully.

The wolf growled. "I invited you in," he pointed out.

"You are nothing—a powerless half-breed. The woman who gave birth to such an abomination must be truly perverted indeed."

He tensed, muscles coiling under him, then sprang. She cried out and struck back at him, flinging him onto the frozen ground. Pain shocked through him, but he staggered to his feet, the taste of his own blood and hers both filling his mouth. His teeth had made a ragged gash in her cheek, but the blood froze solid before it could spill out onto her skin.

Seemingly oblivious to the insignificant wound, she let out a hateful laugh. "You cannot hurt me, beast. I am already dead."

"Then why protest so much?" he asked, and leapt again. She tried to spin away, but his jaws closed over her arm, dragging her down. She hit him again, breaking his hold, but this time they both fell.

"It sickens me that our line, the line of kings, should come to this," Telmonra snarled as she pushed herself up on her elbows. "A sterile half-breed. A beastly abomination. A whore with no love for himself, and whom no one else could ever love. You are nothing without me."

Movement hurt, but somehow he levered himself up until he stood on shaky paws. The cold had worked its way through his fur and was beginning to chill him now, a slow deadening of the senses that leeched feeling from his paws and smell from his nose. "I may be nothing without you," he said, "but at least I have only myself to blame for that. At least my mistakes are mine alone, without your voice clouding my mind."

She drew back in fear as he stalked towards her. "Without me, you have no power. You will lose everything. Remember what it felt like, Yozerf. Remember what it was to be strong, to wield fire and wind like a dragon."

Memories and feelings alien to the wolf intruded, almost dragging him back into Aclytese form. Euphoria, bliss, a sense of his own power that he had never had before. All his life others had taken advantage of him, had dragged him down because he was too weak to fight them. For the first time, the tables had been turned. How could he bear to give that up?

The memory of Suchen came back forcefully. He had almost *killed* her. Almost obliterated the most precious thing in his life. On some level, he realized that, had he gone through with it, the guilt and remorse when he finally came to his senses would have devoured him from within, annihilating all that he was until only Telmonra would remain. No wonder she had been so eager, so reckless in blinding his eyes and mind to what he was really doing.

"So be it," he said, and lunged.

Powerful jaws closed around Telmonra's white throat. She screamed, her hands flailing against him, and he felt fire burn through his fur where she touched. Closing his eyes against the overwhelming agony, he clung to her throat, refusing to let go, until at last the fire consumed them both, and only ash remained on the cold plain, blown away by the wind.

◈◈

Suchen scrambled to her feet when Yozerf collapsed, her heart pounding in terror, although for herself or for Yozerf she didn't know. Cybelen appeared from somewhere and flung herself against Peddock, sobbing and kissing his face wildly. On the other side of Yozerf, the black wolf gathered itself back up, golden eyes hot with rage.

"No, Brenwulf!" Suchen shouted, holding up her hands. A part of her mind was still struggling to assimilate what she had seen: Brenwulf, shucking his clothes in a blur and taking on the shape of the black wolf. The same black wolf, she thought, who had protected her at Nava Yek last winter, when she had escaped the trap that had resulted in Uzco's and Rozah's deaths. At the moment, the implications were nothing she could even think about.

The wolf growled a warning at her, but she ignored it, instead crawling to Yozerf's side. He lay very still, his body completely that of a man once again. Hesitantly, she reached out and touched his face, feeling how cold his skin was. Then, a sudden, frightened realization went through her. "Oh, gods—he's not breathing!"

She grabbed him helplessly by the shoulders, rolling him onto his back. To her intense relief, he suddenly took a deep gasp of air, then another. His eyes fluttered open and he stared at her. But, unlike the dreadful look he had given her moments before, she now saw recognition in their depths.

He sat up slowly and stared about him, like a man waking from a dream. Brenwulf took a step forward, then stopped and growled, all his hackles on end. Buudi approached from the other side, his sword drawn and ready.

Yozerf winced and looked away. "You can put away your weapon," he said quietly. "I am no more threat to you."

Neither of the Sworn moved. Auglar, however drew closer, his blue eyes hard. "I believe that you owe us an explanation," he said.

Yozerf closed his eyes, as if at some sharp pain. "Yes," he said at last, so quiet and subdued that Suchen's heart chilled with fear. "Yes, I do."

❦

He told them everything, holding nothing back. What else could he do, he asked himself bitterly. There was no hope for it now, no web of half-truths he could spin, which would set things aright. Not after what he had done.

Silence fell when he finally finished his explanations. No one spoke; the only sounds were the moan of the wind, the whisper of the leaves, and the distant rumble of thunder. Dimly, he wondered if they would all just stand there forever, a frozen tableau of accusers that would last until the world's ending. Then, very slowly, Suchen rose to her feet. Swallowing his fear, Yozerf forced himself to look at her, but she had already turned her back on him. Her head was bowed, and her arms crossed defensively over her chest.

"Leave us," she said, her voice husky with some powerful emotion.

A little to Yozerf's surprise, the others did as she asked. Neither Brenwulf, Buudi, or Auglar would look straight at him. Fellrant met his eyes briefly, but Yozerf could not read the young lord's expression. Peddock shot him a glare filled with hate and contempt. But, to his shock, Cybelen gave him a look of sympathy, accompanied by a small, sad smile.

Once they were gone, silence again descended over the cemetery. Suchen turned and looked North, as if she could see past the city and over the miles back to Kellsjard. Yozerf's heart pounded in his chest like a trapped bird, and he found that his palms were slick with sweat.

"I'm sorry," he said at last, not knowing what other words might reach her.

She bowed her head a little, golden hair falling even farther forwards, denying him any glimpse of her face. "Why didn't you say anything? Why did you hide this from me?"

"Because I was afraid," he answered, spreading his hands apart helplessly even though she couldn't see the gesture. "Because I thought that...I feared that if you knew there was something wrong with me...that I had something inside of me that I couldn't control...you would leave me. And then, after everything that happened at Nava Yek, I thought that it was too late to tell you. That everyone would be suspicious—why hadn't I said anything before? What really happened to Rozah? I just...I just couldn't risk it."

"I see." Her voice was level, giving him no clues as to what she thought. "So what you are really saying is that you didn't trust me."

"No! No, that isn't what I'm saying at all."

"Isn't it? Listen to yourself, Yozerf. You didn't tell me as soon as you knew that something was wrong because you didn't trust me to stay. You didn't trust my love for you."

Her voice broke on the last words. Pain made a hollow place under his heart, and he took a step forwards, wanting to hold her. "Suchen, I—"

"No. I'm not done yet." She took a deep breath and wiped tears from her eyes. "You said that Telmonra's ghost came back with you that night when you fell and has been with you ever since. Every time we made love, every time I told you something about myself that I've never told anyone else, she was always there, watching and listening without my knowledge.

"And yet you have the gall not to trust *me*."

He stood very still, hearing the enormity of rage and betrayal in her words. She was right, he thought with despair—he had violated her trust, as though it was a thing of no consequence. "I am sorry," he said, at a loss as to what else he could possibly say.

"Get out."

The words made no sense for a moment. "What?"

"I said get out."

He stared at her, thinking that he had to have misunderstood. But she did not return his stare, only stood looking away from him, a small, straight figure against the coming night, and in that moment he knew that he had comprehended only too well.

Moving like an old man, he made his way slowly to the crypt where they had hidden. Everyone else was standing near it, but they moved aside as he came through and did nothing to stop him as he walked past. At the iron gate that divided the world of the dead from the world of the living, he hesitated, perhaps clinging to some desperate hope that Suchen—that anyone—would call out to him and tell him that it wasn't true, that he wasn't being cast out forever.

But of course no one did.

Feeling like a man with a mortal wound, Yozerf gently shut the gate behind him.

Chapter Fifteen

Suchen wept silently for a space of time that she couldn't track. Her sense of betrayal was so keen that it felt like broken glass inside of her, tearing her flesh to ribbons. How could Yozerf, the one person she had trusted above all others, have done this to her? What had he been thinking? How could he have so carelessly damaged their relationship?

He never loved me at all, she thought miserably.

But no, even in her despair, she knew that wasn't true. That in fact Yozerf loved her deeply, desperately. It was himself that he didn't love, himself that he believed unworthy of any affection. That had been why he had kept so many secrets from her—he had thought that revelation would have brought her to her senses and shown him as something she could never want.

Damn you, Yozerf. Damn you, damn you, damn you.

At last her tears were spent, although her anger remained. She didn't know what would come next, didn't know how they could repair their relationship, and for a moment she wondered if she even wanted to do so. But again, the thought was untrue. Despite her anger and her betrayal, she knew that she didn't want to lose him.

Heart heavy, she made her way back through the growing dark to the crypt. The patter of rain sounded in the leaves over her head; a moment later, it had become a cold downpour. By the time she reached the vault, everyone else was inside, looking out towards the rain.

Although she had hoped that Yozerf would be waiting for her with the others, she was not entirely surprised when she found him absent from the crypt that had become their prison. And perhaps it was best if they both had a little time apart to think and to let emotions run their course.

The tableau in the little chamber was odd, although it took Suchen a moment to realize why. Auglar sat atop one of the sarcophagi, Brenwulf close by his side. Buudi was by himself, sitting by the door but staring at his own scarred hands rather than the scene outside. Peddock sat far separated from Auglar, which perforce put him near Fellrant. Cybelen hovered at his side, stroking his arm soothingly, and Suchen saw that the young noblewoman had a bandage around one slender wrist.

Wanting nothing more than to sleep, Suchen nevertheless knew from the tension in the air that none of them would be relaxing anytime soon. She went to stand by Peddock and Cybelen, putting a hand to her brother's shoulder in the only gesture of comfort she could think to make. Cybelen looked up, her large eyes sad. "Are you all right?" she asked.

"No. But I will be." Suchen sighed and tiredly pushed her hair out of her eyes. Outside, thunder rumbled closer. "What happened to your wrist?"

Cybelen made a wry face. "I slipped in the mud and skinned it against a monument. I didn't realize what was happening, so I stopped to bind it." Her hand stilled, then tightened around Peddock's arm. "It frightens me to think what would have happened if not for Brenwulf."

"Yes," said Fellrant, raising his voice so that the entire room could hear, "'if not for Brenwulf' indeed."

Auglar stiffened, then slowly slid off the sarcophagus and turned to face the room. In the poor light of the tallow candles, the dark circles under his eyes were more pronounced than ever. "Say what you mean," he said wearily.

Fellrant rose to his feet, his bearing regal despite his obvious weariness. "Very well, then. You have not only consorted with Wolfkin, but one of them is the brother of your wife. And yet, you do not seem surprised at this revelation. If you had married a demon unknowing, but then cast her out once you learned the truth, that would be understandable. But last I heard, she is in Kellsjard pregnant with your child."

"You have heard correctly," Auglar replied levelly.

"And yet you decided to press your claim to the throne of Jenel," Fellrant mused, lowering his lids over his sharp eyes. "I assume that, had you in fact been crowned king, you would have planned on passing that crown on to a child of your wife's body. A Wolfkin."

Auglar's lips pressed together hard. "What do you expect me to do, Fellrant? Deny it?"

"Yes!" shouted Peddock unexpectedly. He looked up, wild-eyed. "For the gods' sakes, Auglar! How could you even consider betraying Jenel like that?"

"I don't see how I have betrayed Jenel," Auglar responded levelly.

"Don't you? You—you married a Wolfkin, a shape-changer! And as if that wasn't bad enough, you planned on passing off her demon offspring as human on an unsuspecting kingdom! By the time anyone found out, it would be too late!"

"We are not demons!" Brenwulf snarled, although the way he curled his lip over fangs did little to help his case.

"Of course you are," Peddock said shakily, climbing to his feet. "You're unnatural monsters. Abominations. It was bad enough with Yozerf, but at least he didn't have any designs on stealing the throne of Jenel from its rightful human heirs!"

"You will take that back!" Brenwulf shouted, hand going to his sword hilt.

"No!" Peddock yelled back. "No, I won't, damn you! The bond between Sworn and Lord is supposed to go both ways, Auglar! You lied to us, you betrayed us! I wish to the gods that Suchen and I had never set foot in Kellsjard!"

So saying, he pulled away from Cybelen and stalked to one corner of the crypt, standing and staring resolutely at the wall in front of him as if he would follow in Yozerf's steps and set fire to it by will alone. Cybelen stared after him, and Suchen saw tears well up in her eyes.

"He's feeling betrayed," Suchen said quietly, putting a comforting hand to Cybelen's shoulder. "I don't think he ever imagined Auglar would hide something like this. Truth is, none of us did."

"I hope you're right," Cybelen said sadly. Then she pulled gently away and went to Peddock, resting one hand on his back. Peddock turned towards her abruptly and they embraced. From the way his shoulders shook, Suchen suspected that her brother was weeping.

Auglar bowed his head slightly, looking utterly defeated. Like a predator sensing when its prey tires, Fellrant moved in closer. "You can never become King of Jenel now," he said softly. "Unless you kill all of us. But that isn't your style, is it, Auglar? You don't have that ruthless edge, do you?"

"What are you planning?" Auglar asked tiredly.

"If we escape here alive, you will drop your claim to the throne and back me."

A bitter, humorless smile touched Auglar's mouth. "Let's worry about getting away alive first."

Fellrant's eyes narrowed in displeasure, but he made no answer.

❧❧

Rain poured down, as if it would wash all of Segg away into

the sea, cleansing the earth of the city's stain and returning the land to primeval swamp. Gray torrents rushed down the gutters in the centers of the streets, and pools spread and joined until most of the thoroughfares in the Old Quarter were underwater. The edges of roofs became waterfalls, and the river rose restlessly in its banks.

The downpour drove most to seek shelter, so that even the great market was closed. The crows that normally would have bickered over the scraps of food stayed under cover as well, so that only the empty eyes of the hanged men on the gallows looked out over the square.

Yozerf slogged through the otherwise-deserted streets, a pottery jug in one hand. Water splashed over the tops of his boots, soaking his feet, but he did not care. His thick hair hung plastered against his chilled skin, the rain darkening its color to the shade of dried blood. His clothes had long ago been soaked through, and it seemed that there was not an inch of skin on him that was not wet.

Not that it mattered. He took a deep pull from the jug, felt the alcohol within burn a path to his belly. It had been many long years since he had allowed himself to become intoxicated—since he had left Segg, in fact—but at the moment it seemed the only thing he could think to do.

She doesn't love me anymore.

Many bridges crossed the river. Some of them were little more than rude planks nailed together, while others were granite monuments to the ancient architects of the Empire of Kells. Yozerf's aimless wandering brought him upon one of the latter, and he stumbled out on to it to stare at the water below. After a moment, he tucked the pottery jug under his arm and scrambled up on the stone railing, balancing rather precariously on the rain-slippery surface.

So what if I fall in? he wondered morosely. No one was going to miss him, after all. Well, perhaps Londah, he amended.

The last time he had stood on this bridge had been with Ginny. He could not remember what they had said to one another, or where they had been going, only that it had been a beautiful spring evening when the setting sun had turned the very air to a magical shade of lavender. It could not have been very long before she died.

And in all that time since, he still had not gotten it right.

It seemed that he had spent his whole life searching for Suchen, for someone that he could love with an open heart, and who could love him as well. Why else had he not stayed in wolf form forever after leaving Segg? So many years had gone by, and in truth he had given up hope that his future would be any less empty and hopeless than his past...when he had so unexpectedly found her. Everything that he had ever longed for.

And then he just...threw it all away.

His foot slipped, and he came down jarringly on the bridge, sending a bolt of agony up his leg. Wincing, he staggered up and took another long pull on the jug.

I'm never going to see her again. The pain caught him again, unexpectedly, and he doubled over, sobbing quietly to himself. *Oh, gods, how can I live with this?*

There was no answer. The future was a blank to him; he could not imagine living through the next moment, let alone the next day or the next year.

How could I have done this? How could I have hurt her? How could I have thrown it all away so fast?

He hated himself, he thought as he took another generous swallow from the jug. And Suchen hated him, so once again they were in agreement. True soul mates indeed.

Shivering with the cold despite the alcohol in his blood, Yozerf staggered along the street until he spotted a slight overhang where he might be out of the rain. Once beneath it, he collapsed onto the dirt, pulled the jug protectively to his chest, and let oblivion take him.

⁊≈

As the rainy day passed into night and neither of the Aclytes returned, Suchen began to worry. She had assumed that Yozerf would come back eventually, but now she began to wonder if he had taken her words aright. What if he didn't realize that all she had wanted was a little space in which to think? Or worse, what if he was angry, or else decided that he couldn't face her...and never returned?

He'll be back, she told herself. *He won't abandon us.*

But Londah, who had been gone since that morning, did not return either.

"We have to leave," Buudi said quietly. He had not spoken much since the revelations of earlier that day, and Suchen guessed that he was also deeply hurt by the secrets that had been kept, both by Auglar and Yozerf.

Fellrant shifted restlessly, eyes fixed on Buudi, and Suchen wondered if he was considering ways in which to take advantage of Buudi's disaffection with his lord. "What do you propose?"

"Yozerf and Londah are both gone, and we don't know if they're coming back," Buudi replied, still not looking up at anyone. "We have to get out of this city. We can't stay here any longer."

"Agreed," said Auglar.

Cybelen frowned from where she sat once again by Peddock. "It is a great risk."

"No more risky than sitting here and waiting for the lords to find us," Buudi replied, his voice sounding numb. "No more than sitting here until we tear one another into pieces."

Auglar sighed, then straightened. "You're right. We'll buy passage on a ship, if we can. We've lost most of what little we had to Cleistus, but perhaps something can be arranged."

"But what about Yozerf and Londah?" Suchen protested. "We can't just leave them here."

"To Hel with them," Peddock snapped. "I can't believe you would even consider bringing either one of them! Or have you forgotten that your precious Yozerf tried to kill us both only a few hours ago?"

"I haven't forgotten," she said levelly. "But there were extenuating circumstances."

"*If* you believe what he said," Peddock argued stubbornly. "Which, given his history, would be foolish."

"Peddock's right," Auglar put in, drawing surprised looks from them both. "Yozerf lied to us. He concealed a dangerous power from us. We can't trust him."

Suchen bit her lip, torn. "Very well," she said at last. "I will go to the docks with you and see you all safe on a ship. But I'm staying."

"Suchen—"

"I won't leave him!" Suchen closed her eyes, striving to calm herself. "I'm as angry and upset as anyone. But I don't want to abandon him. Not here."

"There's no time to argue," Buudi said grimly. "Let's go. Now."

They gathered what little they had in tense silence, then left the crypt to its ghosts and dust. The rain continued to pour down, reducing the streets to blackened slots, unlit by the usual torches. They moved slowly in the near-utter darkness, picking their way through eerie, deserted alleyways until at last the ocean opened out before them.

The soft sound of boats creaking on their lines came in the night. Auglar stopped and looked around uncertainly, clearly at a loss as to what to do next. The harbormaster could probably help them, Suchen thought—if they dared to approach him.

"What now?" Peddock asked bitterly.

At that moment, a lantern was suddenly unshielded from the dark night only a few feet away from them. The faint light seemed brilliant after the long darkness, and Auglar held up his hand to shade his eyes, squinting painfully against the glare.

"Who goes there?" asked a gruff voice.

"Just...just people looking for passage," Auglar replied uncertainly. "Who are you? Can you help us?"

The lantern drew closer, its bearer invisible in the dimness behind it. "This them?" he asked nonsensically.

"Yes," replied a familiar voice, and Suchen felt her heart freeze. It was Dara-Don.

Buudi let out an oath and drew his sword, Peddock, Suchen, and Brenwulf quickly doing the same. But even as they did so, other lanterns were uncovered, revealing a dozen archers with drawn bows, the arrows pointed directly at their small group.

Dara-Don stepped into the light. His cloak hood was up to keep the rain off, but Suchen could see his broad, familiar features beneath it. There was a tormented look in his brown eyes, but he did not hesitate when he spoke. "Lay down your weapons. They'll kill you if you don't."

Auglar visibly hesitated, then nodded. "Do as he says."

Feeling helpless, Suchen lay her sword down in front of her, only to have a guard quickly kick it away. Rough hands grabbed her wrists, forcing her arms behind her back, and she heard the click of iron manacles. Buudi tried to struggle, but one of the guards struck him hard across the head, sending him to his knees on the wet dock.

Dara-Don walked over to where Auglar was held securely between two soldiers. He looked miserable, Suchen thought. "I'm sorry, Auglar." He frowned, then, and worry started to replace misery on his broad face. "Where are Yozerf and Lord Fellrant?"

Startled, Suchen looked around. Indeed, the diminutive lord was no where to be seen.

"Yozerf betrayed us," Auglar said in a level voice. "And I do not know where Fellrant is."

He must have slipped away in the dark, Suchen realized. *I guess he didn't think much of our plan.*

Dara-Don shook his head. "Don't lie," he pleaded. "It will only go harder on you all."

"As if you care, traitor!" Peddock shouted, straining vainly against the manacles that bound him.

Grief bloomed briefly in Dara-Don's expression, but then he turned away. "Bring them," he ordered the other soldiers. "Lord Igen wishes to see them immediately."

Chapter Sixteen

"Sometimes it seems like nothing ever changes, doesn't it?" asked Ginny.

She was standing on the docks, looking out over the sea. No clouds masked the sky, and the stars shone out in their multitudes. The docks were oddly empty, utterly lacking in ships of any sort, and the only sound was the gentle lap of the water against pylons.

I'm dreaming, Yozerf thought as he joined her. It saddened him, that even in his sleep he could not escape the inevitable fact of her death.

"Sometimes," he agreed, looking down at her. Her curly black hair fell loose to brush the backs of her elbows, and she wore a blue dress that he recalled had been her favorite. There was a look of peace in her brown eyes that he had never seen in life. "Oh, Ginny, I have truly made a mess of things."

She took his hand, her brown skin looking even darker against his pallor. "You have to make a choice, Yozerf. You have to either open yourself completely and let others in, or you have to keep everything to yourself. The half-measure you tried to give Suchen won't work."

He sighed unhappily. "I know. But I was so afraid."

Ginny gently turned him to face her. One hand touched his cheek tenderly. "I know, my angel," she said with a little smile. "But you have to learn to let your secrets go. You have to stop being afraid about what people will think when they finally see you for everything that you are."

Tears welled up in his eyes. "But then they'll leave me. I'm not worthy of love, Ginny. I never have been. And I...I'm so tired of being alone."

"It isn't other people who can't love you, Yozerf. It's you. You have to come to terms with yourself, with what you are. If you don't do that, then you will lose everything."

"I already have." He laughed bitterly. "I'm back to where I started from. No lover, no friends, no money, no power."

"None of that is true. Well, except the no money part." She gave him a lop-sided smile that was so familiar his heart ached, even after all these years. "Telmonra didn't give you anything you didn't already have. She just woke what was already there. It won't be as easy for you to use now, and the power won't be as great. But it's still there."

"You don't know that." Then he shook his head. "Of course you don't—this is just a dream. Just a fantasy. You're gone—you've been gone for years."

Ginny smiled lovingly and caught his face between both hands. "Silly boy," she said gently. "Of course I'm not gone. I'll never be gone, not so long as you keep my memory in your heart."

"Of course I have. No matter how painful."

Grief clouded her bright eyes. "Don't you know yet that I never wanted the thought of me to hurt you? I'm sorry for the things I said and did, Yozerf. It was wrong of me."

"How can you say that, when I was responsible for your death?"

"But you weren't, were you? Neither of us was. And if I hadn't died, we would have been friends again. But there was never time to mend the rift, and for that I'm sorry." Her brown fingers stroked tears from his face. "We loved each other, maybe not as lovers do, but in a deep way that can't be denied. Don't throw away the few good things we shared over all the bad times. It's a bad bargain, Yozerf, and I taught you better than that."

He smiled a little. "You did."

"*Forgive yourself*. That's the most important thing that you have to do. Forgive yourself for all the things, real or imagined, that you've spent a lifetime hating yourself for. It's the only way that you'll ever be all that you were meant to be."

"I'll try," he promised her, not knowing what else to say.

She smiled and nodded. "You are more than you believe, Yozerf. Remember that."

Then Ginny leaned closer, pulling his face down so that she could kiss his forehead. For a moment, he could feel the press of her lips on his skin, as real as anything he had ever experienced. Then a wind rose up around them both, and the scene dissolved into nothingness.

⁓⁓

The soldiers herded their captives up through the steep, rain-drenched streets that stretched from the docks on the ocean to the highest point on the hills. The rain seemed to have effected their spirits, and there was little talk amongst them, for which Suchen was glad. She walked with her head bowed, unwilling to think what might await them at the end of their road. A quick execution might be the best thing to hope for, she supposed. But if that were to happen, then surely the soldiers would simply have killed them all on the docks.

Her feet ached and her hands were numb from the restraints by the time the palace gates finally loomed up before them. Remembering their very-different entrance through these gates only a few days ago, she marveled that fortune could change so quickly. Then, she had believed that they went to a new era, one that would see Auglar crowned King of Jenel. Now, they went only to torture and death.

Thank the gods that Yozerf escaped this, she thought. The desire to see him one last time, to have the opportunity to mend the rift between them, cut so deeply that she wanted to weep from it. It would be enough just to be able to tell him that she loved him one last time.

Rather than being taken to some holding cell, as Suchen had expected, they were instead herded directly into the main body of the palace. Someone had lit all the candles and lanterns, so that the building was illuminated as brightly as day. Guards stood at every entrance, their backs stiff and no trace of weariness in their eyes.

They were led to the great hall, where they had attended the feast. Like the rest of the building, this room was brightly-lit with thousands of candles. The glow caught on the enormous gilded mirrors, reflecting back with increased brilliance. It also glittered on the jewels set in the rings adorning the fingers of the southern lords.

Igen stood at their head, dressed in ermine, a golden fillet about his brow. Directly behind him were grouped one or two lords whom Suchen guessed were his close allies. The rest were a little ways back, and guards seemed to be keeping a covert eye on them. One of these men was Lord Jehnav.

"Father!" Cybelen cried, struggling to go to him. The guards shoved her back roughly. Lord Jehnav's jaw tightened sharply, but he gave no other sign.

Igen stared down at them from the dais, and Suchen saw disgust in his eyes. Certainly the contrast between the perfumed lords in their silks and furs, and the filthy prisoners dressed in rags was sharp. But Auglar raised his head proudly, even as water streamed down out of his wet, dirty hair, and met Igen's gaze.

"Well, well," Igen said slowly, "what a rag-tag lot you are. You have caused me a great deal of trouble these last days."

"Forgive us for not dying conveniently," Auglar said sarcastically.

Igen snorted. "Brave words for a man whose hours are numbered. Where is Fellrant?"

"I don't know."

"I suggest you cooperate. Why endure pain for a man who tried to take your demesne from you?"

"I'm telling the truth," Auglar replied levelly.

"Pity." Igen made a negligent wave with one bejeweled hand. "Then there will be no reason to keep you alive any longer, will there?"

"The people of Jenel will not stand for traitors and usurpers," Auglar said, blue eyes glowing fiercely as he stared fixedly at Igen.

Igen gave the young lord a pitying smile. "The people will stand for whatever we give them. Besides, we are simply executing traitors—the two Northern lords who sought an alliance with Argannon."

Auglar nodded grimly. "So. You will accuse us of your own crimes."

"Of course not. It was the Council who consorted with Argannon, after all. But it makes a convenient excuse."

He must be lying, Suchen thought. *There are Red Guard in the city—someone must be in league with Jahcgroth.*

But if he's telling the truth, if the coup had nothing to do with a plot from Argannon...then it has to be someone else.

Lord Jehnav cleared his throat abruptly. When Igen turned impatiently towards him, he bowed low. "My lord, please...I beg you to spare my daughter. She was just an innocent caught up events beyond her control. Please, let her live."

Igen studied Jehnav thoughtfully. "In exchange for what?"

"My loyalty, lord. I will never speak a word against you once you are king. You will have no more ardent a supporter."

Igen's mouth twisted skeptically. "I see. Perhaps your offer has merit. Or it would...if the girl remains in Nava Nar as...assurance ...of your good faith."

"If that is your request," Jehnav said, bowing low once again.

At Igen's command, the guards unlocked Cybelen's manacles. She hurried to her father's side, rubbing her wrists. The great mirror behind them reflected their forms as they embraced.

At least another one of us will live, Suchen thought, although sne could in truth find only small comfort from it. *A hostage to her father's goodwill, perhaps, but she will live.*

And who knows, perhaps Yozerf will find her and free her. Perhaps she will be able to tell him what happened to the rest of us. Cybelen is perceptive—perhaps she will even tell him that I loved him to the last.

"Enough of this," Igen said, making an impatient gesture. He turned to the rest of the lords. "I have brought these prisoners here because I do not want there to be any mistakes, nor any possibility of wild rumors. It is a pity that Fellrant is not here, but have no doubt that he will soon stand in this place. Watch, all of you, and remember."

Two soldiers came into the room. One carried a crude block of wood, its surface stained with old blood. The other hefted a heavy, double-bladed axe. At Igen's signal, the guards holding Auglar dragged him forwards, forcing him to his knees before the block. Wrapping a hand in his long, black hair, they dragged his head down until his neck was pressed against the dark wood.

"No!" Buudi shouted, only to be punched in the gut by one of the guards. Suchen found herself frozen, consumed by her own helplessness as she watched the headsman raise his axe in preparation for the blow that would take Auglar's life.

"My lords, wait!" Cybelen called out. "There is something I must show you!"

There was no panic in her voice, no trace of horror, only clear command, which was perhaps why the headsman hesitated. Even Igen turned involuntarily towards her.

Cybelen stood upon the dais, just in front of one of the great mirrors. Her father had taken a step back, leaving her alone. The look on her face was one of clear purpose, without fear or uncertainty or doubt. Her right hand wrapped around the pendant about her neck, then yanked on it, snapping the chain.

Brenwulf's nostrils flared, and a look of panic entered his eyes. "No!" he shouted, struggling wildly against his captors. "We have been deceived!"

Lifting the pendant high above her head, Cybelen spun and flung it at the mirror behind her.

The pendant exploded in a flare of ruby-colored light. But instead of sparking and dying out, the glowing light grew, spreading up and down until it entirely covered the surface of the mirror. The reflection of the hall wavered and vanished—and then, a moment later, the glass itself seemed to dissolve. A blast of cold air rushed out, as if through a door that opened onto winter, and for a moment Suchen caught a confused glimpse of a cold, mountainous landscape shrouded in snow.

Then, shrieking their war cries, a host of Red Guard flew through the portal.

The nearest soldiers died before they could react. The guards holding the prisoners abandoned their duty, snatching out their swords and rushing towards the melee. The lords upon the dais for the most part tried to run, only to be dragged down in flurry of silk and blood.

"Protect the prisoners," Cybelen ordered, her clear voice carrying even over the din of battle. A moment later, five Red Guard landed about them with a thunder of wings. Suchen found herself staring up into a bestial, gargoyle-like face, but the crimson eyes that looked back at her were bright with intelligence. The creature lifted its wings, and she smelled its dry, dusty scent.

Brenwulf began howling wildly, tearing so madly at his bonds that Suchen feared he would hurt himself. Desperate, she cast an uncertain glance at their new captors, then edged towards the maddened Wolfkin. When they did nothing to stop her, she went as close as she dared.

"Brenwulf! Stop this!" she shouted, wondering even as she did so whether it mattered, or whether they would all be dead within the hour anyway.

Auglar had regained his feet; now he joined Suchen, trying to block Brenwulf with his own body. Seeing what he was doing, Buudi added his own weight, and the three of them managed to pin the howling Wolfkin between them. Suchen could feel his heart galloping in his chest; his breath came in desperate gasps, and he shook like a horse run too hard. But, after a few moments, his wild struggles ceased and he stood still, head bowed.

The battle did not take long. More Red Guard, followed this time by tall men in armor and heavy furs, flooded through the portal and streamed out of the room. Although there would probably be intense fighting in the halls for some time to come, Suchen knew that the palace's garrison didn't stand a chance. They would not be prepared for an attack from within, an attack that came without warning. The walls of the palace would be painted with blood tonight.

The guards within the room were dispatched quickly, along with most of the lords. Igen lay on the dais steps, his eyes staring blankly at the ceiling, his throat gone. Only Lord Jehnav remained, standing quietly by the mirror-portal, his hands folded before him.

Lord Jehnav...and his daughter, Cybelen.

Fellrant was right all along, Suchen thought, staring incredulously at the young woman she had thought she'd known. *Cybelen and her father were traitors. They just weren't involved with the coup.*

She glanced around for Peddock, found him standing a few feet away. His face was slack with shock, and there was a pleading look in his eyes as he stared in Cybelen's direction, as if he wanted her to tell him that what his eyes had seen was not real.

Grief for her brother knifed through Suchen. In all their long years at Kellsjard, he had never had a true relationship with a woman, had never given his heart to anyone. And now that he had, this was what came of it.

We two must be the most gullible fools in all of Jenel, Suchen thought bitterly.

At some signal that Suchen didn't see or hear, both Red Guard and human soldiers suddenly turned their attention towards the portal. Cybelen moved to stand directly before it once again, then dropped gracefully to her knees, her head bowed.

A shadow formed on the other side, and the air seemed to ripple slightly as a man came through, accompanied by yet more Red Guard. He was an Aclyte, Suchen saw with surprise, although she had never seen one so tall as he. Butter-gold hair fell to his elbows, shining like sunlight around a stern but beautiful face. The eyes that scanned the scene before him were gray—gray as ice, as dragons, as death.

Yozerf's eyes. Londah's eyes.

Jonaglir eyes.

"Welcome to Jenel, Your Highness," Cybelen said reverently.

Suchen stared, shock battling with certainty. This Aclyte, dressed much like the common soldiers around him, was none other than Jahcgroth, the Undying Emperor of Argannon.

And Yozerf's kinsman.

A warm smile spread over Jahcgroth's face as he turned his attention to Cybelen. "You have done well, Kktara. But show me your true face, if you will."

Cybelen—or Kktara—rose to her feet and cast an oddly desperate glance over her shoulder, meeting Peddock's eyes for just a moment. Then she turned back to her lord...and *shifted.*

Delicate white skin faded to be replaced by red hide. Bones mutated, giving rise to wings, fangs, a muzzle. The ragged dress ripped apart as the body beneath it swelled, ropy muscles now covering crooked limbs. When it was over, the beautiful young woman was gone, and a Red Guard stood in her place.

No, Suchen thought, frozen in shock. It was not possible. She had spent the last several days cooped up with Cybelen—she knew the girl, knew her sense of humor, her generosity of spirit. She could not be a monster.

And yet she was.

Jahcgroth nodded, clearly pleased by her new form. "Report, Kktara, first among my Sworn."

Oh, gods...

The Red Guard bowed her massive head. "You observed the coup though the mirror, my Emperor?" she asked in a voice like the rattle of gravel down a hillside.

"The aftermath, yes."

"I went with these ones, and the one you seek. Lord, there is another."

Something like hope seemed to spark in Jahcgroth's eyes. "Another?"

"Londah Jonaglir. Yozerf is her son."

"And yet I do not see either of them here." Although there was no threat in the words, no one could have missed the edge to his voice.

"Forgive me, lord. I did all that I could to protect them without revealing myself, as you ordered. But today there was a...dispute. Telmonra sought to subjugate Yozerf to her will. He broke her hold, and I believe that she has been banished back into the darkness."

Jahcgroth closed his eyes in a gesture of pain. "She never would accept any way but her own," he said at last. "The fault is not yours."

Kktara bowed her head. "The humans did not know of Telmonra's presence until then. There was a quarrel, and Yozerf left. He must yet be in the city. I do not know where Londah is, although I doubt that any ill has befallen her. Her prowess with weapons must be seen to be believed."

Jahcgroth frowned, obviously displeased. "Then we must find them, before something does happen. There will be fighting in the streets, and I will not have my only kin slain needlessly."

"My lord, I believe the fact that you have these prisoners will be all that is required," Kktara said, gesturing towards them with a clawed hand.

Jahcgroth descended from the dais, strolling slowly over to the prisoners. Auglar stared at him defiantly, but the Emperor ignored the young lord. Instead, he reached out and caught Suchen by the chin. Although his touch was gentle, Suchen flinched and scowled furiously at him.

A sudden smile curved Jahcgroth's beautiful mouth. "Ah, yes. I see the spirit that my kinsman is so enamored of. He will come wherever you are, will he not?"

No! No, I can't let him use us for bait to trap Yozerf, Suchen thought frantically. Keeping her expression one of bravado, she snarled, "No, he won't. We quarreled. He won't want anything to do with me."

But Jahcgroth only chuckled. "A good attempt, child. But I

have looked into your mate's mind, and I know that he would not abandon you no matter the cost to himself." He looked up, scanning the faces of the other prisoners. "Nor will he be prepared to listen to me if I kill the rest of you, although that would be the wisest course. Your deaths will have to wait until I have convinced him to join me." Jahcgroth let go of Suchen and turned away, suddenly businesslike. "Find a place to hold them," he ordered their guards. "Make them as comfortable as possible, and see to any needs that aren't utterly unreasonable. Now, we have a kingdom to secure."

Chapter Seventeen

Yozerf blinked awake slowly, his thoughts in a jumble. The stink of cheap liquor burned his nose, and his belly roiled unpleasantly. His body ached from lying on the hard ground, and the sound of falling rain filled up the world. Gradually, he became aware that someone was leaning over him, and he jerked with a gasp, sending a spear of pain bolting through his head.

Londah crouched beside him, her cool face impassive, although he could guess at her disapproval. For a moment, nothing made sense, and he could no longer remember why he was lying in the dirt beneath the overhang of a dilapidated shop. Then he remembered that he had lost Suchen's love along with all the friends he had in the world, and the hollow place that opened under his heart was enough to send him scrambling to his knees to vomit weakly.

He closed his eyes, tasting bile, his wet, dirty hair stuck to his face. Gods, he was a wreck. He wondered what had happened to the jug he had been drinking from, if it had been stolen by another passerby, or if Londah had taken it before he awoke. Not that it mattered—he could always get more.

Then the dream came back to him, sharp and clear as a memory from waking life. He frowned, wondering what it could mean. Nothing, most like—it was only a dream, after all. Then he remembered what the dream-Ginny had said, that he still had the power of wind and fire within him. Could it be true?

He feared to find out.

Sinking back on his knees, he rubbed tiredly at eyes that felt filled with sand. What should he tell Londah, he wondered. Hopefully the others had explained everything before she came looking for him. He didn't know if he could bear to repeat the whole sordid tale.

"When I left yesterday, I talked to everyone I could find about the fires," Londah said, her inflection giving nothing away. "It was said that you were responsible for them."

Yozerf winced. "Yes."

She sighed. "That is why I did not return to the cemetery. I did not want to do so until I had spoken with you. But I was too late."

"Yes."

She said nothing, but he could feel her questions. "They didn't tell you what happened?" he asked, feeling defeated.

"I have not spoken with them," she said, but he could hear something else behind her words.

"Then I don't understand. What do you mean by 'too late'?" His heart sped in sudden fear. "Has something happened?"

Londah looked at him sadly. "Disaster, my son."

⁂

Londah took him to a small, cramped room on the bottom floor of a brothel, yet another of her many bolt holes about the city. Yozerf rinsed his mouth, which rather tasted like the bottom of a boot, with watered wine, then ate a little bread until his stomach settled. Londah perched on a chair, her feet drawn up and her hands about her ankles, listening quietly as he explained everything about Telmonra. His voice caught in his throat when he mentioned that Suchen had thrown him out, but he did his best to sound impassive, knowing that Londah had little pity for love.

And in return, Londah told him how she had finally returned to the cemetery, only to find it empty. The docks had seemed the natural place to look, but before reaching her destination she had spotted a contingent of guards in Igen's livery—guards escorting a band of prisoners up the hill.

"I could not fight so many, so I waited and watched," she said, as Yozerf listened in growing fear. "And then things grew strange."

Somehow—how, neither of them could guess—Red Guard and Argannese soldiers had appeared, issuing from *within* the palace. "They went first to where the city watch was stationed, no doubt meaning to subdue any armed threat. Once they are done with that—and I doubt that it will take long—they will spread out to quell any sign of rebellion. Word has not yet made its way throughout the city—it is too soon—but in a few hours Segg will be completely under their control."

Yozerf sat very still, considering all that she had said. Jahcgroth had planned his attack wisely, he thought. Why waste your armies fighting your way across the whole of Jenel, when you only have to go to the capital city, where all the high nobility have conveniently gathered in one place. "So. Jahcgroth has them now."

"If they still live."

"They do," he said, striving to convince himself as well as her. "I think that Jahcgroth will be looking for me now, and you as well, if he learns that you are here. When I met him before, he seemed...concerned...for me. As if he missed having kin."

"And yet it was he who trapped the dragons in the ice, leading to Caden's destruction."

"Yes." Yozerf shook his head. "It makes no sense to me, either. But I think that he will want to find me. No doubt he knows enough about me to realize that all he needs do is hold my friends prisoner, and then wait for me to come to him."

"A trap."

"Yes."

"Well then." Londah settled back on her heels, a cold smile on her mouth and a feral light in her eyes. "We shall simply have to be more clever than him."

～～

The prisoners found themselves in a small storage room that had been cleared of its previous contents and converted into a cramped, but fairly comfortable, cell. The walls were windowless and of plain stone, illuminated only by a single lantern. Bedrolls had been provided for each of them, along with water for washing off some of the filth, and a good meal that they had to eat with their fingers alone. Two Red Guard stood outside the door, talking in low murmurs that Suchen couldn't make out.

"This is where it all ends, then," Auglar said. He sat on his bedroll, hands clasped loosely before him, head bowed.

"We aren't dead yet," Buudi reminded him. The distance put between them by the revelation that Auglar had married a Wolfkin had dissolved beneath the dangers of the last few hours.

"No. But we are in the grasp of our greatest enemy." Auglar put his face in his hands. "He is only keeping us alive until he traps Yozerf as well. But he cannot afford to let us live for too long, not if he wants to take over Jenel. It would be too dangerous to leave any claimant to the throne to challenge him."

"We may yet escape," Buudi said gently, putting a comforting hand on Auglar's shoulder. "We have to keep our eyes open and seize on any chance that we get."

Peddock sat on the floor, back to the wall, staring at nothing. Suchen went to sit by him, then took his hand in a clumsy attempt at comfort. His fingers were cold as ice. "I'm sorry, Peddock," she said softly, not knowing what else to say.

He shook his head slowly, looking like a man who has taken a grievous wound. "I can't believe it. I can't believe that she's...a monster."

Suchen sighed. "I know. I can't, either."

"All of those times I argued with you over Yozerf...all those times I called him a demon and told you that I couldn't understand how you could love a creature that isn't even human...and now I see. Now I know. It isn't all that damned hard, is it?"

His voice broke, and a tear rolled down his cheek. Suchen put an arm around his shoulders, hugging him fiercely. "Don't chastise yourself. You had no way of knowing. None of us did."

There came the sound of footsteps from the hall outside, followed by the low murmur of voices. Claws scraped on stone, and the heavy bolt on the door slid back. The two Red Guard stood on the other side, each armed with spears longer than a man. Suchen's hopes for escape dwindled at the sight.

In a soft swish of skirts, Cybelen stepped around her two compatriots and entered the cell. She had resumed her human form, even dressed and arranged her hair much as she had when they first met. Her beautiful, gentle eyes were filled with sorrow.

Peddock turned his face away from her. Cybelen winced, then stood with her hands clasped in her skirts, her expression one of uncertainty.

"I wanted to say...that I am sorry," she said finally.

"Then let us go," Auglar suggested wryly.

"I can't." She hesitated, her eyes going to each face in turn and finally lingering on Peddock's averted features. "When I was given this duty, I did not realize that it would be so hard. But living with you all, talking with you...I grew to care for you."

"But not so much that you didn't betray us," Suchen pointed out, refusing to make things any easier.

Cybelen sighed and bowed her head. "I have my duty, to my Emperor and my homeland. You must understand that. Would you not have done the same for Jenel?"

Brenwulf raised his head slightly, his eyes reflecting the lantern-light like those of the wolf. "You stink, Red Guard," he said, his voice little more than a growl. "How is it that I never smelled you before?"

"The pendant I wore. The Emperor sent me not only to observe the lords, but to keep an eye on Yozerf as well. He knew of Yozerf's Wolfkin blood, knew that I would have to hide my...my true nature."

Beside Suchen, Peddock flinched, as if he had been shot with an arrow.

"Jahcgroth wants Yozerf because they are both Jonaglir," Suchen said, wondering how much information she might extract— and what good it could possibly do anyone. "But he betrayed the Jonaglirs, destroyed the dragons that might have kept Jenel's armies at bay. He was responsible for the death of his own kin."

Cybelen shook her head emphatically. "No. It's a lie, Suchen. Telmonra believed that Jahcgroth was to blame. But he was not."

"Then who?"

"Ax."

Silence fell across the small room. Suchen remembered her own dealing with the wizard, who had always seemed nothing but a kindly old man. But Yozerf hated Ax, swore that he was not to be trusted. Could Cybelen's accusation possibly be true?

"You're lying," she said.

Cybelen looked at her sadly. "Why would I?"

"Because if I believe it, then I might convince Yozerf."

"You might. But that is not why I tell you this."

"And why should I believe anything you say? You've lied to us all since the first moment we met, Cybelen. Or should I call you Kktara?"

The other woman sighed. "Cybelen is the name of Lord Jehnav's daughter. She remained behind at his home, carefully guarded, when he set out. I was chosen to join him and take her place."

Suchen's eyes narrowed. "You're one of Jahcgroth's Sworn."

"Yes. He would not have entrusted such an important mission to anyone else." Cybelen took a step back, towards the door. "I...I can't stay. I only wanted to see that you are all comfortable and...to tell you that I am sorry. Truly."

"Can a monster like you even feel sorrow?" Peddock asked coldly. He still didn't look in her direction.

To Suchen's surprise, tears welled in Cybelen's eyes. "Yes," she replied, her voice barely above a whisper. "Oh yes."

Then she fled in a soft rustle of skirts.

Chapter Eighteen

Armored soldiers moved through the rain-drowned streets, their boots flinging up sheets of water with every step. The precision with which they held their ranks spoke of long training, and it was clear that any army of such soldiers would be formidable indeed. About halfway down the street, they paused, and one of them kicked open a door. A man dressed in the livery of the palace guards flung himself out at them, screaming and swinging his sword wildly, no doubt realizing the futility of his defense. Within a few moments, he lay dead on the street, his blood swirling away with the rainwater. No doors or shuttered windows opened to see what passed outside; the citizens of Segg were dug in deep, huddling in fear of their lives while the great fought over possession of them

Yozerf and Londah lay stretched out on a flat rooftop above the street, watching silently while the soldiers continued on their way. They wore their cloak hoods drawn up, both to shield them from the rain and to cast shadows over their faces. Yozerf's nostrils flared, sifting through the confusing morass of scents that wafted up from the street.

"Aclytes and humans both," he whispered of the soldiers. "And there are women among them."

"*Kk'ithii'kk*?" she asked, meaning the Red Guard.

"No. They will be the most difficult to get past, though. Their sense of smell is very keen."

Londah only nodded, absorbing this information along with everything else. Once the soldiers were out of sight, they both rose and moved across the roof in a running crouch, daring the rain as they leapt across to the slick tiles of a pitched roof. The roofs were their only hope of getting near the palace undetected by the squads of Arganese soldiers patrolling the streets. Jahcgroth's subjugation of Segg had been quick and efficient, and Yozerf wondered suddenly how the rest of Jenel might be faring. Was this the first attack—or simply the first one they had become aware of?

Well, he would worry about that when the time came. Right

now, his only concern was to get Suchen and the rest out of Jahcgroth's clutches without being caught himself. That alone seemed so unlikely as to make any plans for the future an exercise in the ridiculous.

They took their time, moving carefully in the pouring rain, hiding whenever the sounds of a patrol echoed from the streets below. As a result, it took them many more hours to draw within sight of the palace walls. By that time, they had been forced to take to the ground, and they hid in the shadow of a gardener's shed behind one of the mansions as they made their plans. Yozerf found himself wondering what had happened to the family within the mansion, if they had been nobles taken into custody by Jahcgroth's minions, or rich bourgeoisie who now had Argannese troops stationed in their house.

Why should I care? he asked himself in surprise. *After all, they are the very class I've always despised. What does it matter what happens to them?*

There seemed no logical answer, only that it did worry him on some level, whether it ought to or not.

Londah drew a small flask from somewhere on her person. She was once again dressed in full Crow Queen regalia, including a wide assortment of weapons and other tools of the assassin's trade. "I use this cream to fool the noses of guard dogs," she said quietly. "Do you think it might work against Red Guard?"

Yozerf took a cautious sniff, then jerked back. Up close, it was a very strong herb scent. "It might," he allowed. "It would work against Wolfkin, at least."

They smeared the cream on their skin, Yozerf trying to ignore the smell as best he could. When they were done, Londah went back to her contemplation of the palace. "I am thinking it might be best to go over the wall," she said.

Yozerf nodded, then touched her arm to get her attention. "Wait, before we plan. I need to...I need to discover something."

"Without me, you have no power," Telmonra had said.

And from one of the dream/memories Telmonra had imparted to him came Jahcgroth's soft voice: *"He told me that, even though I would never lie on the Dragon Stone and bleed my life out into the land, the potential for magic nevertheless existed in me. Exists in all of us, I suppose, but it needs something to wake it up, make it more than mere potential. The ritual that our kings and queens undergo is but one path..."*

And Ginny: *"Telmonra didn't give you anything you didn't already have. She just woke what was already there."*

But his encounter with Telmonra had been desperately real,

while his with Ginny had been only a wishful dream. Hadn't it?

There was only one way to find out.

Very slowly, a small flame bloomed in the darkness, illuminating Londah's face from below. Her gray eyes widened slightly in shock, then fixed on Yozerf. "You still have the power."

"Yes." Yozerf let the flame dissipate, feeling a knot of fear loosen in his chest. "It took more effort than it did before, and I doubt that I will ever regain half the strength that Telmonra gave me, but...yes."

A savage smile slowly crept over Londah's mouth. "Excellent, my son."

⚬⚬

Guards in the livery of Argannon patrolled the walls in droves, their heavy boots ringing off the stone. They were badly dressed for spring in Segg, with their thick cloaks, their armor with layers of padding beneath, helms, and high boots. They paused frequently to drink deeply from their water flasks or swat futilely at the mosquitoes. In addition, the soaking rain made all that they were carrying even more heavy, weighing them down and exhausting them in the unaccustomed heat.

Yozerf and Londah had discussed killing the guards, but realized that an absence would alert the palace to their presence that much more quickly. So instead they waited, watching the patterns of the guards for gaps, until at last an opportunity presented itself. One guard stopped to drink from his flask, while another continued on, spacing them out too far. Using the rain and the night as a shield, the two Aclytes slipped up to the wall. A grappling hook was hastily secured, and two dark forms slithered up and over, disappearing into the garden below only moments before the lagging guard hurried past, trying to make up for his lapse.

They crouched in the formal garden, the elaborate topiaries around them further confusing the eyes of guards and making them harder to spot. Moving slowly and cautiously, they worked their way to where a great tree stood close by the palace, almost against the small window to the room that Suchen and Cybelen had shared. They scrambled easily up the tree, using its thick leaves to conceal them while Londah tripped the latch on the window and let them in.

The small closet was pitch-dark within, and Yozerf conjured the tiniest flame, shielding it with his cloak so that no one could see its glow through the window. The beds, trunks, and other items were all still in place, although someone had straightened the sheets since their hasty departure. Yozerf felt his heart contract with a mixture of fear, grief, and longing.

I failed you once, Suchen, he thought. *But not again.*

They navigated around the furniture on silent feet. Yozerf banished the flame, and Londah eased the door open a slight crack, peering into the corridor outside. She stood still for a long time, listening and looking, until she finally slipped out, signaling him to follow.

The loud tolling of a bell nearly stopped Yozerf's heart. He and Londah exchanged alarmed glances, then faded fast into the shadow of an alcove, striving to disappear. Footsteps pounded along the corridor, and a contingent of guards ran past their hiding place.

Yozerf frowned. Had they been discovered somehow? Would the guards return soon, this time in the form of a methodical search for interlopers?

Or was something else happening beyond the walls, something of which they had no knowledge?

❧❧

Suchen awoke out of an exhausted sleep to the sounds of alarm. For a moment, the clanging of bells and the rush of feet confused her, and she jerked up, reaching for her own sword. But of course no weapon met her searching hand.

Light flared in the little room as Buudi opened the shield on the small lantern. He looked haggard in the yellow glow, his shaggy black hair so shot through with gray now that it was more silver than shadow.

"What's happening?" Auglar wondered, running a hand back through his hair in a vain attempt to smooth it. Worry showed in his pale eyes, emphasizing the dark circles around them.

"An alarm of some sort. An attack?" Buudi speculated uncertainly. "But how could that be? Who knows that Jahcgroth is even here?"

They sat in tense silence after that, listening to the distant sounds of soldiers moving. After what seemed an eternity of waiting, the bolt on their door unexpectedly slid back. On the other side waited an entire contingent of Red Guard, their bestial faces looking even more frightening in the flickering lamplight. Suchen wondered if Cybelen were among them, but was unable to tell the creatures apart well enough to know.

"Out," ordered one in its low, hissing voice. It hefted one of the long spears threateningly. "The Emperor will see you. Now."

They had no choice but to do as they were told. Surrounded by the gargoyle-like monsters, they were marched swiftly through the palace, back to the great hall where they had been taken before. A damp night breeze blew in through the open windows, fluttering the curtains and letting the mosquitoes in. Jahcgroth stood on the dais with a Red Guard and a tall Aclytese soldier. The three of them were hunched over a small hand mirror, and Suchen thought she caught a glimpse of movement within its depths.

He used Dara-Don's mirror to track us last fall, Suchen recalled. *And he said he observed the coup through the mirror here. He must be doing something similar now.*

As they entered, Jahcgroth straightened and turned towards them, his handsome face marred by an expression of annoyance. He marched down the steps to them, long legs making nothing of the distance, until he stood towering over Auglar. "You have lied."

Auglar swallowed, but stood as tall as he could. "I have not."

"Kktara says you knew nothing of Fellrant's whereabouts. But at the moment, I am having difficulty believing that. I give you one last opportunity to tell me of your own free will."

Fellrant? Suchen wondered. *Was he behind all the commotion? But what could he have done in less than a day that would result in such chaos?*

Auglar's face paled slightly, but he did not look away. "Then I suppose you'll have to try some other method, for my answer will not change."

Jahcgroth nodded solemnly. Then, in a movement too quick for Suchen to follow, he clamped both hands on Auglar's head.

Auglar screamed, his body arching helplessly. Buudi cried out, but Red Guard shoved him back, forming a tight circle around the Emperor and Auglar. Jahcgroth ignored them, instead staring fixedly into Auglar's blue eyes, as if he could penetrate to the mind beyond them.

Which, of course, he could.

It did not take long. Jahcgroth withdrew his hands abruptly, and Auglar collapsed. Tears ran silently down his face, but he held his head high. "I am sorry," Jahcgroth said with a surprising amount of sincerity. "You were telling the truth. I should not have doubted Kktara."

Buudi was allowed to go to Auglar, whom he quickly supported against his shoulder. "What is the meaning of this?" he demanded, anger deepening his rough voice.

"The meaning is that everything has not gone according to plan, has it, old friend?" asked an unexpected voice.

Suchen jumped and cast a startled glance across the room. The wizard Ax stood there, robed in white, his blue eyes blazing with anger. Light seemed to shine from within him, and Suchen felt an overwhelming sense of relief.

They were saved.

The Arpannese soldiers reacted immediately, rushing forward to grapple with the unexpected interloper. Ax made a short gesture with his hand, flinging their bodies back to slam against the floor and walls. Power radiated out from him, like heat from a fire.

"Leave him to me!" Jahcgroth commanded sharply, stopping a charge from the Red Guard. Slowly, he and Ax circled one another, their eyes locked together. "So, you are the one who is behind this."

"Of course." Ax narrowed his eyes slightly, and Suchen guessed that the two were testing one another in some mystic way beyond the understanding of anyone not versed in the magical arts. "When I learned that fool Igen had staged a coup, leaving Jenel vulnerable to attack, I immediately went to the nearest thanes and...convinced ...them to rally their troops. They are even now laying waste to Segg under the leadership of King Fellrant."

Ice clotted Suchen's throat, making it hard to breathe. "*K-King* Fellrant?" she gasped.

Ax must have heard her, despite his intense concentration on Jahcgroth. "Of course. I found him in the streets, when you were all on your way to the docks, and I took him to safety. He told me all about Auglar's perfidy. To think that you would have put a less-than-human heir on the throne! You have betrayed Jenel. There is no greater crime. And for that you must be punished."

Without warning, Ax spun and flung a ball of light straight at Auglar.

Wind howled through the room, so strong that it knocked them off their feet. The ball of light passed harmlessly over Auglar's head, struck a tapestry on the far wall—and began to slowly burn through it, sizzling loudly.

Ax and Jahcgroth both froze at the unexpected wind, like hounds striving to catch a scent. "Show yourself!" Ax bellowed. "Show yourself, or else when I find you I will flay your flesh from your bones!"

The two Red Guard nearest the door screamed almost simultaneously. One of them staggered forward, twisting so that Suchen could see the dagger buried in the base of its skull before it collapsed. The other lived only a moment longer, until a sword finished what a throwing knife in the eye had begun.

A dark blur leapt over their bodies, and a silver blade flashed, killing the human soldiers that ran to stop her. Londah let out a maddened war cry, the blood of her opponents streaking her face like barbaric paint. A second group of soldiers attempted to outflank her, but the wind rose again, shoving them back in confusion.

Yozerf appeared in the door, his blood-red hair whipping wildly

around his white face. His expression was grim, tight, as he drew
flame from the air and cast it at the nearest Red Guard. It was not
the firestorm that had been attributed to him when he destroyed
the blood pit and warehouse, but it was enough to fatally distract
the Red Guard from Londah's attack.

Wild joy rose up in Suchen at the sight of him. She pivoted
and kicked the nearest guard as hard as she could; distracted by
the two Aclytes, he wasn't able to avoid the blow. Not letting him
regaining his footing, she moved in to grab a dagger from his belt,
and for a moment they grappled, until Brenwulf joined her. His
eyes were golden, and he snarled furiously. A moment later, the
guard lay dead, and Suchen snatched up his sword.

Brenwulf let go of his human form, shifting before her eyes
into the black wolf. He howled and charged the Red Guard, his
eyes blazing with a hate that was almost madness. Then a knot of
guards came between them, and he was lost from view.

Suchen stabbed the first soldier that drew near, then kicked
his fallen sword over to Buudi. Within moments, they were all
armed and fighting desperately.

Ax cleared a path through the fray, blasting aside anyone who
stepped in his way. Heart in her mouth, Suchen realized that he
was making straight for Yozerf, who was now fighting off soldiers
in a more conventional manner. She tried to scream, to warn him,
but her voice was lost in the din of battle.

But she had not been the only one to notice Ax's movements.
"No!" roared Jahcgroth. Chained lightning leapt from his hand,
striking Ax in the back. The human wizard spun, a mixture of
anger and affront on his aged features, and a moment later they
were once again engaged in a sorcerous struggle.

Smoke began to fill the hall, and Suchen realized that the
tapestry Ax had ignited earlier was beginning to burn in earnest.
Sparks flew through the air, and the gauzy hangings over the windows went up in a *whoosh* of flame. Some of the Argannese soldiers began to panic at the encroaching flames and fled the room.
Locked in their own war, Jahcgroth and Ax appeared oblivious.

Buudi staggered over and grabbed Suchen by the arm. "We
have to get out of here!" he shouted.

She nodded her agreement, and they made their way through
the confusion of smoke, dead bodies, and fleeing men. Brenwulf
loped along behind them, his black fur matted with blood, although
whether or not it belonged to him Suchen did not know.

Peddock and Auglar had already gathered near Londah and
Yozerf. As the last three humans approached, Londah motioned to
them urgently and ran back out the door. They followed, with Yozerf

bringing up the rear.

Even as they raced down the corridor outside, a deep, rumbling boom sounded, and the earth itself seemed to shake. A priceless vase fell off its table and shattered on the marble floor.

"What by Hel?" Suchen shouted, throwing her arms out to keep her balance.

Londah's pale face was grim. Soot streaked her forehead, and dark hollows emphasized her icy gray eyes. "Ax and Jahcgroth—they'll bring the entire palace down just to spite one another," she said.

"Then all the more reason to—" Suchen started, then stopped.

Cybelen stood framed in a side corridor, an expression of pain stamped on her beautiful face. Smoke from the burning palace wreathed her, making her look more angel than the demon her other form would suggest. Her eyes were locked with Peddock's, and the grief in them was terrible.

"Come with me," she said softly, stretching out her hand.

Peddock stared at her, his own hands shaking. What thoughts went through her brother's mind at that moment, Suchen could only guess: longing, despair, love. He broke contact with Cybelen for a moment and met his sister's eyes, and in his gaze she saw both his decision and his apology.

"Peddock, no!" she cried, reaching to stop him.

But it was too late. He clasped Cybelen's hand like a drowning man, entwining his fingers with hers, as if he would never let them go. Her look of pain transformed to one of joy. Then she spun and raced away down the side hall, Peddock on her heels.

For a moment, no one else moved, frozen by shock. Then Suchen made as if to run after them—she had to stop Peddock from making this mistake, had to keep him out of the Red Guard's clutches, had to—

Yozerf grabbed her around the waist, hauling her back. "No! Suchen, don't! They're making for the upper levels. Cybelen can fly, but you can't. You'll be trapped if you try to follow them."

Tears welled up in Suchen's eyes, and she dashed them away. Tearing away from Yozerf, she turned back, leaving her brother to the fate he had chosen.

"Come," Londah said impatiently. If she had any pity for Peddock and his choice, she did not show it. Struggling to put aside her own feelings for the moment, Suchen followed.

They had not gone far, however, before yet another tremor shook the palace, this one stronger than any before. Cracks appeared in the stone walls, and Londah's eyes grew round with sudden fear.

"Run!" she shouted, stopping herself and shoving her charges in front of her.

Something in the ceiling above gave way, and rubble poured down on top of all of them. Suchen flung her arms up, seeing a wooden beam swinging down at her. Then something hit her hard from behind, knocking her to the ground. Closing her eyes, she silently waited to be crushed under tons of stone and wood.

But instead, the tremors died away. Smoke from the fire mixed with the dust of fallen masonry, choking her lungs and making her cough. Climbing shakily to her feet, Suchen turned and saw Londah lying beneath the beam.

"No!" she gasped, reaching for the beam. Then Yozerf was there, perhaps using his magic to heft the heavy wood off of Londah, for it moved far more easily than it should have. Londah did not move, and Suchen saw that one side of her face was covered in blood.

Yozerf dropped to his knees, pressing a hand to Londah's neck. "She still lives," he said, and Suchen could hear the relief in his voice. Yozerf slid his arms under Londah's tall frame, lifting her so that her long, black hair all but brushed the floor. "I'm right behind you—go!"

Their lack of familiarity with the palace, coupled with the smoke and dust, made going difficult. But soon enough, they came to a door leading outside. Even as Buudi reached for the handle, however, Brenwulf suddenly began growling.

Suchen followed his feral gaze back down the corridor, but saw nothing through the chaos of smoke and dust. Yozerf was looking back as well, and Suchen saw his shoulders slump. "Red Guard," he said quietly, cradling Londah's unconscious body closer. "And I suspect that Jahcgroth is with them."

No. No, damn it, we came so close!

"Our only chance is to run for it," she said, knowing that they had little real hope of escape.

Auglar nodded, and Buudi pulled open the door, ushering the rest out before him. Brenwulf was gone in a dark streak, then Auglar, and then Suchen. The cool night breeze was like water on her face, and she breathed in great gasps of air untainted by dust or smoke. The rain had stopped, but the overcast sky was lit by the glare of fire, both from the palace and from the city outside, and she wondered what it meant.

A wide lawn stretched out before them, and on the other side Suchen saw the gates. They were even open, she thought, and for a moment she wondered if they might actually make it after all. Footsteps pounded after her; she turned, expecting to see Yozerf and Buudi. But instead only the Sworn was behind her, and she saw to her shock that he was now carrying Londah's unconscious form.

Nameless dread filled her, and she grabbed Buudi's arm roughly. "Where's Yozerf?"

Buudi's dark eyes glanced back the way they had come. Her heart pounding, Suchen turned back and saw Yozerf standing in the doorway through which they had exited the disintegrating palace. His tall, lanky body was silhouetted against the flames, but his eyes reflected enough of the light for her to realize that he was gazing back at her.

And then he turned and walked inside.

"Yozerf!" she screamed, wondering what madness had taken him. She started to run back, but Auglar tackled her, bearing them both to the ground.

"Let him go, Suchen! He's the only one of us who can hope to hold them off long enough for the rest to escape!"

"No! No, I won't leave him!"

"It's his choice!"

Auglar's fist cracked across her chin. Dazed by pain and shock, she floundered long enough for him to get his arms around her waist and bodily haul her back. Realizing what he was doing, she began to fight him, punching and kicking, desperate to get away, to save Yozerf...

Then, with a roar of flame, the entire wing of the palace collapsed.

Shocked into stillness, Suchen found that she couldn't move, couldn't scream, couldn't do anything but stare at the burning rubble.

"Oh, gods," whispered Auglar.

Yozerf. He was under there, somewhere, underneath the flames and the broken marble. They had to help him...somehow. But her limbs would not move, as if someone had shattered all her bones.

"We have to get out of here," Buudi said raggedly, shifting Londah to a more comfortable position. "Yozerf bought us time. We can't waste that."

"No," Suchen heard herself say, but it was as if someone else spoke through her numb lips. "No, we can't...we can't leave him."

"Yozerf is dead, Suchen," Auglar said gently, putting one hand to her shoulder.

No, that was impossible. "You-you're wrong, Auglar. He can't be..."

Auglar gripped her shoulders and turned her numb body to face him. The grief and pity in his blue eyes almost undid her. "Suchen...no one could have survived that. Not even Yozerf. I'm sorry. But we have to go, or else he will have sacrificed himself in vain. Surely you don't want that to happen."

Somehow, she allowed her friends to lead her away…and yet, it was as if some part of her remained behind, standing there staring at the ruins, caught in that horrible moment forever. Her heart, perhaps, or her soul, or both.

Vaguely, she was aware of passing out through the gates, into streets torn by rioting. Looting was rampant, and most of the Old Quarter seemed to be on fire. Masses of people desperate to escape the city had broken down the main gates, and she and her companions passed out with them, unnoticed by anyone.

Londah revived at some point as they walked down the shell road with the other refugees. Suchen could hear her screams, sobs, and curses, but it was as if they came from the bottom of a mineshaft on the other side of world. Like an automaton, she staggered down the road, following where Auglar led only because she could not imagine having any purpose of her own. After all, this wasn't even really her, was it? It couldn't be, because she was still back at Nava Nar, still staring that burning building, still trapped in that moment.

The sun came up shortly after they cleared the swamps. His face grim, Auglar led them off into the woods, away from the main mass of the refugees. As Buudi lit a small fire, Londah flung herself down on the ground, weeping inconsolably. Suchen sank onto the rough bark of a fallen tree and stared at nothing, able to see nothing save for her last glimpse of Yozerf, standing framed in front of the fire, before he turned and went to his death.

He knew, she thought suddenly. *He knew that he wasn't coming back out again.*

The shell of numbness around her finally cracking, Suchen bowed her head and wept.

Epilogue

Pain.

That was the first thing that the wolf was aware of; pain, and the fact that he was limping through a wood, some instinct urging him on even when he was no longer consciously aware of it. It seemed as if there was no portion of his body that did not hurt; even his paws were tender. The stink of smoke, burned hair, and blood filled his nose, shutting out everything else. His vision was uncertain, the sight through his right eye a blur, the left swollen shut.

The light he could see was strong, late afternoon, perhaps, and the instinct to hide bit at him with sharp teeth. He tried to lift his head and look around, but dizziness overcame him, and for a while he knew no more.

When he awoke again, he dragged himself painfully back to his feet. Either he had been unconscious only a short time, or else a full day had passed, for the sun was in nearly the same position as he had last seen it. His head almost dragging the leaf-strewn ground, he staggered determinedly on, no longer remembering what was left behind him or what he might be going towards. As the light began to wane, he caught sight of a dark opening beneath the roots of a half-fallen tree.

Even though he knew it was likely that something else had already made the space its den, he headed for the opening, long past caring what might await him. The gap was more than large enough to admit him into a wide, but shallow, space beneath the upheaved roots.

As he settled his battered body in, either to heal or to die, he did not care which, he heard the approach of human footsteps. The effort just to open his one working eye was phenomenal, and he wondered why he bothered. It would be far easier to just let the human kill him without seeing the blow coming.

A girl of perhaps eight years crouched outside the den, staring down at him. He could not see her well, either because of failing light or failing sight, but he thought the expression on her filthy, dirt-encrusted face was one of pity. A tiny hand reached tentatively down and stroked his muzzle, then withdrew, congealed blood on its fingers.

"Poor thing," she said in a soft voice that sounded rusty from disuse. She reached towards him again, and might have said something further, but he could no longer hear her over the roaring in his ears. Darkness closed in, and he gratefully let oblivion take him once again.

About The Author

When Elaine Corvidae was eight years old, she came home from school one day and declared that she was going to be a writer. Elaine is not certain what prompted that declaration, but unlike so many other decisions in life, it stuck from that day on.

Elaine has worked as an office assistant, archaeologist, and raptor rehabilitator. She is currently earning her Masters degree in Biology at the University of North Carolina-Charlotte. She lives near Charlotte, NC, with her husband and their three cats, who are just like children, except they never ask to borrow the car.

Elaine is a vegan (strict vegetarian) and interested in animal rights. She enjoys backpacking, wasting time on the computer, good beer, and loud music.

Her first published novel, Winter's Orphans, was the recipient of the 2001 Dream Realm Award and the 2002 Eppie Award.

To learn more about Elaine Corvidae visit her official website at http://www.onecrow.net.

Mundania Press LLC

www . mundania . com
books @ mundania . com

Mundania Press

WOLFKIN by Elaine Corvidae

A kingdom on the eve of war. A queen held captive. A land in turmoil. A shape-changer's heart.

Suchen's life as Steward of Kellsjard is a good one, if uneventful. But the arrival of the exiled wizard Ax threatens to upset her quiet existence. The task he sets for her seems simple on the surface: escort Trethya, a young noblewoman, from the southern reaches of the kingdom back to the safety of Kellsjard's walls.

Soon, however, Suchen and her companions-five warriors Sworn to the service of her lord-discover that the fate of the entire kingdom depends on keeping Trethya alive. For only Trethya is privy to a deadly secret: Rozah, Queen of Jenel, is held captive by her regency council. If she is not freed, the treacherous Council will force her into a marriage with a necromancer intent on making Jenel his own.

Pursued by enemies, attacked by shape-changers, and threatened by hidden traitors, their path seems doomed to end in death. But into this mix comes an unlikely ally: Yozerf Jonaglir, scion of the non-human Aclytese race, heir to a forgotten throne.

Haughty, bitter, and haunted by the darkness of his past, Yozerf at first seems the antithesis of everything Suchen has ever known. Yet from the first, she finds herself drawn to this wild stranger, finding in him an answer to the longings of her own heart.

But is Yozerf the friend he seems to be—or will the dark secrets he hides ultimately destroy them all?

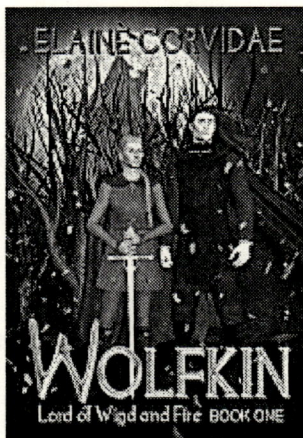

Hardcover . ISBN: 1-59426-055-9
Trade Paperback . ISBN: 1-59426-054-0
eBook . ISBN: 1-59426-053-2

Mundania Press LLC

www . mundania . com

books @ mundania . com

MACROSCOPE by Piers Anthony

Throughout history, man has been searching for better ways to gather information about his universe. But although they may have longed for it, not even the most brilliant minds could conceive of a device as infinitely powerful or as immeasurably precise as the macroscope, until the twenty-first century. By analyzing information carried on macrons, this unbelievable tool brought the whole universe of wonders to man's doorstep.

The macroscope was seen by many as the salvation of the human race. But in the hands of the wrong man, the macroscope could be immensely destructive—infinitely more dangerous than the nuclear bomb. By searching to know too much, man could destroy the very essence of his mind. This is the powerful story of man's struggle with technology, and also the story of his human struggle with himself.

This novel takes us across the breathtaking ranges of space as well as through the most touching places in the human heart. It is a story of coming of age, of sacrifice, and of love. It is the story of man's desperate search for a compromise between his mind and his heart, between knowledge and humanity.

Mundania Press is pleased to bring Piers Anthony's landmark science-fiction novel back into print. Piers has reedited this edition, adding back in what was originally cut by editors, and has included an author's note. Piers refers to this as the "definitive edition."

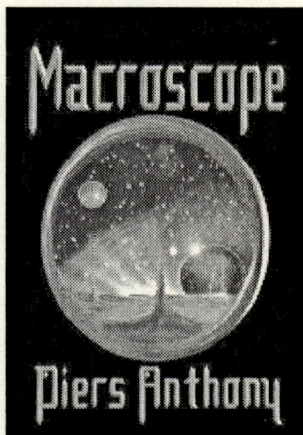

Hardcover . ISBN: 0-9723670-9-8
Trade Paperback . ISBN: 0-9723670-8-X
eBook . ISBN: 1-59426-001-X

Printed in the United States
27836LVS00005B/61-63

9 781594 260582